THE HOUSE OF

CW00539570

Fiona Williams holds a BSc (Hons) in Biological Sciences from the University of Westminster and an MA with Distinction in Creative Writing from Bath Spa University. She is the winner of the 2021 Bridport Prize, Peggy Chapman-Andrews First Novel Award. Originally from south-east London, she is currently completing a PhD in Creative Writing at the University of Exeter. *The House of Broken Bricks* is her debut novel.

FIONA WILLIAMS

THE HOUSE OF BROKEN BRICKS

faber

First published in 2024
by Faber & Faber Ltd
The Bindery, 51 Hatton Garden
London EC1N 8HN
This export edition published in 2024

Typeset by Typo•glyphix, Burton-on-Trent, DE14 3HE
Printed in the UK by CPI Group (UK) Ltd, Croydon, CRO 4YY

*This is a work of fiction. All of the characters, organisations and
events portrayed in this novel are either products of the author's
imagination or are used fictitiously*

A CIP record for this book
is available from the British Library

ISBN 978-0-571-37956-9

2 4 6 8 10 9 7 5 3 1

For my mother and for Jo

Autumn

Sonny

Sometimes there are no dreams to dream. Night-time brings other things, and we must wait patiently until it's over. In the kitchen, chamomile clouds drift across the ceiling, while Mum hides inside her mug of tea, soothed by the lullaby of the washing machine. It will soon be morning. My feet don't make a sound as I slide through the garden on frosted grass. I'm lost inside the blackness of a new moon. Wood pigeons puff themselves up in the cider apple trees and watch me in curious silence. I tread lightly past rushes, the last of the meadowsweet and loosestrife and dying stinging nettles, to where the river twists itself into a silver ribbon. Cold water soaks into my skin. I let it carry me as I listen to the music of the stars and the *kree, kree, kree* of little egrets until, at last, she comes, her tea drunk, laundry basket in her arms, head-scarf tightly wrapped. Like a fearful animal, she tiptoes on slippered feet with her clothes pegs, dark eyes looking inwards. She's too afraid to see how my legs have rooted deep into the riverbed. Eels swim between my knees. When I call for her, I know she sees me.

Tess

There he is again, my mini-me. The soft chestnut-brown little-boy curve of his cheek, and those eyes of his, peering out from between overgrown tangles of dock and ivy, where he plays like he did as a small child. Those eyes flicker as I peg first pants, then mismatched pairs of socks, up on the washing line. They're my eyes, so dark, they're almost black.

It's towels next, which swing back and forth, tainting the chilly air with the synthetic scent of lavender fabric conditioner. It's a struggle to hang up the sheets. My arms have lost their strength and strain to fling them one by one over the line. Steam rises to float away over the river that watches me from behind a screen of butterburs, the leaves no longer green but patched yellow, ragged and torn.

Sunrise appears later and later each day, though at last, the dull red bricks at the back of the house are lit up in startling crimson. There are two suns this morning; one rises low over a stretch of willows that lean as the wind picks up its pace. The other shines brightly out at me from beneath the surface of the water. Together, the light from them is blinding. Still, it's easy to ignore the painful beauty of it and think instead of the frozen chicken thighs defrosting on the kitchen counter that will need seasoning with scallion, garlic, tomatoes and a spoonful of jerk paste ready for roasting tomorrow. Easy to ignore the flock of seagulls already sailing like tiny, brilliant white boats across the

3

floodplain, screeching as they probe the waterlogged grass for worms, or the clouds, purple, and now scarlet, buffeted across the sky towards the distant Quantocks. There is only the laundry, pillowcases billowing, and of course Sonny's face, his sweet lips open as he calls for me.

Max

From the other side of the moor, the church bell at Meare rings six times. I wait behind our house among the tall reeds right at the river's edge. Mud oozes over my frozen toes. Ahead, my brother flashes in and out of sight.

'Maybe we should go back,' I shout. He'll say I'm whining but I don't care. He doesn't answer but heads further into the river to where the current spins, drags and catches things. Floating driftwood and rafts of rotten leaves are tugged down into the darkness. 'Come on, Sonny! It's *freezing*,' I shout again, but my voice is croaky and sounds like someone else's. I slosh through the water after him, worried about the shadows that stretch long fingers along the bank towards us. My stumbling scares a moorhen off its roost. Clucks and coos echo in the damp air. It won't be long before Mum notices we've gone.

'Over here,' Sonny calls, teasing me.

'Where?' As I trip over sunken logs, my breath blows steam around my head. Water laps at my rolled-up jeans and the cold is painful now. 'Sonny?' I yell. But all I can hear is the *rush* of water.

'What on earth are you doing in there?'

Mum's shout makes me jump and I slip, crash onto my knees and soak myself completely. She's high on the river-bank, with her legs half hidden behind nettles. As we clamber out of the water, Sonny's grin vanishes. 'What were you thinking? Get inside!' She chases us through the garden and indoors into the warm, bright kitchen. Dad, still in his dirty outside clothes, sits at the table doing the crossword. He smiles at us as we stand shivering by the Rayburn, dripping water onto the floor. The anger in Mum's eyes looks out at us. 'Off with the wet clothes. Now!'

'Come on, Tess, it's alright. Calm down. Here. Look . . . I've got one for you – remaining, five letters, second letter T,' says Dad, pointing with his pencil at the newspaper. Mum ignores him and comes towards us with a towel in her brown hands. She wraps me up first, like I'm a baby, even though I'm nearly as tall as her. Over her shoulder, I can see a small white moth, a pale tussock I think, fluttering against the steamed-up window.

'You know you're not to go anywhere near the river.'

'We were only mucking about,' I tell her.

Beside me, Sonny nods. 'We're sorry.'

Mum breathes very slowly like she's trying to hold herself still. She does this a lot. 'Go and get changed. It's time for dinner.'

We leap up the stairs, two at a time, our palms streaking along the wallpaper. But once we're safe on the landing, we fight back laughter and shove each other towards the bedroom we share. Inside, we flop down onto our beds, which are identical with matching Spider-Man sheets. Although mine's messy – the duvet's bunched up and covered in books. Sonny's is tidy like all of his things. On the bedside table between us are his reading glasses, the big silver cup he won for maths at school, a photo of us and our cousin Nathan outside an aquarium in London when we were nine, and our whistles with the red, yellow and green ribbons we got that time we went to Notting Hill Carnival. On the shelf above Sonny's bed is his fossil collection. He has way too many. Mum had to put some away in boxes under his bed. I've only got my animal field guides and bird books on my shelf, and the binoculars Aunty Peaches bought me for my last birthday. There's also my jar of feathers, which has fallen on its side. Rook feathers cover my pillow. They look black until I hold them up to the light, then you can see beautiful dark greens, blues and purples. Me and Sonny change quickly, still giggling and poking one another, picking out jeans and identical black and orange striped sweatshirts, before racing back down to the kitchen.

With a finger to his lips, Dad shushes us. He's trying to listen to a gardening programme on the radio. Some man in Hereford is talking about overwintering Swiss chard. Whenever he says something useful, Dad scribbles it down quickly on the edge of his newspaper. I smell cider every time he moves.

'Can you get the cutlery?' Mum asks, glancing at us. She uses her favourite tea towel, the one with the colourful map of Jamaica that's all covered with stains, to lift the hot blackened Dutch pot from the oven. It was a moving-in gift from Nana, bought a long time ago in Brixton Market. I'm guessing at one point the aluminium would have been as bright and shiny as the ones in the Caribbean food shop near Nana's house in Lewisham. As we eat, Dad goes over his plans for the winter planting. He lists hardy onion varieties, Red Baron and Autumn Champion, garlic, leeks, lamb's lettuce, turnips and perpetual spinach. Mum seems to listen, but her eyes keep looking our way and her fingers fidget with the scarf she ties around her afro to keep out the smell of cooking.

'I must get the broad beans in tomorrow morning,' says Dad. 'Anyone going to give me a hand?'

'It's Saturday,' Mum replies without looking up from her plate. 'You know I've got to check on Cyril.'

Dad, busy thinking about seedlings, doesn't hear her. Me and Sonny stay quiet and concentrate on sucking the fat from peppery oxtail bones.

Flicking off the radio, Dad turns to us. 'What about you?'

'Me?' I splutter, spraying bits of rice across the table. Sonny snorts and shoots me a *ha* look.

'No. I was going to take him to Cyril's,' says Mum, jumping up and taking a tray of baked apples from the Rayburn warming drawer. They smell of cloves and cinnamon.

'I don't see why . . .' starts Dad, but then he stops, switches the radio on again and goes back to scribbling on his newspaper. Lately, all their conversations are like this; it's not proper talking at all.

After dinner, Mum goes upstairs with her phone. I can hear her bedroom window opening and know that she'll be sticking her head and arm out into the cold to find good reception. Her voice travels down through the gaps in the floorboards. She'll be talking to Nana, complaining about Dad and how he's got his head in the dirt and never pays attention. It's all they talk about, that and about how lonely Mum is living all the way down here when she should be with Nana and Aunty Peaches and the rest of her family in London. Me and Sonny lie on the sofa and watch Bear Grylls on the telly. This time he's drinking camel pee. We leave Dad at the kitchen table listening to the news with a bottle of beer in his hands.

Later that night, I hear them arguing.

'What are they fighting about?' I ask Sonny.

'You,' he tells me. 'They're worried.'

We lie together in his bed with our noses nearly touching, hidden beneath the duvet. When I stare into Sonny's eyes, I can see my own reflection. Rolling onto my back, I shift my body sideways and lay my head alongside his. Strands of my long sandy hair mix with the dark curls by his ear.

No one believes we're twins. Mum's tired of explaining us to people. 'You can't be twins,' they say, 'twins aren't supposed to be different colours.' Everyone agrees. But we are twins. Non-identical, yes. Different colours, yes, but still definitely twins. People say Sonny takes after Mum because they both have brown skin, shiny brown like a conker. Their eyes are nearly black, and they have black, fluffyish, curly hair. I look like our dad, pale and peaky, according to Nana, with bluey-grey eyes that always look surprised. Everyone says Sonny and I are a *rarity*, something out of the ordinary, *one in a million* apparently. When we were born there was a photo of us in the *Gazette* with a quote from Mum describing her shock: 'We had no idea, their skin colour didn't show up on the scans.' Mum says we used to attract lots of attention when she took us out for walks in our double buggy. If Dad wasn't there, strangers would come to say hello to me and ask if she was babysitting. To prove we were twins, she always dressed us the same, in identical dungarees and matching Babygros. We still like to wear the same clothes, to make sure no one forgets.

Tess

One moment it's breakfast and I'm scooping up stray Coco Pops from the kitchen table, and the next it's gone seven in the evening and I'm clearing away dinner things. Unhappiness settles inside my fingers making them clumsy, so as I wash the dishes, mugs fall, tossing suds onto the draining board. It blocks my ears so they can't hear Richard's retelling of some piece of gossip he picked up from one of his customers as he scrapes the last mouthful of baked apple and custard from his bowl. I watch him laugh and recall the vague memory of how it feels to press my lips against his. Across from him at the table sits Max, laughing the same laugh, his mirror image.

'Mum ... Mum?' His voice, still a child's but already tinged with the threat of adolescence, cuts into my thoughts.

'Sorry, sweetheart. I wasn't listening.'

Max smiles, showing me little-boy crooked teeth, but it's Richard's smile I see when I look at him and Richard's pale blue-grey eyes that gleam with satisfaction as the tale is told a second time for my benefit. Old fears resurface, dark complicated feelings no mother should feel, and I'm taken back to the earth-shattering day his small body, still slick with vernix, was first placed in my arms. *Oh God, how is this boy my child?*

The words hum like angry flies caged inside my head. *I want to go home.* Back to the comforting chaos of millions of people who look like me and who don't care who I am. The concrete landscape there is far too caught up with its own affairs to bother with mine. Here, I'm watched at every turn – over hedges, both neatly manicured privet and unkempt tangles of holly, hawthorn and dog rose, through bleached net curtains that twitch as I take solitary walks along quiet lanes, from across the crowded playground, as I queue for bread in the village's one and only shop or wait for the little bus that appears only twice a day. There's no escape, even in this house, where I must keep away from the back windows if I'm to avoid the watchful gaze of the river.

Sonny

I dream about house bricks glowing tangerine orange in the evening sunlight. Over in Hector's field, the hawthorns are covered in dark red berries. Daddy-long-legs dance robotically across the lawn. In the grass, acorns shine like wet gems. Look – there are earwigs living inside the damsons. See how the dragonflies are hunting the wasps? Behind Dad's shed, the elderberries are going over and turning into hedge currants. Mum better hurry and bring in the laundry. There'll be a frost tonight. After dinner, let's go out into the garden and wave goodbye to the swallows.

Mum says I'm the dreamy one, my head always floating in the clouds, or, as Nana puts it, I'm an old soul on his third round, whereas Max is all corners and straight lines, awkward, unable to fit in comfortably whatever shape the hole is. But people treat us differently because of the way we look. They can't believe we're brothers, not half, step or foster, but full brothers. If they looked closer, they'd see we're really both the same. We smile the same, have the same small teeth that are a bit wonky at the front. We laugh the same too. Mum says she can never tell who's giggling. Most importantly, we're both exactly the same height. I only look taller because of my hair.

Watch me flatten it down with water.

Plus, our feet are the same size, so we can wear each other's wellies. Gloves too, and hats, except I need glasses to read the whiteboard in class. We're the same . . . but different.

It feels weird being called the *black* one. What do they mean? Black, like the chunks of coal we use in the Rayburn when Dad hasn't enough wood? Or black like the ravens that steal the chickens' eggs, and sit and cough on the garden fence?

Sometimes, people say things that hurt, not on purpose, I don't think, just silly things they think are clever or funny. To them, we're a joke. Especially at school, where I'm the only person who looks like me. I pretend it doesn't matter. Like the time Evan said I was the colour of shit because I accidentally hit him in the face with a football. Mr Reid heard and made him sit outside Mrs Haycock's office. I laughed it off with everyone else like I usually do, but I really wanted to punch him.

Mum always knows when I'm upset. Her hugs are sandalwood and vanilla cardigans.

'Don't worry,' she tells me. 'You're perfect. And, anyway, it's the same for me. I'm the only one here too. But see . . . I don't mind.'

But now I know she's pretending.

Mum calls us her *rainbow twins*. She says it like it's a good thing. I'm afraid to tell her that sometimes, not all the time, I wish I looked more like Max and Dad, and less like her. I wish people could guess straight away that Dad's my dad. When I'm out with him in Combe Leigh or Branstock, sitting inside strange pubs or queueing in the post office, they always ask if I'm fostered or just a friend who's come for a visit. Dad laughs it off. When I get upset, he reminds me that I have great-great-grandparents buried in the churchyard. *Old English bones going soft under dark, cold earth.* We've more than three generations now, so I belong here more than most of the other villagers do. But does it count if I only belong on one side of the family?

Everyone knows us here in our village, so no one stares. Not much anyway. According to Dad, we're no longer a novelty. But when I walk with Mum across the fields, out past the chicken farm or Churley's willow works, which mark the ends of our village, onto the footpaths leading to the villages surrounding ours, we're often asked if we're okay or if we need help or directions. Mum smiles, but never shows her teeth, even though they're really white, and puts on a posh voice. She tells them we're fine, only out for a stroll, actually we live not far from here. *Yes, just down the road.* She always says something about the weather, which seems to make them happy. But sometimes, people don't speak to us at all. Their silence watches us as they rake up fallen leaves, weed their flower beds and hang out their laundry. Mum always calls out 'Good morning' or 'Good afternoon.' She puts her arm around my shoulders or holds my hand too tight.

See our hands? They match.

When a black delivery driver turns up at our house, Mum acts embarrassed. She fusses with her hair or picks fluff off her clothes. Then, she speaks with the same voice she uses for

Nana and Aunty Peaches. It's like she's saying 'Yes, I know it looks like I live here, but really, I don't.'

My mum's a chameleon, like the ones in Max's books. When no one else's around, she's a different Mum. She laughs, teeth and tongue all showing, dances to Missy Elliott, shaking her stomach and bottom until Dad grabs her. He always steps on her feet when he spins her around the kitchen. Her voice feels as soft as the lamb's ears plants that grow along the garden path. It's just Mum's voice, her real one, the one she saves for us.

I've not seen her laugh or smile for a long time. She hardly goes out anymore. She stays at home, going only as far as school, the churchyard and the big supermarket on Combe Leigh High Street. She blames the rain and the deep mud that sticks to our boots. Dad's tried to make her laugh, but it's getting too hard, so he's giving up. He's busy doing other things. Sometimes, we hide on the stairs listening to them quarrelling in the kitchen. I press my head against Max's and lean on the warm chimney breast. We've heard these arguments before. Dad's voice is small and quiet. There's the *slip-slap* of Mum's slippers on the stone kitchen floor.

Richard

Richard squats on the heels of his boots in front of the Rayburn and opens the door to the firebox, releasing a blast of heat into the already warm kitchen. Steadying himself, he reaches over to the basket and grasps at logs still slimy and wet.

'You know how I feel.' He tries to keep his voice low, as though talking to a skittish horse. Tess paces behind him, snatching up dirty cutlery from the table and throwing it clattering into the sink.

It has become some unspoken rule; she tends to the inside chores, the laundry, cleaning, cooking and so on, while he takes care of the outside things. There are hedges to trim, the last rounds of blackthorn waiting in the log shed to be split and stacked, fences to mend and, of course, there is his garden, with its constant demand for his time and attention. If someone had told him they would have ended up living a marital stereotype, he would have laughed. The younger, untroubled versions of themselves would have done everything as a team – them against conformity, whether it was outside shoulder to shoulder in the garden pitching hay for mulching, cleaning out the chicken house and pruning back the raspberries, or here in the kitchen, their double act of cooking the Sunday roast perfected, with him whisking batter for Yorkshire puddings while she took care of the meat. Autumn had been a special time. By now, they would

17

have worked their way through the orchard, picking the Bramleys and unblemished pippins and russets, before getting cosy together in the shed, where, between kisses, they wrapped the apples in newspaper and stuck them in an old chest of drawers for winter.

Standing, Richard brushes sawdust and flecks of lichen from his chest and legs, and from his beard, where it clings to the reddish hair, and turns to face the window. Night-time throws the brightly lit kitchen back at him.

'We can't keep pretending this is normal,' he continues evenly, his gaze fixed on his own face – gaunt, almost ghostly, so pale with dark shadows weighing down his eyes. The last fourteen months have aged him ten years.

'Normal? What do you mean – *normal?*' Her voice is quiet, but he can sense danger in it, like feeling a carving knife hidden beneath teaspoons.

'Come off it, Tess. Don't do this. You know what I mean.'

'No, actually I don't.' She abandons the dishes and quickly strides the short length of the kitchen. 'Of course things aren't *normal* . . .' Her voice cracks with the promise of tears.

Richard knows he has to choose his words carefully. 'But love. It's not healthy for Max to carry on like—'

'Not healthy?' She loops around the kitchen – a baited tiger. 'Explain to me how it's not healthy?' She stops behind him, her face reflected alongside his, its features blurred like in a bad photo. 'You want him to be *normal?* Is that it? Is that what you want?'

'For Christ's sake – am I not allowed to be worried too?'

'Oh, don't act like you give a damn,' Tess shouts, returning to the sink and thrashing her hands in the soapy water. Translucent bubbles drift into the air. 'Come on. Let's be honest – all you really care about are your *bloody plants*.'

Richard steps away from the window. 'Wow. Thanks, Tess. Right . . . I can't do this. I've got stuff to do.' She could not be further from the truth, but he does not know what to say to make it right. Guilt is what he feels when he looks at her. Guilt, like bindweed among the cabbages, rooted deep. He picks up his damp coat from where it is draped over one of the dining chairs and heads towards the back door.

'So . . . what? You're just going to walk away?' Tess cuts him off, her soaked dress sticking to her chest.

Richard rounds on her angrily. 'Yeah! Because there's no point. No point, *whatsoever*. You don't want to hear what I've got to say.' He forces his breathing to be steady. 'You want to blame someone. Don't you? Admit it. You want to blame *me*.'

They both stand there and in the silence that follows, Richard can hear the gush of hot water surging in the Rayburn's back boiler. Tess wipes her hands on a tea towel, then presses it briefly to her dress.

'It's this place,' she says in a whisper. 'This godforsaken hellhole.' She glares up at him. 'I fucking *hate* it here!'

He leaves her then, slamming the back door behind him and grabbing his head torch from its hook in the porch. He cannot trust himself to stay calm. There is muck to move – a dozen bags of manure dumped on the gravel opposite the gate by Les earlier in the morning.

Outside, rain falls softly. A moonless night erases the garden, and, beyond, the moor is veiled in darkness. Richard breathes it all in. He loves this place and can remember a time when she loved it as much as he does. But perhaps she is right – he should never have brought her here.

Max

Mum's late for her Saturday morning visit to Cyril. She overslept and her eyes look puffy. After eating a slice of toast, she puts on her thick coat and yanks a woolly hat over her hair. Waiting on the counter is a dish with a portion of last night's dinner in it and a plastic bag containing light bulbs, a pack of dish cloths and a bottle of red wine.

'You sure you're okay to come with me, or would you prefer to stay and help your dad?' she asks us at the back door. Our front door, which leads straight into the living room, never gets used – Mum says we'll track mud into the rugs. Besides, the back door is where the covered porch is and where Dad put up hooks and racks for all our boots and coats. Not that we use them much.

'We want to come with you,' I reply.

'Yes,' adds Sonny.

She sighs. 'Quick then. I'm leaving now.'

We dig out our anoraks from among the heap of waterproofs thrown down on the porch floor and follow her into the garden. Dad's hunched over in the vegetable beds, cutting the last of the pumpkins. Even though they're huge, he can easily carry two at a time. His hands are bright red, which means he's been out here for hours, probably since before daylight. He's usually the first one to wake up. Me and Sonny listen to him creep downstairs for coffee and the morning headlines on the radio. Mum used to go with him. We'd hear whispered laughter trailing behind them. Now she always stays in their bedroom until he's finished his breakfast and left the kitchen.

Dad carries on cutting pumpkins and doesn't lift his head to say good morning. I hope he's not cross with me for not helping him with the broad beans.

'No. It's because of the argument last night,' Sonny whispers as we pass Mum's empty flower garden and jump over the wooden crates stacked along the path leading to the gate. 'The Veggie Man' is painted on each of them in thick black letters, same as the words written on both sides of Dad's van. Steam rises from a mound of horse poo piled up by the fence and the stink fills the cold October air.

We walk up to Cyril's house, past Barbara next door in the Gables, Marge in Willow Cottage, then Riverside, where the truck driver lives, who we never see, and last, Mr Brewer's bungalow. There are only houses on one side of our road, with the river running like a secret behind them. Opposite, there's nothing but withy beds and fields until we get to Winslow Farm. Sometimes I wish we lived in the middle of the village like all the other kids at school, either in Salter Close or on Puttford Lane. But Dad says he likes old houses best and prefers it out here on our sleepy road. I dawdle by Hector's field, where sheep graze between the brambles. It won't be long before the blackberries rot and have been spat on by the devil. The road's quiet, but I can still hear tractors revving up at the farm and wind quivering the bird diverters on the power lines. Soon it will be winter, and all the pastures will be empty. Sonny walks up ahead, humming to himself and kicking wasps off the windfall apples.

Cyril's house is bigger than all the other riverbank cottages and is covered right up to the roof in ivy. Dad says at one time it used to be a little shop and post office, but now we've got a proper village shop, Ted and Janet's, next to the pub. As we step round pots of dying herbs on the porch, the starlings hogging the bird feeder fly off chattering. I search for fallen feathers, while Mum gets the spare key from the rusty old biscuit tin hidden under the small bench where Cyril likes to sit when it's sunny.

'Cyril? Are you up? It's only us,' she calls as she opens the front door.

Inside's cold and dark. The blinds at the windows are half pulled. Me and Sonny help ourselves to Cyril's posh almond biscuits while Mum puts our dish of leftovers on the cooker, unpacks the carrier bag and fills up the kettle. She moves about the kitchen putting plates and bowls away in cupboards and wiping up crumbs. Dust floats into the air and circles the faded wooden parrots swinging from the ceiling. Antiques fill the wide dresser that takes up a whole wall. There are mugs with knobbly handles, a large wooden Indian god with an elephant's head, expensive-looking blue and white china plates, and a tobacco jar that apparently came off the *Titanic*. I skim my hand over a tempting collection of golden animal figures Cyril brought back from Colombia. He's also a fossil collector but has passed on all his best bits to Sonny, apart from his enormous megalodon tooth, which Sonny really wants but Dad reckons must be worth quite a lot of money.

'Go and find Cyril,' Mum tells us. 'And don't touch anything.' She always warns us not to play with the ornaments or the awards and trophies sitting on the shelves, even though she knows it's impossible. It's like a museum in here, full of really cool things Cyril found when he went travelling. He used to be an actor, in real movies, but now he's too old and so spends all his time writing rude poetry.

Out in the hallway, the lemon-yellow walls are covered from floor to ceiling in old film posters. Most are black and white, but there's one in colour that shows a young Cyril with a thin moustache wearing a fancy black suit. His arms are wrapped around a laughing woman in a really tight red dress. Me and Sonny find him sitting at the enormous wooden table in the corner of the sitting room, so still and huddled under his blanket, he's almost invisible. His thin hands grip tightly at the arms of his reclining chair. Spit bubbles trail down his chin. On seeing us, his eyes flutter and he waves a hand towards the table. He needs something urgently, but I can't move. I'm frozen, hypnotised by a rattling sound coming from his chest and by the small gasps he makes as he tries to breathe. It's as though he's under water. My heart beats really hard. I've heard this sound before. Cyril points at the table with weak jabs of his finger. He's desperate, but I can't do anything except hold my breath and stare as his face sags. His lips are turning blue. But Sonny doesn't seem to care about the sounds Cyril's

24

making or the way his eyes have rolled back till there's mostly white showing.

'Quick – his inhaler must be here somewhere,' he tells me. 'We need to find it.' The table is untidy and we search under tablet packets, flung-open books and newspapers and wads of dirty tissues. 'Here!' Sonny spots the inhaler hidden behind a mug of cold coffee. I put it in Cyril's shaking hands and we watch as he gulps and gulps at it. Blood rushes pink back into his cheeks.

'You alright in here?' asks Mum, coming into the room carrying a tray. 'Max! What's wrong . . . ? Cyril?' She runs over, spilling tea into the carpet. Sonny steps aside to make room for her.

'It's okay, Mum. He's fine now.'

'Cyril? Are you alright?' She puts her hand on Cyril's shoulder, which seems to make him unfold. His back, neck, arms and legs stretch out, sort of like a brand-new butterfly, and he seems taller and not shrunken at all.

'Stop fussing,' he replies. 'Of course I'm alright. Did you bring my wine?'

We're trapped here till lunchtime, when Mum reheats last night's dinner, filling the whole house with the spicy smell of oxtail. It's the only real meal Cyril's likely to have all week. He usually lives on crusty bread, olives, tins of mackerel in tomato sauce and butterscotch mousse. He's never very hungry. He says Mum's cooking is the only thing that excites him. Before he fell ill, he used to make us pancakes stuffed with tinned peaches or fruit cocktail, dusted with icing sugar.

While he was in hospital, Mum popped over to water the plants and feed Brutus, his cat, who got killed by a car in the spring. Now Mum comes most Saturdays, usually in the morning, before the carer's visit. Cyril says Mum's a natural nurse like most Caribbean women. Mum does this pinched thing with her mouth whenever he says this. Dad reckons Cyril would be better off in an old people's home.

'They'll have to carry me out of this house in a box,' Cyril tells us.

Me and Sonny balance on the arms of the sofa while he reads Mum his latest poem, something about the 'moist, yielding cleft of Lo'. He shouts to make himself heard over the sound of horse racing on the telly, which he won't turn off. Mum hasn't been able to get him to change out of his pyjamas, but he's agreed to wrap himself up in a long silky dressing gown. He uses the corner of it to wipe his mouth. As he reads, thin white hairs sway about on his head. I gaze, yawning, through the patio doors out into the garden. There's a wren hopping about like a mouse in the dandelions. It hasn't noticed, but there's a large rat watching from a broken drainpipe. There's still the bright orange of nasturtiums. Wind sends winged sycamore seeds spiralling to the ground.

'So how are you managing?' Cyril's asking Mum. He gives her a look that means he wants to say more but can't because we're in the room.

'Why don't you go outside for a bit,' she suggests to us. 'But please stay in the garden.'

26

'We will,' I reply.

Once outside, me and Sonny run down the long path swatting the poppy seed heads to release showers of tiny black seeds. It's been raining and the stone slabs are slippery with soft green moss. The air makes my face wet. I kick aside piles of yellow-brown leaves, uncovering twisting knots of earthworms and a glossy devil's coach horse beetle.

'Why didn't you help him?' asks Sonny. The damp lays a halo of droplets on his curly hair.

'I dunno,' I say as I wedge the toe of my boot into a water-filled crack in the paving. 'That sound he was making. Made me feel weird.'

'But he could've died.'

I follow Sonny down to the bottom of the garden, where the enormous gunnera leaves have burst through broken panes of glass into the greenhouse. He's right. Cyril could easily have died. He's got a disease that eats away at the insides of his lungs. The tubes in there are getting narrow and sealing his breath up. He's getting worse and worse every day, bent double all the time, spitting and coughing. Mum says he's living on borrowed time.

We climb the small steps leading up from the garden to the riverbank and lean over the gate. Everything's grey and it's hard to tell land from sky. From the opposite bank, cold wind blows off the moor towards us. The river's rising, as it always does this time of year. Soon it will burst its banks and flood the spillway until it can't take any more. Sonny lifts the gate latch, frightening a heron hunting in the rushes. It flaps away on noisy wings. Looking back, I can see the dark shadow of Mum's face close against the glass of the patio door.

'We'd better not risk it,' I say.

The next few days are filled with endless rain. Water drops fall like bombs exploding on the path. Dad's empty plant pots fill and overflow, sending a tidal wave through the garden down to the road. Halloween comes and goes without pumpkin carving, the same as last year. But at least this time it's half term, so we don't have to listen to everyone at school gloating over their pillowcases full of sweets and going on about who wore the scariest costume to the village spooky disco. I know Mum feels guilty about it and although I tell her that now I'm ten, I'm too old for trick or treating, deep down I'm disappointed.

Dad's busy, so I hardly see him. When he's not making deliveries, he's in the garden getting everything ready for the flooding. He hardly talks, but he must feel guilty too, because at dinner he offers to take us to the village bonfire on Sunday evening if it stops raining. He asks Mum if she fancies coming, even though we know she won't want to. She hates going to outside things at night-time.

'This isn't still because of what happened at that wassail, is it?' Dad asks her. It's as though he's forgotten how upset she was. Me and Sonny haven't. That's when Jane Harris got drunk and tried to take Mum's photo with her phone. She told Mum she needed to smile more as no one could see her in the dark.

28

Mum's fork pauses over her roast potatoes. 'Let's not do this now. Okay.'

'Look, I know Jane was out of order, but you know she didn't mean anything by it,' says Dad. 'And anyway. That was years ago. You can't let little things like that stop you doing stuff.' Mum puts down her fork and turns my way.

'Max, have you looked at the book Mr Reid gave you? Remember you need to take it back to school on Monday.'

'Uh-huh,' I reply. It's a book about bird migration routes. I've read it twice already. Dad lowers his head and carries on eating.

When Sunday evening arrives, the rain has eased off, but it's super-windy. I worry the mountain of wood that's been heaped up on the playing field will blow all over the place. Mum goes upstairs with her computer so me and Sonny go with Dad, who makes us stop first in the Bird in Hand for a pint.

'Just something to get me warmed up,' he tells us. 'Won't be long.' But by the time we reach the bonfire it's already been lit and there's a crowd standing around a fold-out table where the church ladies are selling hot chocolate. This year they're raising money to build a disabled toilet at a school in Botswana. Les Pollard is here. He's got a large metal pot filled with mulled cider balanced on a tiny camping stove. Dad heads straight for him.

Fiery embers from the bonfire rise and flicker against the jet-black sky. Lots of the kids from school huddle in groups away from their parents or run about screaming.

'Come on, let's go and check it out,' says Sonny, leading me into the darkness.

'Where you off to?' calls Dad.

'Just over there. Going to see who's here.'

'Okay. Be careful not to get too close.' He means to the fire, which gives off so much heat my forehead sweats inside my hat. Me and Sonny make our way over to where Mason, Evan, Oliver and Daniel from our class are stood with Henry Taylor and some of the older boys. At first, I'm glad to see them, but as we get nearer, I start to change my mind. They're Sonny's friends, really, not mine.

'Maybe we shouldn't leave Dad by himself.'

'He'll be fine. Come on,' Sonny replies, speeding ahead of me. The boys look up at us as we get closer. Sonny grins, not caring that he's leaving me behind. Then, all of a sudden, he's gone, and I stand here alone like an idiot. Evan gives me a *what do you want* look and the others completely ignore me. Sonny's laughing somewhere, but rather than face them, I carry on walking and pretend I'm only heading this way to make a circle round the bonfire. Dad's waiting by the main gate. I spy him downing another mulled cider as I walk my third circle, scuffing up clods of wet grass with my wellies. It's always so easy for Sonny. Everyone at school loves him for being different. They all want to hang out with him.

30

Tess

Slice onion, not too thinly, fry in butter until golden. Rain pours down in slanted sheets against the kitchen window. I hear childlike feet on the landing upstairs, giggles and whispering. Lauryn Hill sings 'When it Hurts so Bad' on the radio. My tears fall on the chopping board. Crush three . . . four cloves of garlic. There's no more fresh ginger. No beef, only venison, a roe deer shot last week on Shepherd's Drove by Les's son Redford. I must see if I can get more goat for curry.

Yet another morning of waking up alone with only a cold space in the bed beside me. Brown the meat . . . wonder if I should've done rabbit instead. Add turmeric, curry powder. No scotch bonnets or pimentos? Mixed herbs will have to do and maybe a pinch of cayenne. There was the sound of him tugging on his boots in the porch.

Where's the veg? Got carrots, quarter of a crown prince, no bell peppers or green beans. There's the last of the curly kale – could just pick off the brown bits. I hear children's footsteps on the stairs, leaping the final step. Thuds in the hallway. Tin of chopped tomatoes. Shall I pad it out with butter beans?

So many unkind words, so many accusations, threats. *I can't stay here.* Chicken stock cube. Rice or potatoes? I've had enough of goddam potatoes. *The Simpsons* is on TV in the living room. There's no point talking about it; he already

31

knows what I think. Tears season the rice water. Lid on, leave to simmer for an hour. More amber flood warnings on the radio.

Sonny

The sweet smell of rain moves through the house. There's a storm coming. It wakes the dead, who yawn and stir inside the soil to wait with dry throats. Out on the moor, the starlings come home to roost. Keep one eye open in case a sparrowhawk takes your head. Did you hear? A chicken farmer in Larkhill killed himself with a shotgun. Shrews shrink into their winter skins. Under the water, brown lily leaves float like submarines. Collared doves fight over winter wheat seeds. Don't forget to close the door to the woodshed. Toads follow the yellow light of the hunter's moon. Mum's planning her escape while Dad hides inside a coffee fog reading the parish newsletter.

It's dimpsy outside. Rain falls into a blue garden. Now the wet days are getting colder, the more Mum talks about moving. She does this every year and, usually, we laugh about it and tell her to stop being silly. Why would we want to move away from here? But not this year. Dad chooses not to hear her and Max acts as though she's speaking to someone else. When she's not thinking about London, she's dreaming about owning a house in Jamaica.

Oh, Sonny. I'd give anything to swap this awful mud for dry red dirt, the sandy kind that stains the soles of your feet. Instead of hemlock, ragwort and deadly nightshade, and those horrible shaggy inkcaps overflowing with slime, we could have butterfly jasmine, bougainvillea and candy-coloured hibiscus petals. Instead of cowering indoors because of this constant drizzle, we could stretch out barelegged beneath a shocking blue sky, a hot sun baking my skin a deeper, darker brown. There'd be no more frost or numb toes swollen with chilblains. No more Raynaud's freezing the third finger of my left hand. No more being left out in the cold. Imagine . . .

Her thoughts come to me in bursts. They slip out of her as she searches in her wardrobe for a thicker jumper. She sighs them out at breakfast over porridge. Listen – she's sprinkling them around the kitchen, like paprika over raw chicken.

Most evenings, when Dad vanishes, she sits staring at adverts for white-gated beachfront houses on her laptop. I sit next to her on the sofa, my arms wrapped tight around her stomach.

'But Mum, you don't know anything about living in Jamaica.'

The only sky she really knows is the smog-grey one that looks down on busy streets filled with red double-decker buses. All she can remember is her old backyard, where she and Aunty Peaches used to play when they were little girls, sucking on cola ice lollies and pestering the ants. Her sugar cane comes peeled and split, £3 a bag in Deptford Market. She brings home her Caribbean treasure from our London trips but moans, in Nana's voice, that her guineps, naseberries, custard apples and spiky June plums are undersized, force-ripened, lacking in flavour.

I wonder. 'But how do you know?'

Mum went to Montego Bay when she was seven and swam in a warm sea in a frilly pink swimming costume. I've seen the pictures in her old photo album. She tells us stories about the farm where Nana grew up, how she roamed the bush with her sisters and brothers eating juicy sweet mangoes and roasting songbirds on sticks. She tells us how they drank milk from their own goats, baked their own bread, grew their own coffee, callaloo, yams and bananas.

'But that's the same as us?' I tell her. We drink milk fresh from the cows at Winslow Farm, bake our own bread, grow our own apples, strawberries, carrots, potatoes and tomatoes, roam the fields, climbing stiles and running through hay meadows. She's forgotten she used to love it here; all she ever wanted was to be surrounded by *bush*, like her grandparents. I remember hearing her say this down the phone to Aunty Peaches. It's the reason she left London in the first place. She loved to tell us about when she met Dad, how he'd lured her away when she finished university. How it hadn't taken much to persuade her. She was supposed to have become an architect and design city skyscrapers. But he told her about the wild flowers, honeysuckle, bees in the apple orchards, the sweet smell of withies, about growing rhubarb and making sparkling elderflower wine. She said it sounded like *The Darling Buds of May*. She used to laugh at this part of the story, and me and Max laughed too, even though we didn't know what she was talking about.

Richard

Sacks of potatoes jiggle in the back of the van. Richard checks they are still tied shut and not spilling out their contents. Rain spots the windscreen and in the wide beam of the van's headlights, he catches the white streak of a low-flying barn owl. It is later than he thought. Tea will be on the table getting cold and Tess will be angry *again*. Really, it would be easier for him to not go home at all – easier for both of them. Dangling off the passenger seat is a large bundle of leaves, spinach, Richard had hoped, but apparently not, according to Janet at the shop. The seed packet had definitely been labelled 'Matador Spinach', but something about the way the leaves grew off the main stalk seemed more like a weed. Still, it smelt and tasted right. He prayed no one would notice, but Janet would not take them, said they would not sell because people do not like anything different. It is a shame for them to go to waste.

Richard tucks the leaves under his arm and dumps a carrier bag of cider bottles inside the porch beside his wet boots. He sniffs – *curry venison* – recognising the smell immediately. Tess, engrossed in front of the stove, does not seem to hear the back door opening. Richard watches her sip at the spoon in her fingers to see if the curry needs anything. Though it is gone seven thirty, the table is not yet laid and the sound of Max chatting to Sonny emanates from the living room.

'Alright?' Richard ventures, readying himself for her rebuff. When there is none, he holds out the leaves. 'These any use to you? Some sort of spinach . . . I think.' It is only when she turns that he notices the bottle of wine beside her on the chopping board – one of the gooseberry batch they brewed quite a few years back. He is shocked, both to see it, thinking they had polished off the lot in pretty much one go, and by the fact Tess is drinking by herself in the early evening.

'It's callaloo. You know that.'

'What?' He looks at her, bewildered. Soft tufts of her afro have escaped the front of her headscarf.

'That . . . in your hand. Callaloo. You've eaten it before. My mum sometimes cooks it. And you had it at Ronnie's. Remember? You said it tasted better than spinach.'

'Oh yeah – callaloo.'

'Where'd you get it?'

'Eh? Oh . . . problem with some of the seeds . . . what are you drinking?'

Rather than being angry, she seems embarrassed as though caught doing something forbidden.

'Ah . . . I was going to do rabbit, but it needed wine. Found this at the back of the pickle cupboard.' She squints at the bottle. 'Wasn't sure it was still good, so I . . . I forgot how strong it is.' She lets out a laugh and quickly covers her mouth with her hand. Richard takes another wine glass from the dresser.

'I haven't forgotten.'

38

They stare at each other until she breaks away to find cutlery and heap steaming rice onto plates. Richard waits for her to settle before sitting down. 'And of course I remember Ronnie's. You kept me dancing for hours.' Tess's lips soften into a bashful smile.

'I did, didn't I?'

'Who's Ronnie?' Max asks, eager to join in.

'It's a place, not a *who*. I'll take you there one day.'

'You will?'

Tess turns her smile on him. 'I promise.' Satisfied, Max eases contentedly back into his seat.

They finish the wine and Tess does not protest when Richard tops up their glasses with cider. He leans in closer as her body relaxes beside him. Her leg, under the table, feels warm against his.

Max's cry wakes Richard at some point in the night, but Tess is already out of bed and covering her nakedness with her dressing gown. Confused, Richard is left with the cooling sensation of where she must have been lying on his chest. Max shouts out again, and there is Tess shushing him back to sleep. Richard rolls over on his pillow, disheartened that the evening is to end with another episode of Max's night terrors. But then, why would this night be any different? When he next opens his eyes, dawn lights a pale blue strip around the curtains. He is alone – Tess never made it back to bed. Richard can tell by the set of her face when she comes down to the kitchen that she is upset. She does not even glance at him, let alone say good morning.

Tess

'Tessa, please don't tell me you're staying down dere?' As usual, my mother's voice is full of anxiety.

'It's fine, Mama. Really,' I tell her, leaning my head out of the open window as the line begins to crackle. It's freezing. Wind and rain blast the desolate wilderness that surrounds this house. With my free hand, I tighten the cord of my dressing gown. I wish I'd bothered to dress properly. Little by little, my standards are slipping. The cold pinches the tips of my fingers as I grip at my phone to stop it from plummeting into the garden below.

'Can't you convince him?' Undeterred, she presses on.

'I don't think so, Mama. It's gone beyond that.'

'Well, you cyaan stay dere. Don't him know dat enough is enough?' she shouts and the repressed patois in her voice leaps out with sudden alacrity. 'Dat place is no good, you hear!'

I remember when I first told her I'd be moving down here, the way she flipped between fury and defeated resignation. She had good reason to be upset. I'd just finished my last semester, had a sought-after internship at an architectural firm waiting for me in Southwark, with the promise of a fully funded Masters when it was over. None of the family was pleased, particularly my sister and all those expectant aunties in Jamaica.

'I know, Mama. But what can I do? He doesn't want to talk about it anymore.' How can I tell her he doesn't want to talk to me at all? How, almost instantly, the tenderness we felt the other night evaporated, burnt up by our relentless quarrelling. All that's left is an urge to run away. 'Jesus wept, child, why your ears so hard? You cyaan stay dere. It's . . .' Mama's voice disappears.

'Mama? Mum? You there?' I push my chest further out of the window, ignoring the pain as the rough wooden sill presses deeper into my stomach. 'Can you hear me?' I ask the silent phone. As if it wasn't already enough, the rain turns to sleet and sends drops of ice drumming down onto my head, wetting up my hair through my headscarf. I'm sick and tired of this constant battle with the phone reception. Even the mobile company, who begrudgingly admits we're too remote for 3G, recommends we get a landline. A landline – another thing that can't be talked about, that's too expensive, seeing as the phone company would need to connect us to the telegraph pole at the end of the road. It feels deliberate. He's in league with this place, both determined to keep me locked away here forever.

I should call Mama back. She'll be trying to reach me from her end, but today, as on most days, it feels too hard. I'm tired of talking. Richard's right, there's nothing left to say. I'm even more tired of crying – I'm not even sure what I'm crying about.

In the kitchen, everything is as it should be – the lunch dishes have been washed and tidied away, the floor mopped, and the Rayburn replenished. A plum cake sits cooling on the counter.

Dinner will be ready within an hour and, right on schedule, the room fills with the soothing scent of roasting chicken and woodsmoke. Thankfully, unlike the rest of the house, it's warm in here. I wipe down the table for the third time today. My fingers move on autopilot while my eyes watch the rain filling up my dreary garden. It's not much to look at, even in summer, just a small narrow patch out of Richard's way where I can grow two rose bushes, one yellow and one peach, some dahlias and a few patches of forget-me-nots. He calls them useless plants that don't bear fruit. When we moved here, he wanted the space for vegetables; the business was taking off and not an inch of soil could be spared. But he relented eventually, bought me a bag of bulbs but then joked they might be shallots. They grew into small orange irises, which cluster brightly along the path. They always remind me of Mama, of the concrete paving in our old backyard and its chaotic assortment of pots and tubs bursting with colour. Now, in my garden, there are only dying stalks protruding through the rising mud.

'Mum, is there anything to eat?' Max's voice calls out from the living room.

'Just an apple, nothing more. Your dinner's nearly ready,' I answer, snapping back my gaze, glad of the interruption. He appears in the doorway, looking more like his father every day – not just his white-boy colours, the floppy, light brown hair, too long now so it hangs in waves past his ears, or the ever-changing blue-grey eyes, but something in the way he stands, in the angle of his head over his shoulders. Sometimes it hurts to look at him. He grabs two apples from the fruit bowl, one for him and one for Sonny.

'How you keeping?' I'm startled by Marge's throaty voice. She's out for her walk, on doctor's orders, although it only extends from her front door as far as our side fence, and then back again into the safety of her overheated kitchen. Her large ruddy face appears as I drag two full recycling boxes down the garden path. The *chink-chink* of bottles is unmistakable. Marge leans on her walker and surveys me with knowing eyes. 'Oh. I'm fine. How are you doing?' I stand up to greet her with what I know is a strained smile.

Marge shoves her walker over to the gate, nearly stumbling over Angus, her grossly overweight Jack Russell, who has stopped to sniff at lumps of horse manure that have fallen in the road.

'Fine, huh? You sure 'bout that?' she asks, her eyes sweeping over the contents of the recycling boxes. 'Thought I heard shouting the other night. Could've been tawnies, though, carrying on in your orchard.'

I pull my smile tighter.

It would be such a relief to confide in her, so easy, but for the years of Mama warning me to 'Never tell dem people your business'. As far as my mother's concerned, no one here can be trusted, Richard included. Although, of all the neighbours, Marge is perhaps the most welcoming and kindest, well, apart from Cyril, of course. She's seen me at my worst, when all I could do was weep onto her cardigan.

'Looks like we're in for a big one this year,' she says, gesturing with a swollen hand to where water pours out of the French drain. 'Has Richard sorted out the house?'

Avoiding the intensity of her gaze, I pick at strips of black paint flaking off the gate. 'You know Richard, he won't worry until the sofa floats away.'

'Ah, you'll be alright. Richard's one of us marsh folk, he knows what he's about.'

One of us *marsh folk*. Yes, he is. He was born in this swamp, only a few steps away in Rose Cottage. And me? The way the people here bang on about belonging, it's like I'm a foreigner – an immigrant.

'And Max? He alright?' Marge continues.

On reflex, I look back at the house and, for a second, I see my son's face peering down from the upstairs window. But it's a school day. Max won't be home for hours.

'Max? Oh, he's okay. You know how he is.'

'Poor lad. He's been through a lot. Hopefully, the counsellor will sort it all out.'

My fingers freeze in their exploration of the gate. The thought of Richard broadcasting our personal troubles makes me feel lonelier than ever.

'Yeah. Hopefully. Look, sorry, Marge, got to dash. Got porridge on the stove,' I tell her with as much brightness as I can muster before I turn away and head back up the garden path.

Max

The river rises and rain hammers on the roof each night. One morning, we wake up to find the moor has turned into a huge lake – our very own Okavango Delta, but without zebras and buffaloes. Finally, the wind's calmed down and small waves roll through the orchard and over the veggie beds onto the back of the house. We all stand upstairs at the landing window watching seagulls swimming above the nettles. I've got my binoculars and my best bird identification book ready, in case something rare turns up. But Dad says I've got to wait. There won't be anything interesting until after the water dries up and leaves behind lots of dead insects.

The flooded riverbank pushes damp into the downstairs walls making white mould grow behind Mum's painting of hibiscus flowers. The whole house smells musty, like dirty laundry mixed with stale bread. Gigantic tiger slugs slither out from invisible cracks between the floorboards and the skirting. They prowl the house when we're asleep, streaking the rugs with slime.

'Oh God. This is awful,' Mum says again and again.

Dad tells her not to worry; our house has been standing here with its backside embedded in the riverbank for more than three hundred years, withstanding more than the occasional flood. Although he also says this could be worse than the big one in 1926, when the only way to escape the village was by boat.

On the other side of the road, the puddles in Hector's field grow and multiply. It's a sign our little row of houses is struggling to hold back the river water. Helicopters hover over us like African black vultures. Our lake is on the six o'clock news. Roger Winslow's on telly too, stood outside the farm complaining about the lack of dredging.

Cyril says he's more worried about running out of wine than about his house flooding. He gives me a pull-out aerial shot from his newspaper. I put it up on my pinboard next to my WWF poster of a Tibetan snow leopard. Our house is a smudge of brown and red, but I recognise the white of Dad's new polytunnel. It arrived a few weeks ago in a gigantic cardboard box. Most of it is still in bits, but part of the cover is up and weighed down with sandbags.

Dad can't do any gardening now the floods have forced him to stay inside the house. We're not used to having him in here all day taking up space on the sofa. I ask him to play draughts, but he says he's too distracted. He's had to call his customers to tell them there'll be no more veggie deliveries until the roads reopen. He left the van in the King's Arms car park at the top of Warren Hill.

Mum hangs out of the upstairs window with her phone talking to Nana who's terrified we're having another disaster. It's not going very well – Mum ends up crying. We even get a call from Grandma and Grandad Hembry in Portugal. They only speak to Dad though, not to us, and want to know about their house they rent out on Withy Grove.

At first the floods don't bother me. The water stretches

out as far as Meare. All the lanes are closed, so there's no school. Me and Sonny sit on top of the stone wall separating us from Barbara next door. Sunlight sparkles on the lake's surface. Mr Reid says that two hundred million years ago the moor used to be a tropical sea with plesiosaurs and ichthyosaurs and ammonites. We can hear geese arriving from Greenland, a train crossing the Woodholt viaduct, Angus barking over at Marge's. Tied to the jetty at the back of Cyril's house is *Bernadette*. She bobs up and down in the current.

After five days, Dad takes up the rugs. They're packed away upstairs with the books from the bottom shelves of the bookcases. He checks outside the house to make sure the drains are clear and free of rats' nests. There are power cuts. Mum leaves candles and a box of matches ready on the upstairs landing just in case. The internet plays up even more than it usually does, and we can't watch our favourite telly programmes. Ellie from school and some of the other people living in the council houses in Salter Close are evacuated in the middle of the night to the village hall. They have to carry all their stuff on their backs like tortoises. Both me and Sonny begin to feel afraid.

'Right, enough of this. Come on. Let's check on Marge,' says Dad. He tells us to put on our wellies and waterproof trousers. We slosh through ankle-deep water up to Willow Cottage, which smells of dog food and sausages. Water's running out through the door that's been left open so Angus can easily get out into the front yard. He whimpers as we

49

come up the path and presses his wet nose against Dad's leg. Like our house, Marge's house is crooked like a squatting toad with its back legs bent into the riverbank. But unlike our house, which Dad made bigger by adding on an extension, the front door in Marge's house opens straight into her kitchen, and there isn't a back door at all.

Something meaty is frying on the stove – a pink something that swims about in hot cooking oil.

'That smells good. What's for breakfast then, Marge?' asks Dad. Marge chuckles.

There are grease stains on the walls. If I press my fingers against them, they come away sticky. Marge, who's as wide as she's tall, leans with one hand on her walker. The other hand uses a spatula to lift thick gammon slices out of the pan. Angus knows they're for him. He waddles in from outside with dribble running from his mouth.

'You still afloat then, Marge?' asks Dad.

'It'll take more than a spot of water to slow me down,' she replies. Sonny laughs. The joke is, Marge is the slowest person we know. It takes her ages to get from one end of her house to the other. She lives downstairs all the time because her legs are too swollen to make it up to her bedroom.

Dad takes the broom and sweeps out the water collecting in the passageway. He has to take up the rubber mats Marge puts down to give Angus something to grip on to. Sweat shines above his eyebrows. As usual the radiators are on full blast. Me and Sonny shake off our coats and settle down to wait beside the kitchen counter. It's piled high with dirty dishes. Our backs press against large jars of syrupy sloe gin and a bowl of medlars. I watch, hungry, as Marge pulls the gammon steaks apart with her fingers. The heat doesn't bother her – she says she's got asbestos hands. Every now and then she pops a piece into her mouth. Angus doesn't want to wait. He starts to bark and tries to climb his feet up Marge's legs, but he's too fat to lift his body off the floor.

'Hush now, 'ere you go,' Marge tells him as she scrapes the meat into his bowl. It's gone in seconds, followed by half a jam doughnut. Marge eats the other half, licking the sugar off her lips.

'Got enough food in?' Dad asks and sticks his head inside the freezer. 'You got a couple of chickens in here, a few packs of sausages and a bag of something, could be pheasant, could be blackberries. There's a loaf or two, tons of veg and plenty of stewed apple.'

'Is that all?' says Marge. 'Well, it'll have to do. I heard there's nothing left in the shop.'

'I can't imagine they've run out already,' Dad replies.

'It's true. The shelves are all empty,' I tell them, pleased I know something they don't. I heard Mason's gran telling Mum yesterday. Marge winks at me and takes a large bag of fruit pastilles out of the drawer. Sonny always chooses the red ones, whereas I like the green ones best. Marge grabs them by the handful, not caring about their colour. She tells us she takes them for her diabetes.

''Ere, help us into the other room,' she says.

We back into the corners of the kitchen so Marge can shuffle herself and her walker out through the narrow passageway. She's wearing men's rigger boots because they're the only things she can squeeze her massive legs into.

'Should've worn my roller skates,' she says, looking down at her feet and laughing. I bring her handbag full of her emergency supplies in case she falls: a second packet of fruit pastilles, her mobile phone, her Piper Alarm and a copy of the *TV Times*. The sitting room is covered in orange and brown swirly wallpaper that matches her cardigan and trousers. The weather forecast is on telly, with lots of red triangles telling us about flood warnings all over the country. We can hear the boiler grunting under the stairs. It takes Marge a long time to sit down, lowering herself slowly onto the sofa. While Dad heads outside to check the gutters, me and Sonny squeeze ourselves in on either side of her. She smells of fried meat.

'So, how's school?' she asks, opening the second packet of sweets.

'Okay, I s'pose.' I don't want to talk about school.

'Those kids still being mean to you?' I nod a little.

'Don't pay any attention. Backwards, the lot of them.' She gives me a hug, squashing my head into her soft belly. Sonny looks at me over the mountain of her body. My eyes are stinging, but I don't want to cry.

'Now, now. No need for that,' says Marge, patting my knees. 'Take a breath. You'll be alright.' For a while we're all quiet, listening to the boiler and Dad whistling in the front yard. 'Come on,' she says eventually, her mouth bulging with fruit pastilles. 'Let's see what's on the other channel.' It's *Judge Rinder*, Marge's favourite. We're only halfway through when Dad shouts it's time to go.

On our way out, we stop to pick the last few blackberries. They're the biggest and tastiest on the whole road. Dad reckons it's because Marge's septic tank is buried underneath them and has never been emptied. He says it's best not to think about it. As we pass the Gables, bramblings chitter in the hedge. Barbara sticks her head out of her kitchen window. It's dark in her house, so I can't see her properly, only her bright pink plastic fingernails curving over the windowsill. She's been spying and knows we've come from Marge's.

'Richard. When are you coming to check on me?' she calls to Dad. She never says *please* or *thank you*.

'That damn woman,' says Dad under his breath. 'Go on. You head back home. It's nearly teatime. Tell your mum I won't be long.' But me and Sonny know he'll take ages. After Barbara, it will be Mr Brewer who needs his drains unblocked or maybe Janice Fisher at the top of the road in the corner house needing Dad to check her internet aerial again. We also know Mum will get cross and have to scrape his cold dinner back into the pan. Dad doesn't even get paid for helping. He says it's good to be neighbourly. Barbara gives us a small wave, but me and Sonny don't wave back. We hate her.

Sonny

Sunlight flashes like lightning on the surface of the water. Between the roots of the crack willows swim golden rudd with copper fins. Listen – there are mice scrabbling under the floorboards, slugs so big they set off the mousetraps. Dad stokes up the fire in the Rayburn. Smoke takes his words and turns them into ash. I brush my fingers over the mould growing around the windowsills. There's the smell of damp. Wet coats are drying on the landing radiator. Badgers climb the hills at Turlough Woods. It's time to rescue the ants! Icing sugar drifts around the kitchen. Quick – stick your tongue out. Mum's making apple drop scones for breakfast.

Rain drowns out their fights and from everywhere there's the sound of running water. During the daytime, it's easier to ignore. It's hidden behind Mum's radio music or the chatter of the telly. But at night it trickles through the walls, turning our tiny house into a boat. When I close my eyes, it feels as though the bricks are tilting, lifting, and I'm floating free to rock gently in the river's current.

Our house is so old. Dad says it's been built and rebuilt, bits knocked in and out, reshaped and added. When no one's looking, the rooms turn themselves into cabins. We're safe in here, in our very own ark, but Mum can't sleep. In the middle of the night, her shadow hangs about by the landing window. Listen – I can hear her sneaking downstairs to the kitchen.

Baking is the only thing that calms her. Cakes and trays of muffins and biscuits tumble out of the oven, too many for us to eat. She worries the water will never stop rising.

'Oh, when will this end?' she thinks aloud. 'I don't know how much more I can take.'

I don't know how to answer her. Dad doesn't either; he's too busy thinking about old floods to see what this one's doing. He hasn't noticed the way the river's creeping up the back of the house and swallowing the broken bricks.

All I want is for things to go back to the way they were, when they laughed, held hands, and hid secret kisses behind their bedroom door. Me and Max would squeeze inside their hugs and guzzle up the warmth. Now there are no more cuddles. My quiet feet follow the rhythm of *silence-shouting-silence* trying to figure out where they've gone.

Richard

It is not yet 5.00 a.m. and still dark outside, a rare quiet time before the house wakes up, when Richard comes as close as he can to something that resembles peace. The rain, petering first into drizzle, has finally stopped. Nursing his second mug of black coffee, he sits at the kitchen table, uncomfortable in sweaty anorak and waders, and only dimly aware of sparrows rousing under the eaves. His thoughts focus on the shock-waves of last night's fight still echoing through the house.

He had been late and tea was ruined, his cold, food-laden plate abandoned on the kitchen counter. Tense, he drank one too many IPAs, but later, when they were alone, he followed her into the living room to try and make amends. On seeing Tess curled on the sofa under one of the boys' fleecy blankets watching *A Place in the Sun*, Richard was floored. She looked so much like Sonny. He floundered before her upturned face, not knowing what to say and settling on what in hindsight had been a stupid suggestion – that it might do Max good to have some father and son time, that maybe he could take him for a quick trip out in *Bernadette*, seeing as the weather was now calm and the moor completely in flood.

The harsh whip of her anger was unbearable as she hurled accusations of his thoughtlessness, his inability to take anything seriously, escalating in strained whispers to his failure, both as a father and, without question, as a husband. Well, those were not her exact words, but how else was Richard to take them? It was clear, she felt nothing for him but bitterness. Not that he had made it easy for her; he was not cut out for heartache or tension. Far easier to sit alone in his shed with an empty stomach and listen to the news on his radio, finding solace in a world in chaos – at least two hundred presumed dead in a landslide in Pakistan, more disruption as heavy rain moves up across the north of England, three children burnt alive in a house fire in Macclesfield – his own worries are nothing in comparison, though the pressure of them threatens to engulf him.

On the table, the standby light on Tess's laptop blinks. Richard stares at it, unseeing, and tries to ignore the constant twitch of his right eyelid; it will soon stop, Dr Frencher told him over a year ago. Normally, Tess took her laptop up to bed, reluctant to sever her lifeline to the *real* world. She used to laugh at his unwillingness to use technology, but he trusts his hands, the soil and common sense to find an answer to most things. When Richard lifts the laptop open, the screen's bright light dances long shadows across the kitchen walls. A pixelated image of a young black woman materialises, incongruous, with one half of her head covered in short fuzz and the other with long straight hair that falls well past her shoulders. Yet another of Tess's YouTube hair videos, this one apparently teaching viewers how to achieve a silky, relaxer-like finish with a hot comb in under thirty minutes. Richard remembers when they first moved into the house and Tess's worry about finding somewhere local to get her hair done. Back then, she wore it in fancy braids, Senegalese twists, she called them. It was like another language. A subdued walk down Combe Leigh High Street confirmed she would have to do her own hair from now on. For a while, she relied on hair videos, trying to learn how to braid and do roller sets, but somewhere along the way she gave up and chopped it all off into a manageable afro. Richard was proud of her practical approach, but dared not say; he knew it was more than her hair she had severed.

There are other windows open. Scrolling through, Richard sees a price list for a new hairdresser in Peckham, a recipe for authentic Jamaican red pea soup, an email to Yvette, an old friend, which Richard passes over – he does not want to know what Tess says about him – and, last, admissions info for a secondary school in New Cross, only a fifteen-minute bus ride from Tess's childhood home in Lewisham.

Richard shuts the laptop and gets to his feet.

Max

After three weeks, the floods dry up. It's taken much longer than we thought it would. Dirty rubbish has been left behind on everyone's driveways. Twists of barbed wire, bits of black plastic from last summer's hay bales, rotten fence posts and even a bright blue pedal car are stranded in the flower beds. There's a fishy, dustbin truck smell that reminds me of when we went crabbing at Exmouth. There's the same scream of seagulls. The neighbourhood starts a clean-up crew and Dad's happy to be busy again.

Les comes over in his tractor. His house is the only one on the wrong side of the river, so always gets it worst. But him and his family are really tough. Dad says that's because they're proper marsh folk. They don't mind wading about in knee-deep, dirty water. All their plug sockets are halfway up the wall so they can still watch telly. Les brings his biggest trailer, ready to carry the rubbish away. He also brings two rabbits, which he leaves hanging on our gate. Later Mum will skin and gut them, cover them in breadcrumbs and fry them like Kentucky Fried Chicken.

Dead badgers look like rolls of muddy carpet chucked by the side of the road. I count six between our house and the pumping station. One's a huge dog badger. Its skull's been squashed flat by passing cars and jackdaws are fighting over its brain. Ballooned rats are fished out of wet sheds and thrown into the river. I hate the thought of them floating along downstream. After breakfast, Mum sends us to let the chickens out to scratch about in the sludge.

It's strange seeing cars on the road again. The village shop's open, but they haven't got any bread. Dad restarts his veggie business, but there's not much to deliver, only knobbly carrots, pumpkins, cabbage and turnips. The apples wrapped in newspaper have gone bad, and so have the sacks of potatoes.

Me and Sonny walk along the squelchy riverbank, picking up bits of shell from battered freshwater mussels. We stuff as many as we can into our coat pockets. Animal tracks are pressed into the soft mud leading down to the water – rats, water voles, mice and a heron.

'Look. What do you reckon made those?' Sonny points at prints that look like they were made by a cat, but much bigger.

'Could be a dog.'

'Nah. There's no way a dog could get past Barbara next door.' He's right, nothing gets past her. Four-legged animals on the riverbank get shot at with an air rifle loaded with Blu Tack. Dad says it's why we can't get a puppy.

The bus is running again, so Mum decides to go into Combe Leigh to get some shopping. We've run out of everything. Dad gets back from his deliveries just as she's leaving.

'Quick,' he says when she's gone. 'Let's take the boat and see what treasures we can find.' I'm not sure I want to go, but it's been ages since Dad wanted to do anything other than gardening. 'Come on. You'll enjoy it. I promise.'

Sonny doesn't want to go. He'd rather stay home and watch us from the riverbank. Knowing him, he'll go straight up to our room, start looking at his fossils and forget all about us.

Me and Dad hurry up the road to Cyril's. We don't bother to knock but go straight into his garden through the side gate and up onto the riverbank to untie *Bernadette*. We're not allowed to take her out when Mum's around. She'd go mad. She's told us not to go anywhere near her, not under any circumstances.

'It'll be fine, Max,' Dad says when I hesitate.

'Are you sure?'

'Yeah. I'm sure,' he tells me.

Cyril's jetty is still underwater. I step onto it slowly and grip the mooring pole with both hands. My boots skid and slide on the wet wood, which wobbles like it's going to tip. I'm scared of slipping. What if I fall off the edge into the blackness? I hold the pole tighter, but Dad unwraps my hands and helps me into the boat. The bottom of *Bernadette* is filled with water, so he bails her out with an old plastic milk carton. Green slime has grown all over the wooden seat and there's only one oar. We never did find the other one.

'You okay?' asks Dad. I nod, but I think I'm going to throw up. Dad pushes us away from the jetty and pulls with the oar, first on this side, then on the other. It slices through the water. The river's quiet. There's no sign of the mallards. Dad takes us across to the other side, then on, over the opposite bank, which is still covered in flood water. Withies scratch like fingernails along the bottom of the boat, and a magpie swoops low over us before disappearing into the willows. Behind us, I can't see Sonny anywhere.

Dad stops paddling once we're over the moor and lets us drift. Grassy mounds rise up out of the water and there's something moving. Small creatures, voles, I think, and tiny shrews are stuck on rafts made of twigs. As we get closer, they scrabble into the boat and climb and tumble and dart about between our legs.

'What are they doing?' I shout, snatching my feet up onto the seat. There are tons of them. I can't decide if I like the feel of them running over my wellies. They squirm about squeaking, all wet brown fur and big black eyes. They're not afraid of us at all, just like those animals in the Galapagos.

'Poor things,' says Dad. 'They must have been stranded out here for days. They're lucky they've lasted this long.' He smiles. 'I remember seeing this when I was about your age. I was out with my dad after the floods.'

'Out with Grandad?' I can't imagine Dad being ten. I can't imagine him sitting in a boat with Grandad Hembry. Dad laughs and I watch his breath puff into the air. I haven't heard him laugh in ages.

'Your grandad said they were vermin and tipped them all out.'

'Tipped them out? But ... but that means they must've ...' I swallow so hard my throat hurts.

'I know,' replies Dad, staring out across the water. 'Your grandad was a hard one. He never did see the point of

64

animals you couldn't milk or eat. But don't worry, we'll drop this lot off somewhere.' He ignores the scurrying and paddles *Bernadette* over the grass to where the river squeezes under Pike Bridge. The water's lower here, or maybe it's the earth that's higher. We stop in a clump of reeds. It's the only bit of bank that stayed dry, so it's spotted with mole hills. As we climb out, our boots sink into the soft earth. Dad's strong enough to tip the boat onto its side so I can shoo the creatures out. They run all over each other before dashing off into the rushes. Sonny will be so upset he missed this.

'I guess we'd best be turning back,' says Dad.

I nod. 'We ought to get home before the bus.'

Dad smiles but his eyes have stopped looking happy.

We head downstream, past the back of John and Edith's at the end of our road. They've got loads of old TVs heaped up in their garden covered over with black tarpaulin. As we get closer to Les's place, we can hear shouting. Dad paddles hard onto the bank and leaps from the boat, which glides through the wet grass after him. I clamber out too and start running. Alan Pollard, Les's brother, is lying on his back in the shallow water. It looks as though he's trying to pull an old wooden gate out of the river.

'Help,' Alan's yelling. 'That you, Les? Get over here and help me. What the . . . ? Bloody hell, hurry up.'

Alan's face is normally red, but today it's grey and he looks terrified. There's duckweed caught in his long, wispy side-burns. The gate's lying half in, half out of the river.

65

'It's me back. I've pulled me bloody back,' he shouts.

''Ere, let's get you on your feet,' Dad says. He changes his voice, so he sounds the same as Alan. He always does this when he's talking to the neighbours. Mum can never understand what they're saying. Alan swears loudly when Dad holds him under the armpits and tries to lift him. It takes four goes before he's upright.

'Hope the gate's worth it,' says Dad.

'Les told me he'd seen it in the river. Thought it too good to waste. No, weren't the gate. Was summat in 'em bushes. Wait . . . there it is! What the bloody hell's that?' Alan moves so suddenly I'm sure he'll fall down again. Dad and I can't see anything, although there's the flash of something that could be a blackbird.

'You been on the cider already?' asks Dad, laughing.

'Was just a nip, for the cold.'

Dad walks over to the hedge and parts the bare hawthorn branches to prove there's nothing in there to be afraid of. Then he helps Alan stagger back towards the house.

'I'm buggered if I don't need me a drop of brandy,' Alan tells us. 'For the shock an all.'

We leave Alan and go back to pull the gate completely out of the water, dragging it over to lean up against the house wall. I don't know how all the Pollard family fit inside this house. There are Pollards all over the village and even more in Woodholt. Dad says they're all related somehow, either by blood or marriage. There are more Pollard headstones in the churchyard than any other name, although there are quite a few Haycocks and Winslows. Oliver at school says that to belong to this village, you have to have more than three generations in the graveyard. That means we belong as well, even though no one here believes it.

'Where have you been?' asks Mum quietly when we walk through the back door. She's crouching in front of the food cupboard stacking tins of coconut milk. She looks small and tired, wrapped up in her fluffy green scarf. Sonny sits watching from the kitchen table. I listen to Dad. He tells her we've been to Cyril's, that he needed help moving his dresser back downstairs, that we got stuck clearing muck and debris out of his greenhouse. I've never heard him lie to Mum before. He says it so quickly, I almost believe him. Mum doesn't say anything. Our clothes are wet and dirty and covered in mud, and my hands are sore from the cold and from pulling at the gate. Mum keeps stacking and doesn't turn to look at us. Dad disappears out the door. She looks up then. We know he won't be back until I'm sent to tell him tea's on the table.

'Go on, Max. Get changed,' Mum says to me, hiding her head inside the cupboard again.

Sonny follows me up to our room. He sits on the end of my bed and fiddles with my pocket microscope. There's wet mud around the tops of his socks. I tell him about the voles and shrews and their twig rafts, about Alan drinking too much and being frightened of a hedge. He's quiet, busy examining the knee of his jeans under the microscope lens. There's a small rip. He fluffs up the edges of it with his finger.

Most likely he's cross because he missed out. He could've come if he'd wanted to, but he says he doesn't like going in *Bernadette*. I hope he's not going to sulk about it all evening. It's only four o'clock, but it's already getting dark.

'I don't know why Dad didn't just tell Mum where we'd been. He could have at least told her the bit about Alan.'

'He knew she'd be furious, that's why,' replies Sonny, looking through the microscope at one of my kingfisher feathers. He turns it over in his hands.

'Do you reckon he lies to her about other things?'

He shrugs. 'Probably.'

Sonny

Dad teaches us how to fry puffball mushrooms in butter. Beech leaves are the last to fall. Listen – it's only clinker rattling down the chimney. There are too many house spiders. Do you see long legs poking out from behind the photo frames? Don't disturb the goldfinch eating seeds on the lemon balm. Woodlice hide under the bookcase. I wipe dust off my coelacanth fossil. Mum's ragga thumps through the house vibrating the cobwebs. Tonight, we're having macaroni cheese with ketchup, and apple and almond crumble with custard for pudding.

The end of autumn brings a freezing fog that appears in the night, hiding everything. When morning comes, it's still so thick I can stare at the sun without squinting. It's a pale yellow hole in the middle of a sheet of grey. I sit on an upside-down flowerpot in Dad's shed watching a garden spider swollen with eggs hurry along its silky thread.

Dad's finished building his new polytunnel. It's grown into a giant white grub at the far end of the garden next to Barbara's wall. No one's been invited inside. Max stays out of its way, knowing there'll be chores if he gets too close. I sneak around it on feathered feet trying to peek through its gossamer doors. Mum won't go near it or Dad's other greenhouse. I'm the only one who helps. I like the feel of dirt between my fingers.

Here inside Dad's shed smells of rust. Tiny beads of condensation drip from the tin roof above our heads. Dad moves seedlings into a cold frame that's being warmed by a small paraffin heater. For each one he writes out a name on a thin white label, then lifts the tiny plants, one by one, from their trays. He holds them between his finger and thumb, gently separating their roots, before burying each of them in their own little pot. Hunger growls inside his belly like a bad-tempered dog. He's not eating, too busy lately to come in for lunch or dinner. He uses an old paintbrush to sweep away the extra soil, spilling it to the shed floor to join the metal filings and sawdust.

An icy wind puffs through gaps between the wooden slats, bringing me far-off voices. Listen – sounds like they're calling me. But it's too cold out there. Here, Dad's closeness warms me. I try to breathe in his heat. There's more grey hair above his ears than there used to be. Even his blue eyes look grey. He moves around the shed as though his boots are too heavy. There are packets of seeds on the worktop: runner beans, beetroot, courgettes, coriander, some saved from last year wrapped in folds of kitchen tissue. When I'm bored, I like to mix them up, turning pumpkins into melons, leeks into onions. I know it's naughty, but Dad says everyone likes a surprise once in a while. Outside, the wind clears away the fog, and through the shed's filthy window I see Mum, waiting by the side of the road for the bus into town. Max stands with her, skidding his boots over the ice.

Today, I choose to stay here with Dad and sniff the coffee

that curls steaming from his flask. I've spent a lot of time in this shed, helping with potting and watering, fixing punctures in our bike tyres. Dad seems calmer. He's whistling a tune I've not heard since I was little. I see he's a chameleon too; here's a different Dad to the angry, silent one who lives inside the house. I brush soil from my feet and watch him get ready for his deliveries. Brussels sprouts are cleaned and trimmed and packed into crates filled with hay, and there are blueish eggs from our chickens. Ice is scraped off in horizontal lines from the van's windscreen. Dark clouds have rolled in, cutting the day short. While Dad struggles with the ignition, I try to blow steam onto the rear-view mirror and press my fingerprints onto it.

In the Bird in Hand, the clock ticks loudly. It sounds like a heartbeat. Brian, the latest landlord, stands in front of the muted telly watching football. Dad takes his pint to his usual corner over by the window. I sit beside him and think of the taste of fizzy, sharp, sweet blackcurrant and soda. Look – my hands are not very clean. I've left smudges on the table.

When me and Max were little, Dad would bring us here after playing in the park, for a bowl of vanilla ice cream crowned with a biscuit wafer. He would shout our order over the ring of men circling the bar and heads would turn to look at us. There'd be chuckles and rude comments. Women would ruffle my curly hair, never Max's, call us 'love', and slip us pound coins when Dad wasn't looking. It's only now I see the anger that crept across Dad's face, hidden by his loud laughter. I'm being quiet; I can pay closer attention. After all, Dad always told us 'Words are just words'. Then, I loved all the fuss and loved listening to our *one-in-a-million* birth story being tossed like chicken feed around the bar.

Today, only an old fat cat sees me sitting here. It's watching me with its milky eyes as it dozes by a hissing fire of wet willow. After a few whispers, Brian lets Dad buy a couple of bottles as takeout. He drinks them in the van, parked underneath the yew tree with the poisonous red berries that grows just inside the churchyard. His phone is ringing, but it's lost somewhere underneath the loose change, foil strips of painkillers and bunches of keys. He ignores it. He's good at ignoring things. We'll sit here for a while, him swallowing his beer, me watching the watery sun sink behind the church weathervane. We do this a lot. Then, usually, it's home again and I leave him to hide inside his shed, but today, I feel something 'ping' inside him, like a tiny seed splitting apart. He glugs the last of his beer and starts up the engine.

Max

Me and Sonny kneel on his bed and look out of our bedroom window at the fields across the road. We're bored. There's been a hard frost, crisping up trees and shaping the mud and grass into sharp white spikes. If we hurry, we can stamp our boots through all that whiteness before anyone else does.

'Come on, Sonny,' I say, quickly pulling a fleecy hoodie on over my pyjamas. We tiptoe onto the landing, so Mum doesn't hear us leaving.

It's chilly in the kitchen. The logs in the wood basket are still speckled with ice and the Rayburn's smoking, which means Dad's about somewhere. We stay silent until we're past his shed, where there's a light on. Everything under our feet crunches. The chickens run across the path flapping themselves warm. We run through the garden, snapping off small icicles hanging along the fence, and cross the quiet road to climb over the gate into Hector's field. The sheep resting under the oak tree scatter. Thin sheets of ice cover the rhynes. We leap over them easily, throwing our arms forward to stop ourselves from slipping. Cold wind finds a way under my clothes. Huge networks of ponds have been left behind by the floods. One has at least ten swans crowded into it, but they're just boring mutes, no whoopers or Bewick's. Here, there's barely any frost and the paths are sloppy with mud. There's the strong smell of mushrooms. I think of Alan Pollard and whatever it was he saw in the bushes. Predators need cover,

73

so we dip down along hedges. Tufts of badger hair cling to the barbed wire. I hear a little owl peeping nearby and the far-off mooing from cows up at the farm. A rabbit shoots across the path, making us grab at each other in fright. We hunt for signs: tracks in the frost, bloody entrails, bits of bone. But all we find are the slotted prints of deer and smelly mink droppings.

'Maybe we should head over that way?' Sonny points to where a trail leads across the boggy field towards a dark clump of trees. They're elm trees, all of them dead with stiff branches wrapped in brambles.

'You don't really think there's something out there, do you?' I ask, ignoring the trail and marching ahead through withered goose grass. Something about those trees frightens me. What if there *is* something out there watching us? What if it's one of those escaped panthers they show on telly? I imagine yellow eyes hidden in the burdock.

Sonny laughs and says I'm crazy. 'Well, I ain't afraid of no puma!'

'Panther,' I correct him. It irritates me when he does this because we both watch the same nature programmes.

'Panther puma, puma panther,' he sings. 'Pantherpuma, pumapanther.' He's trying to wind me up, but I smile anyway.

'Pantherpuma pumapanther,' I join in. The shadows fade as we both stumble about laughing. But suddenly, a great black shape tears through the hedge a few feet away. I choke on my laughter. Fear feels electric under my skin. The beast is followed by a lady we've never seen before in a furry hat

74

and pink wellies. She gives us the same look Mum does when we're being silly.

'Come on, Walter,' she shouts to her fat black lab as she and her dog head across the field.

'Pumapantherpantherpuma,' shouts Sonny after her. As she turns back to look at us, we burst out laughing again and run off as fast as we can. We don't make it very far, only to Shepherd's Drove. My toes are numb with cold, plus I'm starving.

The creature in the hedge is all I can think about. What if it's real? I think up traps and snares during assembly at school. Mr Reid says he'll have to speak to Mum if I don't make more of an effort to concentrate. I tell him about me and Sonny, about the paw prints we found on the riverbank, about Alan, and the yellow eyes watching through the leaves. He asks me to stay in at break time to talk about it properly.

Tess

School calls, asking for yet another meeting. I want Richard to come with me, but at pickup time he's nowhere to be found. So I go alone on potholed roads, taking the long way round to avoid sodden fields. Soft mud that's accumulated in deep troughs along the verge wrenches at my wellies. The weather has changed – heavy rain exchanged for biting cold. There's little daylight left. Cars on the school run race through leftover puddles, spraying dirty water up my legs. Amy drives past on her way home with Mason, going so fast she doesn't see me recoiling inside the dark hood of my coat.

I'm late, so thankfully, by the time I arrive, the playground's empty and I'm spared the usual awkward glances. There's the lonely sound of my boots stomping across the tarmac to where lights are still on in the office. I falter at the door. *Why isn't Richard here?* Mrs Welsh, the receptionist, handbag and coat balanced on her arm, looks up as I enter.

'Ah, Tessa. Good. Mr Reid is waiting for you.' She ushers me up the narrow stairs, past charcoal sketches of Chinese terracotta soldiers. There's one by Sonny, his name spelt out at the bottom in careful, neat pen. Black fingerprints smudge the edges of the paper, whorls, rings and delicate concentric loops. I long to press my own fingers onto them and feel for his presence like a blind man searching for meaning in braille.

Through the door's glass panel, I catch sight of Max sitting sprawled on a large beanbag in the book corner, reading. He smiles on seeing me, unperturbed. Inside the starkly lit classroom, once again, Mr Reid beckons for me to sit opposite him on one of the uncomfortable, too-small students' chairs, a page of typed notes ready in his hands.

Sonny

As the wind brushes past, the plastic walls of the polytunnel whisper their secrets. They promise warmth, happiness, protection from the cold. Dad hears them echo inside his glass cider bottle. Thoughts of winter vegetables and fussy customers are pushed aside. There's no time to sit inside the shed reading the newspaper. Don't worry, I tell him, I'll help. I can fetch the wheelbarrow, find the secateurs, the good ones with the red handles, not the old green ones that are stiff with rust. I can collect the wobbly plastic towers of seed pots from under the garden sink. We can't rest. Can't you see? Angry words are weeds. I watch them grow and spread through the house like couch grass. While Dad daydreams, Mum takes the broom and sweeps them out the front door. I must hold on tight, else she'll blow away with the dust.

Max

Sonny's ignoring me today. He's hanging about in the kitchen with Mum while she gets tea ready. It's usually me in there, getting under her feet while she tries to get things done. But lately, he's always there, sniffing at the Dutch pot, hovering around and taking up her attention. Over the buzz of the radio, I hear her talking to him about potatoes.

'What do you think?' she's asking. 'Mash or chips?'

I could go and find Dad, but he's been gone all day. I know he can't still be out dropping off veg. Maybe he's gone to the pub and got stuck talking to Brian. He must've forgotten the time, or is too busy playing pool or darts. I'm not sure. Somehow this feels different.

Earlier this morning, I spied him in the garden walking around in small circles while talking on his phone. Normally he can never find his mobile as it gets chucked into the footwell of the van or is lost somewhere in his shed until Mum forces him to look for it and tells him to stop being unreliable. But this week, his mobile has rung all the time. It rings from the back pocket of his jeans, ready to be answered in a flash. It must be customers, but I don't know why so many would be calling. Maybe Dad got their orders mixed up, but when I ask him about it, he tells me to mind my own beeswax. He rushes off to shuffle about by the compost heap, where I can't hear what he's saying.

Thinking about Dad makes my head hurt. I stare at myself

in the mirror on Mum's wooden chest of drawers, smoothing my messy hair behind my ears. I wish it was curly, like Sonny's. It's losing its golden colour. I've got my winter coat on according to Mum. What she means is I don't look brown at all. Not like Sonny, who's still toasty. With him there's no confusion.

For me, everything's confusing, not just the colour of my skin. There's the silence, then the shouting, Dad ignoring us, Mum crying she wants to move back to London or run away to Jamaica. She only says this late in the evening when she thinks we're sleeping. During the daytime she acts like everything's normal.

I grab my binoculars from the shelf above my bed and point them through the landing window. I look out across the moor to where there's a long, narrow stretch of water. It's a slash of bright sunset colours against the shadowy grass. My eyes run along its edge hoping to see glossy ibis, black-tailed godwits, greenshanks, maybe even red-beaked oyster catchers or shovelers. But all I can spot are a few wading terns, some lapwings and a cormorant spreading its wings out to dry. Next door, Barbara's trying to tip water out of her wheelie bin onto the riverbank. It's too heavy for her, so her skinny stick arms drag it back to its little cubby hole beside the house. I can hear her swearing from all the way up here. Her back is so twisted, she can't look at anything but her boots. I can't work out how she sees where she's going. Mum says she's got something called scoliosis. But Barbara says that's nonsense, there's nothing wrong with her, she knackered her back looking after her husband in his final days. She tells everyone he was a huge man, and there'd been too much lifting and turning. But Marge reckons Barbara's lying, that she slowly poisoned him after she found out he was having an affair.

Daniel's dad had an affair, with the tall woman with ginger hair who used to work at the feed mills. Now him and Daniel's mum are divorced, and he's moved into a flat by the big play park in Combe Leigh. Daniel goes to stay with him every other weekend and in the school holidays. He thinks it's great because now he has two bedrooms and his dad buys him loads of cool stuff to make up for it. I can't believe he got an electric scooter for his birthday, when I don't even have a regular one. It must be really weird though, your mum and dad living in different houses. Inside my tummy feels sick as though there's a rock in there or something.

We're sitting down for tea when the van finally parks outside the gate. Dad doesn't come in. Instead, we hear his footsteps heading straight through the garden and behind the house towards the polytunnel. Mum stops eating. She breathes really loudly, then stands up, takes her plate over to the bin and chucks her chips away.

'Tell your dad his dinner's in the warming drawer,' she says as she disappears into the living room. We hear her switch the telly on. Me and Sonny look at each other, too nervous to say anything.

'You alright in here?' Dad asks when he finally comes in through the back door. Cold night-time air fills the kitchen.

He washes his hands at the sink, drying them on Mum's favourite tea towel.

'Dad, where have you been?' I ask him. He doesn't seem drunk. His face is its normal colour and there's no cider or beer smell coming off him. If anything, he looks happier than usual.

'Oh, nowhere important. Had to sort out a new order of manure. There's a bloke in Larkhill that's offered to bring over a trailer load when he's next passing.'

'It took ages,' I complain, filling my mouth with peas.

'Suppose it did. These things do sometimes. Can't be helped.' I glance up from my plate, but his face is turned away so I can't see his eyes.

'Your tea's in the Rayburn,' I tell him, but he knows that and has already stooped down to fetch it.

Mum surprises us when she comes up to say goodnight, asking if we'd like a bedtime story. I can't remember the last time we had one. Not since we got old enough to read books by ourselves. Her and Dad used to shoo us up the stairs, so they could cuddle in peace on the sofa. Mum sits on the end of Sonny's bed, her fingers gently stroking the duvet.

'What do you fancy?' she asks eventually.

'Can we have The Water-Babies?' asks Sonny.

'The Water-Babies,' I echo.

'Really?' Mum hesitates. We know it's for kids, but it's still one of our favourites. We love hearing about Tom and the evil Mr Grimes. Anyway, most of our other old books have gone to the charity shop. 'Okay,' she says eventually. Cooking smells float down from her jumper as she reaches up her arms to get the book off Sonny's shelf. I think of all those good chips in the bin. I don't think Dad's seen her yet. They've been avoiding each other, hiding in different rooms. I guess he's gone back outside.

As Mum reads, she keeps blowing her nose on a tissue she keeps up her sleeve. But that doesn't spoil the story. I'm little again and loving this feeling. Her voice sinks into me, making me sleepy. Sonny's silent, his face squished against his pillow. He might be sleeping. I try to stay awake so I can see the pictures. Mum puts her tissue down and turns the book my way whenever she comes to one. The last thing I remember seeing is Tom, completely covered in soot, frightened by the face looking back at him in the mirror.

Tess

When I was a child, Mama told me duppies dwell in the roots of cotton trees. Here, there is only the alder, who Richard calls swamp dweller, King of the Water. The grassy border between the orchard and the riverbank is carpeted in his brittle orange leaves. They crackle beneath my boots as I stagger back to the house under the weight of a full log basket. Not long, I tell myself; soon this hardship will be over. No more waking up to a cold house – a flick of a switch and I'll be warm. No doubt I sound ungrateful. Isn't the charming chocolate-box cottage complete with open fires the dream? But then I only have myself to blame. Be careful what you wish for, they say. Although maybe it's all the fault of those books; too much Enid Blyton can't be good for anyone. It's so easy to be lured in by what seems the perfect fantasy, when really it's nothing but a bad dream.

Chicken merry, hawk deh near.

Yes, Mama, you were right. At least she hasn't gone as far as to say 'I told you so.'

Max

Last night I dreamt I was swimming. I was a water-baby, legs and arms twisting, diving between wide feathered leaves. Maybe it was a giant kelp forest. The water was so clear. I saw small fish darting by. I saw a pike exploding to the surface, a bullet of silver and green. Sonny swam beside me. Stroke for stroke, we glided. Until darkness spilt. Through the murk, his legs shot him forwards. Reeds clung and pulled, reaching out greedy fingers. I struggled to keep up, but he was gone. I called after him. Bubbles burst between my lips.

I'm tired all day. Mr Reid's telling us something about Stephenson's Rocket, but the words won't stay in my head. Even the writing on the whiteboard's blurry. I can't stop yawning, so after break time he lets me sit on one of the beanbags in the book corner and look at the animal encyclopedias. I have this uncomfortable feeling, like something bad is happening, but I don't know what it is. Sonny says he can feel it too. Things aren't how they used to be. It's like they hate each other.

This morning at breakfast, there was silence, and when they did speak, they were extra polite. Dad said he had to go and see a man about a rotavator, that the van would be full of gear, so we'd have to walk home from school. He told Mum not to bother with a plate, he'd grab some bread and cheese when he got back. Mum didn't say anything, just handed out gloves and hats.

She's waiting by the gate when we finish school, with only her eyes peeking over her scarf. Mason's mum is giving her a hug, but Mum shakes her off when she sees us coming. We take the road, rather than cutting across the fields. But it's already dark by the time we reach the houses at the edge of the village and Mum has to use the light on her phone as a torch.

'I'll never get used to there being no street lights here,' she says.

'If there were street lights, we couldn't see the stars,' I tell her. We look up. Me and Sonny know where to find Orion's Belt and the saucepan ones, though we forget what they're called, and Cyril showed us how to spot the fuzzy Seven Sisters. He said they're there, but you can't see them if you look directly at them. They hide in plain sight at the edges of your eyes.

'I think I've had enough of stars,' Mum replies. I've left my gloves behind at school, so I bury one hand in hers and stuff the other into my coat pocket. On the radio they said it's going to be the coldest winter in a decade. My school shoes slip on ice, making me grip her tighter. We forgot to pack wellies.

'I can't believe your dad's disappeared again.'

She's right; it's not like him to leave us to walk home by ourselves, not at this time of year.

There's no one else about, only a few cars, other mums rushing home after the school run. Mum used to have her own car, a small red one with a chipped windscreen, but it stopped working and there wasn't enough money to fix it or buy a new one. We reach the corner house and turn onto our road, passing the quiet yard at the farm. Bright lights are on in the barn. Once we leave them behind, the hedges seem even blacker. Mum's phone battery dies.

'It's okay,' I tell her. 'We know the way.' It's freezing and my cheeks are stinging. There are no houses on this bit of the road, just fields on both sides, so it feels massive and empty. It's like the whole world's gone indoors. The only sound is of us breathing. As we walk by the withy beds, something big crashes in the hedge. We stop. My heart's thumping.

'It's probably a fox or a badger. Everything sounds louder at night,' says Mum. These are Dad's words, but they're easier to believe when he says them.

'Pumapanther,' Sonny sings quietly, but now it isn't nearly so funny. We hurry, almost jogging till we see the lit-up windows at Cyril's house.

Tonight, they have the biggest argument ever. It's awful. Mum's screaming, not caring if we can hear. Sonny and I whisper to each other in our bedroom. We're wearing our camo pyjamas and are squeezed like sardines into my bed. He feels warm beside me and smells of grass.

'What d'you think's going on?' I ask him. Sonny shrugs, wriggling his feet out of the bottom of the duvet. 'Is it something to do with us?'

'Don't think so. But I guess it could be something to do with you and the fact that you're a weirdo,' he says, laughing.

'If I'm a weirdo, what does that make you?' I ask, digging my elbow hard into his chest. He thumps me in reply, and I thump back, thrashing about hitting and punching and kicking until a glass of milk gets knocked off the beside table and smashes against the wall. Immediately, the shouting downstairs stops.

Winter

Tess

The coach lets us off at Victoria Station and, in an instant, we're overwhelmed. Above, the wide-open sky has shrunk into a remote pewter strip. Although I'm a native, this crush comes as a shock. I turn back to look for Sonny, but then I remember – of course, this time it's just me and Max. I stall, hypnotised, as people swarm around us, by the red flare of buses jostling with gleaming black cabs, the screech of brakes, cyclists bright in lurid high-vis vests, shouts, swearing, laughter, the clash of so many different voices. Max grasps tightly at my arm, afraid of losing me in the crowd. *I've forgotten why I'm here.* But then a switch turns on inside me and I'm back, breathing hard at the fume-filled air, sidestepping my way through the throng like it's a well-rehearsed dance.

Christmas lights sparkle on the shopfronts – so this is what festive looks like?

I try not to think of the house I've left behind, empty of celebration. Richard didn't even blink when I told him I was leaving for a few days. Maybe I'd hoped for surprise, resistance, disappointment, anything, but he merely nodded as though he didn't care either way.

Outside the Tube station, a man with long greying locs plays Whitney's 'Where Do Broken Hearts Go' on a tarnished saxophone. I give Max a pound coin to drop into his crumpled hat. My son's blue eyes are wide, and the cold

95

brings a flush of colour to his pale cheeks. As we head down on the escalators, we both stare like tourists at adverts streaming past – a new sushi chain, sleek hot yoga studios, art exhibitions and West End musicals – a far cry from the village plant sale and am-dram productions. On the platform, Max cranes his neck to look down on the tracks in search of Tube mice.

'Mum. Mum. Did you know they've become their own species now?' he informs me.

'Really? No, I didn't know that.' I shake my head, only half listening.

'It's because they've spent so much time in this new habitat that they're different from all the other brown mice. You know? The ones that live above ground. I wonder if they can still see or if they've gone blind like cave salamanders.'

I let him prattle on while my thoughts drift along with the warm, dry air pushing through the Tube tunnel.

I haven't told Mama the real reason for my visit: to tell her I've finally come to my senses. Though it occurs to me – do I need to ask for her permission? Surely not. It's *my* room, after all, in *my* family home, and it's not too far from the school in New Cross. The perfect new start.

As always, the Tube is packed. Instinctively my sight turns inwards to shut out the curious glances that often come my way when I'm alone with Max. For his sake, and my sanity, I've learnt to ignore them. Instead, I let my eyes wander through the carriage to a woman leaning against the handrail opposite, who is similar to me in nearly every way – same skin tone, height, possibly weight, except . . . I look at her with interest. *Or is it envy?* Note her skilfully contoured face, the sculpted eyebrows, French manicured nails, the expensive leather handbag and woollen coat. Her relaxed shoulder-length hair shines with a glossy blackness that matches her kitten-heeled patent shoes. Max smiles at her, but she doesn't smile back. For a second, her eyes meet mine, then they flick to Max and back to me again before sweeping away. Dried mud encrusts the sides of my old boots and streaks up the legs of my jeans, and there are unidentifiable stains on my waterproof jacket that no amount of presoaking will erase. Clusters of sticky burrs cling to the fringes of my scarf. While her head is turned, I try to tug them off, but I'm not fast enough; her gaze returns, and she watches as I cram them into my pocket. Max looks at me with approval. We both know you shouldn't throw sticky burrs away – they're tenacious weeds that could put down roots anywhere. I smile at him, trying not to focus on his dirty trainers.

Post-Christmas shoppers filter down from the plastic glamour of Oxford Street to the platforms at Charing Cross Station. We join the stampede as it surges along and switch onto an overground train heading south of the river, crammed among a kaleidoscope of ethnicities. Whenever I'm back, it strikes me – no one here realises how rare and valuable this mixture is. Exhausted, Max slumps heavily in his seat. Over his head, a woman – who could be Filipino I guess, an au pair maybe, who seems to be sitting with two neat blond children – makes a show of looking first at him and then at me, then

97

she rolls her tired eyes as if in sympathy. It takes a second for the penny to drop – of course, she thinks I'm his nanny. *I'm sure it's what they all think.* Something inside me flinches.

Next, we take a bus, with its littered floor sticky with dirty tissues, newspapers, food wrappers, globules of spit and greasy fried chicken carcasses. We climb the stairs and collapse into the seats right at the front and stare out at the red blur of brake lights. By the time I get us home, it feels like we've journeyed across continents.

Sonny

Can you hear the cold sound of winter approaching? The house fills with voices that shriek like the wind. Sunlight sleeps through days crowded with darkness. Mind how you go – ice has polished the garden path. There's a mum-shaped hole at the centre of the universe. No one's here but wild geese. Dad's world shrinks to the size of his shed, where I try to show him the peacock butterflies hibernating under the windowsill. All he sees are seeds waiting to be planted, bills piling higher and higher, and the mum-shaped hole. But we mustn't moan. If we're quiet, we'll soon hear 'Auld Lang Syne' being sung in the village square. Outside the King's Arms, the Black Knight is killed by St George. Where's the doctor to bring him back to life? Let's warm our toes and stare at the faces in the fire. Old men talk of roasted badger hams and scrumpy warmed with ginger.

Tess

Mama's frying fish. The burn of scotch bonnets stings inside our nostrils the moment I turn my key in the front door.

'*Tessa*? You finally here? I thought you got lost.' She comes flying down the passageway to greet me. Flour coats her hair, ageing her.

'Yes, Mama. I know it's late. It was such a long journey.' My words fall out in a rush.

'Never mind. Never mind. It's okay. You here now.'

I allow myself to be pulled into her arms, where I let out a breath I've been holding on to for far too long.

Finally, she sees Max hidden in the doorway behind me.

'Max . . . let me look at you. You grown so tall. Boy, you take everyting from your father, don't you?' She says this every time she sees him. 'Come. Shut the door, don't let in the cold.'

We follow her past the sitting room, with our leather sofa, loud TV and our old plastic Christmas tree smothered in tinsel, into the stuffy kitchen, where Peaches stands at the counter slicing hard-dough bread. Her hair is tightly braided back away from her face into small, neat plaits that hang all the way down to her bottom. She looks younger than thirty-seven, much younger than me. No one would guess she's three years older.

'Hey, Sis. You okay?' She puts down her knife, then comes and hugs me hard. 'What took you so long? Please don't tell me you took a coach again.'

'Peaches. I've just walked through the door and already you're starting on me. You know the coach is much cheaper.'

'But I'd have bought train tickets if you'd asked. You'd have been here hours ago!' She pushes me away from her so she can glare down, exploiting her extra couple of inches. 'Tessa, why do you always make your life harder than it needs to be?' She knows I can see through her big-sister bossiness to the protectiveness underneath.

'Well, we're here now. No Tayo?' I ask. Peaches narrows her eyes and returns to slicing the bread.

'No. His turn to be on call. He had Christmas and Boxing Day off. Like he doesn't already do more than his share.'

Max, still wrapped up for the cold, fidgets in the sudden heat of the kitchen. Without Sonny by his side, he seems so . . . misplaced.

'Where's Nathan?' he asks, with what I can tell is trepidation.

Peaches gestures towards the ceiling. 'Upstairs.'

'Max. Come. Give me your coat. Go up and find him?' says Mama, who takes his coat and hangs it with mine in the cupboard under the stairs, where we keep the bottles of bleach and vacuum cleaner. Max gives me a pleading look.

'Go on,' I whisper. He slopes off, leaving me to pray that Nathan goes easier on him this time.

'Girl! What happened to your head?' Peaches demands as though she's only just seeing me. She wipes butter from her hands with a piece of kitchen tissue and reaches over to scrunch at my hair.

I jerk myself away. 'I know it looks bad. I don't know what to do with it.'

'What do you mean? I told you last time. Get it relaxed. It'll be easier. Stop worrying about whether it's *unnatural* or not. Relax it yourself and don't leave it on for long. Take a load of box kits back with you,' she replies, like it's the simplest thing in the world.

'I told you. I can't use them. They're not compatible with the biodigester.'

'The bio what?' She still thinks I'm messing with her.

'Biodigester. Septic tank. It doesn't like chemicals.'

Peaches laughs and looks appalled at me as if I'm speaking in tongues.

In the chipped old blue serving dish, Mama lines up red snappers that have been fried until their tails are crispy and stiff. Remembering that I can't take heat the way I used to, she scrapes the scotch bonnets to one side, leaving the rings of sweet onions, then orders me to wash my hands. She tuts at the chewed state of my fingernails. It's always been my job to make the coleslaw. I retrieve the grater from among the pans in the cupboard under the sink. Carrots and cabbage live on the rusty vegetable carousel pushed into the far corner of the counter next to the salad cream, Maggi, malt vinegar and hot pepper sauce. Net bags of garlic still hang from various hooks, along with dried bunches of thyme from the pot in the garden. As I place a bowl on the counter, my fingers search for where the Formica has bubbled and burst into tarry rings under years of scalding mugs and Mama's hot Dutch pot.

Peaches and I work side by side and while I grate the carrots into long, thin shreds, I feel myself slide seamlessly back into the presence of this house. Mama makes me a hot cup of Milo. She rubs my shoulders as she's passing and tucks in the label of my jumper, which must have been poking out since I got dressed this morning.

Max

Mum's old house hasn't changed since she was small. There's soft carpet everywhere instead of hard floorboards. On the walls are lots of paintings, mostly of jet-black women in bright, colourful clothes who look like they're dancing. In Nana's bedroom, there are a few in swirly gold frames like the ones in the Combe Leigh antiques market showing green hills and fields, and either sheep or cows or pigs. Nana says they relax her, so I can't understand why she won't come and see the real thing. I tell her about the sheep that live opposite our house in Hector's field, but she just says 'That's nice, dear'. As well as paintings, Nana has tons of ornaments. She used to collect them, and people kept giving them to her as presents. White and blue china people sit on shelves holding lambs or fish or drinking from tiny china teacups. When we were little, me and Sonny used to take them down to look at them. My favourite one is still the large glass lionfish on the coffee table. Above the electric fire in the sitting room are photos of Grandad. He looks sort of like Mum and Sonny. Mum says she can still see him in the green leather armchair sipping rum and milk, and reading his newspaper.

When it's dark, foxes bark outside in the garden. Dad says there are more foxes living here than there are at home. I guess they must like the city as much as Mum does. In her old bedroom there's a small fold-out bed waiting for me.

While dinner's cooking, I look through Mum's old books on the bookshelf. We've most of them at our house: *George's Marvellous Medicine, Brambly Hedge, The Children of Green Knowe, Stig of the Dump,* and *The Secret Seven.* It's funny knowing Mum reads us the same stuff she read when she was little. There's also a 1998 calendar on the wall with photos of endangered animals – December's snow leopard is just like my WWF poster. Bored, I fiddle with dusty beads, buttons, necklaces and broken earrings. Her old knick-knacks, she calls them. I don't know why she doesn't throw them away. It's not like she needs them anymore.

We're only here for a few days, but I'm ready to go home now. Nathan is being an idiot as usual. He keeps calling me the *albino.* When Dad calls to check if we've arrived safely, he tells me to ignore it, that Nathan's only showing off. I guess. Sometimes he can be nice. Like one time, he gave me a fake copy of *Call of Duty* even though it's too old for me and I don't have anything at home to play it on. Everything feels weird without Sonny. I'm still upset he had to stay behind, even though this time is my turn. He thinks Nathan's ace. Maybe it's good he didn't come, because last time, they both went off without me, and Aunty Peaches wouldn't stop going on about how Sonny was so handsome.

Tess

Both boys come down for dinner; Nathan, the rapster teenager in a man-sized burgundy tracksuit and shockingly white
trainers. He's gone and got himself a grown-up barbershop
fade and had his high-top pulled into tiny twists. The hint of
a moustache shadows his top lip. Beside him, Max looks
washed out, insubstantial somehow, and strained. His eyes
are over-bright as though he's been crying. Keeping my face
neutral, I beckon for him to come and sit by me, so I can
squeeze his hand under the table.

'Hi, Aunty,' says Nathan, coming to give me a kiss on the
cheek. He pulls out a chair and sits with his long legs spread
out on either side.

'Hi yourself,' I tell him. 'So how you been keeping?'

'Everything's cool.'

'And how's school?'

'Fine. It's school, innit,' he says, shrugging his shoulders
and flicking out his phone.

'Put that away. You know it's not allowed at the table,'
Peaches tells him before turning to me with a broad smile on
her face. 'Don't let this boy fool you,' she says, digging at him
with her elbow. 'Go on. Tell Aunty your good news.'

'What good news?' I ask. Nathan perches his phone by the
side of his plate.

'Ain't nothing much,' he says.

'What do you mean, it *ain't nothing much*!' Peaches

screeches as she leaps up from her chair. 'Can you believe it? All the hours I spent nagging this boy to look at his books have finally paid off. He got a Year 9 scholarship! He was first on the reserve list. Starts All Saints next September.'

'Yes! I knew you'd get it.' I pull him into a hug.

'It's no biggie,' he replies, but I can see from his face that it is and for a moment he transforms back into the hopeful little boy he's grown out of.

'Course it is! You worked so hard for this. Don't forget that,' I tell him.

'Well, what choice did I have?' he replies, straightening himself back into his chair. 'True say, we don't all have white privilege.' He casts a sidelong glance past me at Max. Through the dining-room wall comes the murmur of the television – sounds like a soap, *Coronation Street*, perhaps, or *Emmerdale*.

'Don't start with dat nonsense again,' warns Mama. She taps him on the head with her fork.

'Oi, Nana, stop that. You're messing up my hair. I ain't said nothing that didn't need saying.' Nathan laughs but has the decency to look sheepish. Beside me, Max stares at his plate. Mama eyes him before pushing herself to her feet and disappearing back into the kitchen. She returns with a dish covered in foil, which she peels back to reveal layers of golden saltfish fritters.

'Max. See what me make for you? I know these your favourite,' she tells him. Max looks into the dish and then up at Mama.

'Thanks, Nana, but they're Sonny's favourites, not mine. I'm the one that likes the sugary dumpling things.'

At the mention of Sonny's name, Mama's face looks pained, as though years of tiredness trapped behind her skin have finally struggled to the surface. I know what she's feeling, what she always feels whenever anyone talks about her beloved grandchild who she says is the image of my father when he was younger. My heart goes out to her; the fritters were supposed to be a peace offering.

'So, Tessa, how are things really?' Peaches, astute as ever, deflects the attention onto me.

Conscious of Max, I shake my head. 'We're all fine. The flooding is over so it's pretty much life as normal.'

'Yeah, as if life down there could ever be normal,' Nathan scoffs, his eyes fixed once again on his phone. I ignore him and try to bring some lightness to the conversation.

'Well, I can always come here if I *need* a culture fix,' I say with an abrupt laugh. 'In fact, I was . . .' Peaches and Mama exchange a look that makes me stop mid-sentence. I know what they're thinking – I'm a fool who should never have moved so far away in the first place.

Max

The Return of the Jedi is on telly this afternoon. I really want to watch it, but Aunty Peaches is taking me and Mum out, her treat, seeing as we missed Christmas dinner. Even worse, I've just realised I'm going to miss the New Year's Eve fireworks on the playing field this evening. Sonny will get to see them without me.

Nana puts leftover fried fish back inside the fridge, saying, 'Why are you going out in this cold when there's plenty needs eating here?' She looks over at Mum, who's all dressed up in a green sparkly jumper and Aunty Peaches' high-heeled shoes. 'Fine. But don't stay too long. I don't see you enough as it is.'

Nathan doesn't answer when Mum calls up to him. He's probably got his headphones on, listening to music.

'Jus' leave him,' says Nana as she takes our coats and scarves out of the understairs cupboard.

When we get inside Aunty Peaches' car, Mum pulls down the flap that protects your eyes from the sun. There's a little mirror there, which she looks at while making an *O* shape with her mouth and covering her lips with reddish lipstick. She never wears lipstick at home, says there's no point – who's there to look pretty for? It makes her look younger. She acts younger too, laughing and talking about people she and Aunty Peaches used to know at school. They talk non-stop, while Aunty Peaches takes us to a part of London I don't remember, though Mum's sure I've been here before. We're walled in by traffic, and pigeons are the only birds I can see in the sky.

'Oh no, what a shame!' says Mum.

'What's a shame?' asks Aunty Peaches. She drives too close to the car in front of us.

'My bakery's gone. You know the one? The *bakery*! The one we used to go to after netball.'

We all look. Mum's bakery has turned into a shop with flashing disco lights selling mobile-phone accessories.

'Peaches – oh my God! Isn't that the club we used to go to? Ah . . . what was it called? Shine something . . .' Mum points to an old brick building, where the doors and windows are covered with wooden boards. Someone has drawn graffiti all over them.

'Which one? Oh there – that was Moonshine.'

'Moonshine. That's it! Wow, I miss that place. We used to dance all night.'

'*All night*,' Aunty Peaches sings. 'Yeah. We did. Remember that time we missed the night bus home and Dad was waiting up for us? Man, he was furious.'

'Oh my God. Yes. That was *your* fault. And then Mama confiscated my white catsuit and threw it in the bin.

'Ahh . . . your white catsuit. I remember. Well, that outfit was dangerous. All those boys . . . all those flashing lighters.' They laugh like they've forgotten I'm in the car.

'Mum? Where are we going?' She hasn't told me yet. I wonder if it'll be McDonald's or Burger King. There's

Biddy's Burgers in Combe Leigh, but it's not the same thing.

'I'm taking your mum to her favourite place,' says Aunty Peaches. Mum twists her head round so she can see me.

'Max, you're going to love it. We used to go there every payday or whenever—'

'No, *you* used to go there,' Aunty Peaches says. 'You and that Yvette.'

'Yeah, yeah. Me and Yvette were addicted.'

'Mm-hmm – and not just to the food.'

'What you talking about, woman – of course it was for the food.'

'Yeah, right,' says Aunty Peaches and they both start giggling again. They're worse than me and Sonny.

Mum's favourite place turns out to be Ronnie's. Inside, plants have been put everywhere to make it feel tropical. Brightly painted tables and chairs full of people fill up one side, and in the corner is a small stage where Aunty Peaches says they used to have live reggae music.

'Don't they do music anymore?' Mum looks disappointed.

'Nah,' answers Aunty Peaches. 'Stopped that a while back. Sometimes there's a DJ at the end of the month, but it's mostly house and garage nonsense for the youngsters.'

Everyone in here is black like us, but I don't think Mum's noticed.

'Do they still do the jerk kingfish?' she asks and picks up a menu. 'Had that the first time I came here with David. Well . . . that was a meal.'

113

Aunty Peaches' eyebrows rise up her forehead. 'I'm sure it was.'

Mum lifts her menu in front of her face. 'Don't look at me like that,' she says, which makes Aunty Peaches smile with her lips pinched together. This makes her face look thinner. Then I remember – Peaches isn't even her real name, it's Veronica, but everyone's called her Peaches since she was a fat, round baby.

'Don't look at you like what? You can't hide from me, Tessa. You know, it's funny you mention David. I was thinking about him the other day.'

'I don't know why . . . Max, is there anything on here you like the look of?' Mum passes me her menu.

'I heard he's started his own business. Might be worth looking him up if you ever decide . . .'

While Aunty Peaches is talking, I search to see if they have any chicken wings, but the only ones I find come with something called kimchi.

'Mum. There's nothing on here I like.'

'Uh? What's the matter? Oh, there must be something, Max. Here, let me look.'

Mum's jerk fish isn't there, neither is the honey barbecued pork or fried bammy. 'Oh. How disappointing. I really wanted you to try them.' There's nothing on the menu that Mum remembers. It's not even Jamaican food anymore but a mix of Caribbean, Asian and normal stuff, so there's lobster nuggets and curry chicken steamed buns. Mum doesn't know what to order.

'Tessa, things change, you know,' Aunty Peaches tells her and chooses for us.

When we walk back to the car, I whisper, 'It wasn't that nice in there anyway, Mum. The food wasn't as good as yours – and did you see? All the plants were made of plastic.'

Richard

Blood drips into the kitchen sink. Richard turns on the tap, letting the frigid water anaesthetise his torn knuckles. So much for his plans to get the steel retaining posts in for the raised beds; he knows he should have got the lump hammer from the shed, rather than trying to use the back of the mattock – the wrong tool for the wrong job. It had slipped round as he held the post, scalping his fist. He could always call it a day, take a craved-for break in front of the TV and watch *The Return of Jedi*, his and Sonny's favourite film, but outside, the sky is darkening. Those old railway sleepers still want moving from where the workmen repairing the level crossing had deposited them over the fence in exchange for Richard's help with scraping up some fallen ballast. Somehow, he will have to haul them, heavy and slippery though they are, all the way to the polytunnel, where they will make rough but perfect borders for his new beds.

Gingerly, Richard lifts a thick flap of skin. Blood wells up and spills darkly over the back of his hand – it probably needs a stitch, but he does not have the patience to wait around at the surgery, which will undoubtedly be busy after last night's new year's shenanigans. Tess would fetch the first aid tin, give his hand a careful clean and dress it properly, then pester him for days afterwards with the tea tree oil and clean plasters but, as his mother would have done, Richard reaches down into the cupboard by his knees for the Dettol.

He pours a capful over his hand, wincing at the pain but more at the smell, which makes him recall how she always diluted it first in warm water. Dabbing his childhood wounds with wet cotton wool was about the only motherly thing she ever did for him. His relationship with his parents had always been quite businesslike. When Tess said years ago how kind his parents were to help them with the house deposit, Richard cringed inside, remembering the typed contract for repayment with interest. The family farm hadn't long been sold – quite soon after his and Tess's wedding, so his father could whisk his cherished wife away to the Algarve. They kept just one of the thatched farm cottages on Withy Grove to provide themselves with a rental income. It is no wonder, Richard feels, as an only child in a village where everyone boasted at least a handful of siblings, he grew up lacking in confidence and rather quiet and self-contained. Least now, his parents only have themselves to worry about.

Spots of blood trail across the kitchen floor from the sink to the back door. Richard must have put his hand down on the table without thinking because there is blood too on one of Sonny's Spider-Man comics. Richard quickly wipes it away with his sleeve before it dries. Really, he ought to use this break in his work to call Tess, but then she could call him if she wanted to talk. When she left to catch the coach with Max, Richard tried to kiss her goodbye, out of habit more than anything, but she turned away at the last moment and he did not pursue it, knowing it was because of him she was leaving in such haste, him and all this arguing. No doubt her sister will be encouraging her to get a divorce.

Richard inspects his knuckles. The bleeding has stopped but deep inside the wound is peppered black with dirt. He gets himself a couple of plasters and heads upstairs to the bathroom to look for Tess's tea tree oil.

Max

Nana watches *Judge Rinder* just like Marge, but it's all so boring. I miss being at home. The chickens will be wondering where I've gone. I beg Mum to take me to the Natural History Museum, but she says there won't be enough time. She reminds me, the last time we went we had to queue for over two hours just to see the dinosaurs. People sat on the floor eating sandwiches because the café was full. I thought it was epic. Sonny made us spend ages looking at fossils of sea animals. My favourites were the birds and insects.

Instead, Mum takes me to the fruit and veg market to get cooking supplies. We go every time we come to London. It's loud and Mum walks too fast, but she never crashes into anyone. Everyone keeps shoving past me. All the stalls sell the same things. I can't tell them apart, but Mum goes to the same ones Nana uses. Mum says if I don't moan, she'll buy me a saltfish patty and a can of grape soda when we've finished. We meet lots of people she knows. Some are her friends from when she was young. Some are our family. They're all really happy to see her so it's impossible to tell which ones we're related to. Most of them seem to know me even though I don't remember them. They stroke my hair, laugh about the colour of my skin, give me mint balls to suck and tell me I look nothing like my mum. An old lady, who Mum calls Aunty even though she isn't, says it's such a shame I didn't come out looking more like the other one.

I pull hard on Mum's arm and tell her the smell of traffic is giving me a headache.

'Tessa Sullivan? Is that you?' asks a man. He's really tall and wears a furry green trapper hat that's exactly the same as Dad's. We've been queueing inside the Caribbean food shop for ages. It smells strange in here, a bit like Mum's curry powder.

'David? Oh my God!' Mum's voice sounds really strange and fluttery. She smiles a real smile, not her normal pretend one.

'I knew it was you. What are you doing here? I mean, apart from buying plantain?' he asks, laughing so we can see all his teeth. Mum laughs as well and they hug each other, holding on for a long time.

'Well, er . . . I'm home, for a few days. You know, to see Mama and Peaches and some of the old crowd. Wow . . . how long has it been?' They both laugh again, until he sees me and asks Mum who I am. 'Oh, yeah, this is Max, my . . . son,' she replies. His eyes, which are nearly black like Mum's, open up really wide.

'Your son? Yeah. Yeah. I heard you had kids. Twins, wasn't it? I guess you're not a Sullivan anymore?'

'We're Hembrys,' I tell him.

'Is that right? Hembry? Okay. Okay.' He puts his hands in his coat pockets and his eyes move back to Mum. 'Tessa. Man, it's so good to see you. You haven't changed a bit, well . . . maybe apart from the hair.' He smiles, but his mouth has gotten a lot smaller. Mum looks embarrassed and pats her afro.

'My hair? Oh yeah. I'm just on my way to get it done,' she lies.

'Cool. Cool. Ah . . . So, how's Mama? I haven't seen her in a long time.'

'She's good, you know. Really good. She'll be so happy when I tell her I've seen you.'

'Cool. Give her my best. It was good to see you. Yeah. Good to see you. Right, I suppose I'd better be going.' They say goodbye, but now neither of them is smiling.

Later, when we're sitting with Nana on the sofa, Mum tells her about the man in the shop. I wish they'd stop talking. There's a nature programme on telly about wolves hunting caribou, but I can't hear a thing. Nana's made roast bread-fruit. I dunk big wedges of it into my chicken gravy.

'No, him never stay with Marcia. That girl was bad news. She went and got herself pregnant for Gerald,' Nana's saying.

'She got with Gerald? But I thought . . .' replies Mum.

'No, but by the time that happen, you already gone. He come and ask for you a few times, and his mother used to ask after you in church.' Nana sighs. 'But once you set your eyes on Richard, that was the end of everyting. I've never seen you so determined.'

Mum's quiet for a moment so I can finally hear what David Attenborough's saying. But just as he gets to the bit where the caribou calf is separated from its mother, Nana starts talking again.

'Him doing really well, you know.'

'Who? Richard?' asks Mum.

'No, David. Him turn property developer. Went and buy up some houses in Deptford. Fix them up real nice. I heard he's making quite a lot of money out of it. I know you don't want to hear it, but if things had been different, the two of you would have made a good team.'

'What's this?' Aunty Peaches comes into the room. She's been in the bath and smells like flowers.

Mum gets up from the sofa with her empty plate. 'Right, let me make a start on the dishes.'

'We jus' talking about David,' says Nana.

The next day, Mum's gone for hours. She doesn't tell me where she's going, only that I should behave myself and listen to Aunty Peaches. Some of Nana's church friends come to visit and take over the sitting room. I'm trying to watch *Ben 10*, but they switch the telly over to *Oprah*. I sneak away upstairs. Maybe Nathan will let me into the spare room he claims is his.

'Can I come in?' I ask outside the door. I know he'll say no, but without Sonny here I've got no one else to talk to. I jump when the door's yanked open. Nathan just leaves it like that and goes straight back inside.

It's ages before he says, 'Come on then if you're coming.'

Music plays from a small black speaker that's linked to Nathan's phone, which he's holding over his face so he can look at it while he lies on his back. Next to him on the bed are loads of manga comics, really cool ones, all covered in Japanese writing. They're new, so must have been a Christmas present. Nathan sees me staring and does the tiniest nod with his head, which means, *Yes, you can look at them.*

'Ahh, tune.' Nathan's eyes don't leave his phone, but his free hand smacks the duvet in time to the music. 'Tell me you know who this is?'

I sit on the end of the bed. 'I don't know,' I tell him. Although the song does sound familiar. I think it's something Mum sometimes listens to.

'What? How can you not know? You sure you're my cousin?' Nathan leans up on his elbow. 'It's Beenie Man. He's a classic! Here . . . listen.' He taps super-fast at his phone. Another song comes on that I've never heard before. Nathan turns the volume up, but not too loud else Nana will come stomping upstairs to tell him off.

'Right – what d'you think of this?'

I like this song better than the first one. It makes my feet move by themselves.

'Yes,' says Nathan, nodding as though he's pleased with me. He plays me song after song until there's a knock on the door and Mum pokes her head in. She's had her hair done and looks completely different.

'You boys okay in here?' she asks. Her voice is soft.

I tell her 'Yes' and Nathan just shrugs, but he doesn't kick me out. I get to stay with him till bedtime.

'Laters, cuz,' he says when Mum calls that it's gone ten

o'clock. He reaches down into his bag, then slaps two packs of strawberry bubblegum into my hand – one for me and one for Sonny.

Tess

Mama wraps thick crescents of roast breadfruit in cling film for me to fry when I get home and stacks them on the kitchen counter beside tins of ackee, paper bags filled with whole nutmegs, bammy and coconut drops, and a pile of semi-ripened plantains. Inside a large Tupperware tub is at least three meals' worth of stew lamb, not too spicy but hot enough to save me from the winter chills. From the back of a cupboard materialises a small rum-soaked Christmas cake that was baked for me several months ago.

'Tessa, you sure you cyaan take some of the pork belly?' I shoot my mother an incredulous look but as usual she's not to be denied. 'And Aunty Meryl did make some sorrel drink for you to carry.'

'Mama, yes, I'm sure! *Look* . . .' I thrust my open hands at my overloaded bags. 'I can't fit anything else in there. We're on a coach, don't forget – how am I going to lug everything? And Mama, please, I've got to hurry! We need to be gone in the next half hour.' My mother kisses her teeth to show her dissatisfaction, making me realise there's no point in me holding off any longer. 'Anyway . . . thing is. There's no need for me to take too much. I'll be coming back sooner than you think.'

Peaches catches this last statement as she hurries into the kitchen. She's running late and is already supposed to be halfway across London where she's to meet Tayo before heading to his parents' in Walthamstow. 'You coming back? When?' She and Mama give each other that secret look again. 'What is it?' I demand.

'It's just. Well ... Mama?' Hesitation widens my sister's eyes.

'What?' I shout as I'm reminded of when my dad fell ill, and how Mama and Peaches tried to keep it from me as though I was still a child who can't handle reality.

'Mama, you're going to have to tell her.'

'Tell me what? Peaches? Mama!'

'Calm yourself, Tessa. It's nothing to get worked up about,' says Mama. She's covering the cake with foil and finishes her task before continuing. 'I'm planning to sell the house and move back to Jamaica.' She says it serenely, like she's talking about selling an unwanted car.

'What do you mean, you're selling the house?' My voice is shrill.

'I told you she'd get upset,' Peaches interjects.

'Mama. What do you mean, you're selling the house?'

'But Tessa, it's not like it was when you girls were at home.'

I will myself to breathe. They always talked about moving *back home* – their mantra, a family catchphrase spoken in the cold of every winter when a bus turned up late, or after a fall-out with one of the neighbours. I thought it was a game we played. Images of white-gated, beachfront apartments flicker inside my mind. I thought it was something I wanted, but now it's here. No – I don't want to build a house *back home*.

Max

Mum's crying when it's time to leave, but Nana tells her to stop her nonsense. It's Sunday, so the Tube isn't crowded. I want to ask what her and Aunty Peaches were fighting about, but I can tell Mum isn't in the mood for talking. To make her happy, I hold her hand all the way to the coach station, even though people are looking. I love it when she pulls me close and we pretend we're invisible. On our coach, there are no other black people, only me and Mum. As we drive out of London, I press my forehead against the window, but can only see lots and lots of buildings. I keep looking until they fade away and, at last, I spot a deer. A little muntjac is standing in a green field, watching.

Sonny

In winter, tawny owls fly closer to the house. They are calling in the orchard. Under the trees, brown leaves have rotted to sludge. Worms burrow deeper to where the earth's warmer. Careful of the frozen mud heaped high on the verges. Conkers are trapped under the ice. See how the wind pricks our skin with goosebumps? At night, handfuls of white glitter moonlight fall into the freezing water. Look – there are silverfish sleeping behind the curtains. Chrysalises stick like thorns above the door frame. Sadness sighs under chairs and through window cracks.

A new Mum returns from London, one with long plaits that swing from side to side when she moves her head. This Mum wears bright red lipstick and draws black around her eyes. She kisses her teeth loudly, bangs pan lids and slams the fridge door. I wait until she's tired herself out, then I wrap myself around her and try to find my Mum hidden inside.

I walk with her out across Hector's field, over the broken-down stile and into the frozen meadow. Owls are half asleep in the willows. Sleet rides the whirlwinds that whip around us and washes her city make-up away. We hold hands because she doesn't like it out here. I can feel her warmth through her gloves even though her fingers are cold. She's afraid of cows, of barking farm dogs, of bumping into unfriendly people or taking the wrong footpath and getting lost. Our boots slip on ice and mud. It's better to lean against each other than hold on to thorny brambles. We leave our house behind and come out past the allotments on the track by the church, where frost spreads like icing sugar in the yew tree. I show her the empty rooks' nest still lined with fluff and the grey-green lichen that grows on the churchyard headstones. We walk for miles, until that new Mum finally fades away. The tight braids frizz and have to be taken out. See her soft fluffy afro? Ah – here's *my* Mum back again.

Comfort used to be the feel of David Attenborough's voice in the evening after school, Sunday jerk chicken with homemade Yorkshire puddings and gravy, the shape of our family squashed into Dad's van with boxes of veg balanced on our knees. Now everything inside this house feels itchy, as though the air's full of unsaid words that tickle like sawdust. Everyone plays let's pretend. Dad doesn't seem pleased that Mum and Max are back. He pretends the last few days without them have been normal. He's not interested in Mum's bags of food. Although today I catch him making a hard-dough bread cheese sandwich with a few drops of hot pepper sauce instead of chutney. When he comes in late for tea, he watches Mum out of the corners of his eyes as he reaches for his plate in the Rayburn, sees her change from new back to old, or is it from *old* back to *new*? But he doesn't ask her how she got on, if Nana's well or if Aunty Peaches and Uncle Tayo say hello. He pretends they aren't his family too.

It's no wonder Mum thinks Dad doesn't care. She doesn't know that while she and Max were gone, he barely came inside the house. Perhaps there was something in here he was afraid of.

An argument bounces off the walls their first night back, about a silly thing – Dad packing away the Christmas decorations two days before Twelfth Night. Mum drags boxes down out of the loft and back into the living room. The tree's already been turned into woodchip, but she climbs on chairs and pins glittery things to the wooden beams. Her anger shatters baubles, spilling glass splinters all over the rug. But me and Max don't mind. We pretend we're small again and run laughing through the house, although we haven't long to enjoy the shimmer of fairy lights – only forty-eight hours before they'll be taken down again. Watch how they sparkle like tiny galactic nebulas. They help us forget how rubbish Christmas was this year – no laughter, no paper hats or crackers, no sherry trifle and Jamaican chocolate tea, no playing Scrabble and Dad cheating with his two-letter words, no snuggling together under blankets to watch *Home Alone*.

Richard

Unsure of how he came to be there, Richard finds himself in the doorway of the boys' bedroom. Normally, he avoids the room at all costs, simply refuses to see it, turning straight out of his and Tess's room onto the landing and either ducking into the small bathroom or hurrying directly downstairs. Max no longer invites him in, but it is still Tess's domain, a place of scattered school clothes, dirty cups and bedtime stories. There is always something pressing to do elsewhere that stops Richard from lingering.

Inside the room, nothing has changed. Sonny's bed is made, and the duvet, dark navy and splattered with white stars, is neatly arranged, matching the one on Max's bed. Richard knows Tess comes in to tidy as soon as Max leaves for school. Muted winter sunshine glances off the silver cup Sonny won for his progress in maths at the end of Year 4. Beside it sit his reading glasses, a black plastic pair, still practically new, that were prescribed for close work, looking at the school whiteboard or when using computers. This had been the only difference Richard noted in his sons – Max's vision is twenty-twenty, primed for spotting near-invisible creatures that no one else could detect. Richard tries hard not to brush against anything, worried the muck on his hands and clothes will contaminate this scene, this time capsule, this . . . shrine. His whole presence in the room feels awkward. The air is cold, still. Richard closes his eyes and, for once, allows himself to imagine his sons' voices, their bickering on the stairs, Sonny crowing as he beats his brother to the top step. Is it so mad to think he is still here, in this house? Richard finds it hard to believe the past year even happened; perhaps he dreamt it all. Governed by the garden's cycle, it is easier than he likes to admit to pretend life continues as normal, each month following the last, ignorant of his inner turmoil.

There have been so many arguments, but Tess refuses to see reason and continues to wash Sonny's sheets and pillowcases, even though Richard has urged her to pack his things away. Surely it cannot help, leaving everything as it was. Max does not make matters any easier, switching between the beds whenever the mood takes him, wearing both his and his brother's clothes indiscriminately, and continuing to blame Sonny for the untidiness, the smashed crockery, fossils and feathers strewn all over the floor. Deep down, Richard fears his son's behaviour and the way they have to tiptoe around him, perpetuating this painful charade, but who can blame the kid, struggling with so much and with no other way of processing any of it? The topic of counselling has been abandoned; Richard is too afraid to broach it. He understands; therapy is not the Caribbean way. Maybe Tess is right. Why should Max stop speaking to his brother, when it is the only way he can cope with the grief?

As Richard retreats out of the room, he senses Tess moving beneath him in the kitchen, fancies she listens to his tentative footsteps and turns those disappointed eyes of hers upwards.

Since returning from London, she has not spoken to him, except to berate him for packing away the Christmas things. He had thought she would not want them left up. Why would they want to be reminded of past Christmases that had no hope of being repeated?

Tess

It's grown too cold to dry washing outside. There's not enough sunlight to melt the thick layer of ice covering the length of the garden fence. Evening hurries to arrive the moment the morning has passed. I share wet clothes out among the lukewarm radiators in the living room, in the bedrooms, and up on the landing, where they'll sit damp for several days. School trousers are needed for the week, so they take priority and earn prize position on the Rayburn's hand-rail. Upstairs, there's dry laundry to put away: tea towels, solitary socks, Richard's old bobbly jumpers that smell of potatoes, jeans with frayed rips at the knee. I change the duvet covers and pillowcases in the boys' bedroom, taking care that they match down to the position of each pillow – a ten-minute job that takes me more than half an hour. Out on the landing, I pause to stare at the river.

Yes, Mama, who cyaan hear mus feel.

To escape from myself, I take to the fields. There's nothing out here today, no birds, no animals, people . . . nothing. I feel conspicuous, but still I stagger on regardless.

Richard tried to teach me the names of the trees, and of the plants threaded through the hedgerows. I warned him he'd be wasting his time, but he was so eager to share his precious home with me and make me see it like he did.

'And this. It's a sycamore. Here. Tess, are you looking? See how the leaves grow in clumps? They're shaped a bit like a maple's, but maples don't grow round here. And here. You should know this one. This is an oak. See how the branches are twisted and hook back on themselves? And there's a silver birch, do you see its trunk? An easy one for you to remember. Now the ash is smooth barked. See? With symmetrical pairs of leaves.'

'And what's that?' I asked, moved by his boyish enthusiasm.

'Ah, that's hazel. See how straight it grows? There'll be nuts in the summer. You've got to try them before they turn brown.'

So many names, my brain couldn't hold on to them all. But I remember the taste of my first wild hazelnut, a cobnut, Richard called it. He cracked the green shell in his teeth to reveal a soft white kernel that was creamy, almost like pine nuts or almonds. Turned out I loved foraging – sweet chestnuts, damsons, pignuts, blackberries and, best of all, whortleberries that stained the pink of my palms purple.

Today, the leafless trees are unrecognisable and band together to form a single hostile mass. To avoid them, I strike out across the cut withy beds, where the hedges thin out. My teeth catch at my lips, which are raw and flake from the cold. I try not to lick them; it only makes them worse. Maybe I just hate walking out here alone. It's easier when someone else is with me, makes me feel braver somehow. Somewhere across the fields, there's a dog barking. Sharp winds distort any sounds. Wait – is that shouting or is it merely the whirr of swans flying overhead? Fear eventually overtakes me, turns me around and sends me tramping back the way I've come.

Sonny

Can you feel the river tugging under icy stones, through webs of widespread willow roots, past sleepy leatherjackets? There's been no rain, so the water level lowers. Ripped tyres, coils of pig wire and bits of bikes rise from the mud and just below the surface, there's the remains of that old steel barge no tractor was able to pull out. Under his hill, Merlin waits until it's time to burn the ashen faggot. There was no one to toast the New Year but *Allium porrum, Lactuca sativa, Solanum tuberosum*. Cold kills Dad's seeds inside their plastic shell. His heated lamps don't work. But don't give up! Let's make tiny blankets out of spongy, green moss, go a-wassailing and scare away the wind. Out in the fields, a mother fox cries. Look, Mum, never mind your frozen toes. Don't you see the old man's beard, all fluffy in the hedgerow? Or the soft hazel catkins? They're winter's secret flowers, you know. Never mind the voice on the other end of Dad's mobile phone. I can hear his heart racing. He doesn't see me treading along the rows with my small garden fork collecting fallen lumps of coal.

Richard

Taking care not to wake Tess, Richard sits gently on his side of the bed and reaches down to peel off his damp socks. His back, sore from digging manure into the frozen potato beds, aches from his shoulder blades down to his waist. There are not enough hours in the day and no matter how much he gets done, the white arc of the polytunnel is a constant reminder of all the hard work still waiting for him.

Plants have always come easy, their needs simple – water, food, light, warmth. He never has any trouble, apart from the odd spot of blight, but now he is out of his depth. He does not claim to be a businessman and loathes anything resembling paperwork, whether it be bureaucratic red tape, financial forecasting, or simply making a list of customers who have yet to pay. Gardening, well, vegetable growing to be precise – he cannot be doing with flowers – is all he really knows. Of course, Richard thinks as he massages the calluses on his palms, he will need to broaden his selection; he cannot keep selling the same uninspiring cabbages and turnips if he is to make a profit.

'She's leaving.'

Tess's voice startles him.

'Who's leaving?' Richard asks quietly, sliding into bed and staring at the complex red and green pattern on the headscarf covering the back of her head.

'Mama. Christ, who else would I be talking about? She's going back to Jamaica.'

'Really? That's a surprise, but, then … I guess we knew she'd go back eventually.' Tess does not reply, so Richard tries again. 'It'll be good for her though. Won't it? I mean. Isn't it what she and your dad always wanted?'

The small gold clock, the last of their wedding gifts, ticks into the silence.

Tess

My phone rings while I'm at the feed mills, where I struggle to cradle a twenty-kilo bag of layers pellets, a canister of red mite powder, fat balls and a bag of mixed seeds for Cyril's bird feeder. Really, Richard should've come in the van, not me, cycling with the rickety trailer for two and a half miles in the icy cold. But the chickens are hungry and can't wait. My movements are watched by a handful of other customers, who apparently enjoy the spectacle of a black woman buying farm products. Thank goodness they can't see my cheeks burning. Ignoring my phone, I stagger over to my bike and heave the bags into the trailer, but it continues to ring as I cycle back along the road. The sound is loud in the quiet, in that dismal end-of-January slump that keeps everyone indoors, apart from the occasional car and a large speeding muck spreader that flicks fresh cow shit onto my path. I'll never get used to the smell. Sweat seeps under the double layer of my headscarf and hat to trickle down my nose. Above, the sky is a subdued pinky-yellow as though it might snow.

'Tessa. What happened . . . ? Did David call you?' Peaches' voice is hard to make out; there's music in the background, loud and tinny, drum and bass maybe.

'I can't believe you gave him my number. You didn't even warn me!'

'I thought . . . talk to him . . .'

'What?' I move closer to the kitchen window to get better reception. 'I can't hear you – what is all that noise?'

'I'm out. Picking up a few bits in the sales. Hang on, hang on. Let me get into the changing rooms. It's madness out here.' There's the sound of scuffling and my sister asking if she can try on six items. Finally, the music quietens. 'Yeah, yeah. I should've warned you, but Tessa – you'd have chickened out.'

'You told him I was looking for a job.'

'Well? Aren't you? Look . . .' Peaches' tone softens, and I can tell she's trying hard not to set me off. 'Tessa. I know you want to come back. You can't let Mama leaving stop you.'

Outside the window, a light dusting of snow falls onto the wheelie bin waiting by the gate. It's rare to get snow here, something to do with being in a shallow valley, I think.

'Tessa?'

'Hmm? Yeah, I'm still here.'

'Come on, girl. I know it's a shock. But it's not the same for her here without Dad. That house is worth a lot now, you know. She'll be able to live out there in comfort.'

It's cold enough for the snow to settle. I watch, engrossed, as each flake floats down and collects here and there in perfect crystalline clusters.

'*Tessa?*' My sister's frustration cuts through the silence.

'Sorry. I'm . . .' The words trail off. I struggle to focus, to pull my eyes away from the picture-book scene unfolding in the garden. Snow fills the creases of the fence and hides the matted tangle of dead plants smothering my flower bed. My hand presses against the chilly glass of the window as though it's an invisible forcefield I could step through.

'Tessa – what is it? And please don't tell me you're fine when you're obviously not.'

She's right. I'm not. 'I'm . . . I'm not coping.' There. I've said it, but I don't know what I'm expecting her to say. Sympathy is not her strong point. Besides, we've been brought up to fold up any discomfort and pack it neatly away.

'Course you're not coping – what did you expect? Look at how much you've lost! And you're still there – stuck in that mouldy house. Bloody hell, man. You don't even have a career to lean on. There's nothing for you down there! *Jesus Christ*, Tessa. I blame those stupid books you used to read. Who d'you think you are? One of those Larkins or something?' My sister huffs in that dramatic way of hers.

'Look, Peaches. Just go. Okay. Go and get back to your shopping.'

She draws a deep breath. 'I'm sorry. Don't be angry. Tell me . . . what did David say?'

I make myself put away my indignation because I know she means well. 'Not a lot. I didn't talk to him for long. He thinks he might be able to find me something.'

'*See*. I told you. Look. I know it's complicated, but at least say you'll think about it. Okay? Oh, dammit. Look, Sis. Someone's lurking outside. I'd better go before they think I'm in here stealing something.'

Her words stay with me for the rest of the day. My head fills with them as I strain my way through dinner and

Richard's empty chair. I can hear them as I sit with Max on the sofa in front of the living-room fire watching reruns of *Blue Planet*.

It's the middle of the night. I creep downstairs wrapped in my dressing gown when everyone's asleep. Better to be up and busy than lying there frustrated. The house is so still, I can almost hear the murmur of the river through the bricks. The flagstones in the kitchen are glacial beneath my bare feet. My slippers are upstairs. I'm quieter without them. There's still some heat left in the Rayburn, but not nearly enough, so I shove in wood until the log basket is completely empty. Outside, there's not a drop of light in any direction, as though the entire world has disappeared. We could be the only people left, alone in this house, oblivious. It's the same routine, a furtive cup of tea, followed by some sort of baking. My new habit. I'm good at it now. Stealthy. I cream sugar and butter, crack eggs and sift flour without making a sound. Not that I need to worry; once asleep they don't wake up until morning. Tonight, I decide on blackberry muffins and take from the freezer a couple of bags of misshapen fruit, picked most likely by Max at the end of summer from the brambles that border the sheep field. They begin to thaw on contact with the batter. I fold in air with my large metal spoon, one eye on the clock. All these cakes and I can barely eat them. Mama thinks I'm losing weight, says this life doesn't agree with me, that I'm losing the coveted Sullivan backside and hips. Mama says a lot of things, so does Peaches. Maybe they're right.

Oh, what am I thinking?

Thirty minutes until the muffins are done, so I sit and sip my tea and stare at the reflected woman in the window.

Is this really what I've become?

Finally roasting hot, the Rayburn drums into life and thrusts boiling water through the narrow copper pipes leading out of the kitchen, along the hall skirting to the tepid radiators. It taps quietly in an animated rhythm that disturbs the silence. Sometimes it feels like this house is alive. The warmth brings with it the honeyed smell of baking that makes my eyelids heavy and reminds me of sleep. I'm taken back to past summers, spur-of-the-moment picnic teas in the orchard, the boys keeping wasps off the jam sandwiches and all those plump, juicy blackberries that overflowed from empty ice-cream tubs and left our fingers pricked and sticky.

A creak on the stairs brings me back. I freeze, my mug at my lips. For a moment I think it's Sonny, awakened by a bad dream perhaps or by the low rumble of the heating. As a baby, he was the one who stirred most often during the night to summon me from my sleep, more in need than Max of a feed or cuddle. If it is him, I won't send him back to bed. He could keep me company until the muffins are ready, and then we'd eat one each with a spoonful of cold custard straight out of the tin, our secret. I wait, but no one comes. It's only the wooden treads stretching as the house warms up.

A flawless black Range Rover grinds onto the small rectangle of gravel opposite the house as I mop the kitchen floor. I'm tired and not in the mood for her today. The slam of Amy's car door shuts out the blare of Beyoncé and panics the sparrows, who pick through patches of snow on the garden path. She's had her hair done and is no longer a blonde, but a dark burgundy brunette.

'Tess, love.' She bursts into the kitchen through the back door and heads straight for the kettle, tracking dirty boot prints across my clean floor. No one stands on ceremony here.

'Hi, Amy, how you doing?' I stash away the mop but use my foot to push a piece of damp kitchen tissue after her.

'Having a bloody nightmare. Stupid washing machine has packed in. I've ordered a new one, but it won't be here till Friday. What the hell am I supposed to do in the mean-time?' Amy pushes her large all-season sunglasses up to form a headband and helps herself to coffee and a muffin. 'I won't be able to pick up the kids today. Sorry. Got to go into town this afternoon and find a pair of shoes for this ball. God knows what I'm going to wear. Was thinking of my red velvet dress but might have to buy something new. Mum's going to grab Mason for me. Will you be alright?' She sinks into a chair at the kitchen table and shoves aside a stack of unopened envelopes that I noticed this morning were all addressed to Richard.

'Yeah, don't worry. We'll manage,' I tell her, even though it probably means another walk home in the dark. 'So, when's this ball then?' I sit down beside her, glad of the company after all.

'First Saturday in February. Can't wait. I'm desperate for some excitement. You coming this year?'

Am I going to the annual Farmers' Ball? To stand insecure and nervous in a draughty village hall festooned with streamers, among middle-aged men in black tie and identical women in identical cocktail dresses making polite forced conservation, which always seem to centre around who I am, and where I've come from, and what a lovely curvaceous figure I have.

'No, doubt it. You know it's not Richard's thing,' I say as I stare into my tea.

'Richard? No, definitely not. Oh, I wanted to ask. What was he doing in Branstock the other day? Saw him coming out of the post office. I'd just finished having lunch with Graham's mother. We went to the Granary, it's been refurbished – simply wonderful. I called out to him, but he didn't hear me. What's wrong with the postal service here? I could have sworn there was someone else in the van, but he took off in such a hurry, I couldn't really tell.'

It's like being hit. Pieces of a puzzle that have been eluding me suddenly fall into place.

'Branstock,' I repeat. Amy nods, her mouth full of coffee. The newly dyed hair sways and brings out the green in her eyes. 'Nice colour,' I tell her, desperate to steer her off this topic.

'My hair? Oh yeah, isn't it lush? Had it done a few days ago. I'll lighten it again in the summer. They've got a new girl in the salon at the top of the high street. You know the one? She's brilliant, a dab hand at tinting. Felicity, she's called. You should definitely pop in and see her.'

'Thanks for the tip.' I give her my best pretend smile, the one I usually reserve for special occasions. After all these years, she still doesn't understand – this Felicity would have kittens if I walked into her salon and asked for a tint. 'You look great, it really suits you.'

'You think?' Amy tilts her head from side to side. 'Not that Graham's noticed. He's so busy with the new barn. Can you believe the parish council rejected the planning? Said the roof's too high. Reckon it was that spiteful Mrs Bulmer. It's only cows, for God's sake, not like she's going to be over-looked by actual *people*.' Amy stretches out her long legs, clad in their customary uniform of super-tight skinny jeans, and looks around the kitchen. 'Blimey, Tess, how do you keep this place looking so spotless? Thank goodness I've got Irina coming tomorrow morning, our house is a tip.'

I laugh despite myself. Poor Amy. We're poles apart, yet somehow, we've become good friends. Perhaps it's the fact she moved here from a council estate in Battersea when she was eight. Not that anyone would know. The London in her has been too diluted.

'So, how's Ginny getting on? She enjoying herself? I still can't believe she's at uni. What's she doing again?' I ask, leaning over in my chair to chuck a few more logs into the Rayburn.

'Neither can I.' Amy brushes away crumbs caught on her sequined jumper. 'Makes me feel so old. She's doing political

science. Crazy. S
took her back u
Birmingham's fan

I allow myself t
and not her daug
surface, and I'm te
that would mean co
and I can't bring my
What a change for k
fun she must be hav
so far away?' I say i

'Nah, not really,' i
me and her dad have
to as long as she do
bring home a black bo
Tess, *you* know what
again at half term. Lei
They've got two mass

I've stopped listenii
she said? My ears fil
into something accepi
something. But what?
a black woman with
something . . .

'I love H&M. Still c
Leigh,' I reply as I ris
mugs to the sink.

Max

Dad's late to collect us after school, so me and Sonny have to wait in the playground with Miss Simmonds. She's the new Reception teacher since Miss Thompson got married and moved to Scotland. Miss Simmonds makes me help her tidy away the PE balls and skipping ropes, even though it's getting too dark to see. My fingers are so cold, they're tingling. She pulls up the sleeve of her coat and checks her watch.

'This is the second time this week. I think we might need to have a word with your mum,' she says. It's actually the third time, but yesterday Mr Reid was on duty, and he doesn't mind. Miss Simmonds looks at us as though it's our fault.

'Sorry about that,' says Dad when we climb into the van. There are important-looking papers spread all over the seats.

'What are these?' I ask and pick up one that has a huge red 'URGENT' written at the top.

'What? Oh, nothing. Just stick them down by your feet. Come on, else your mum will be worrying,' Dad tells us.

Dinner's waiting on the table when we get in, chicken and rice. Mum's version doesn't taste nearly as good as Nana's. There isn't enough gravy. At least there's treacle sponge for afters.

'It was photo day today,' I tell her. I know she forgot, even though I reminded her about it ages ago. Usually, she fusses about us being extra tidy. But we're always smart, not like some of the other kids who get away with wearing sweatshirts and trainers. Mum says it's important we make a good impression. On photo day, everyone has to wear proper school uniform with the proper logo on it. Last year, Mum took me to get my hair cut in Combe Leigh at the barbershop with the massive black-leather swivel chairs. The barber kept looking at me and Mum in the mirror and asking if Mum was *sure* she was my mum. He thought it was really funny, but me and Mum didn't laugh. Then he cut my hair too short, so I looked like Caleb in Year 4. Ruby said we could be brothers, which made me furious because Caleb's really annoying and he's white, whereas I'm not, and I've already got a brother. Sonny's never been to the barbershop. Mum cuts his hair herself with special clippers she got from Argos.

First, we have a photo taken by ourselves. Then Mr Reid calls up everyone who is a sibling before the whole class takes one together. It's always easy to find Sonny in the class photo, but I'm invisible.

'So, how did you get on?' Mum asks. She pushes her rice about with her fork.

'Alright.' My mouth's filled with bits of chicken bone. Sometimes, I wish she'd cook chicken with no bones in like Mason's mum does.

'Come on. Hurry up,' says Sonny, who's already finished eating. Quickly, I scoff down the rest of my food and ask if I can leave the table.

In the living room, we lie on the sofa and watch a *Scooby-Doo* film, a cartoon one, not the rubbish one with real people in it. Afterwards, I look at the new book I got for Christmas. It's brilliant. There are chapters on mammals, birds, reptiles and insects. The pictures are really good, with lots of close-ups. Plus, it has a whole section on identifying animal tracks. I took it into school after the holidays, but nobody wanted to see it. They only wanted to talk about Evan's new air rifle and how he went with his dad shooting jackdaws. Ellie said it's cruel to kill animals, but Evan just called her a stupid vegan.

I take my book over to Cyril's in the morning. The cold has made his lungs worse, so he isn't allowed out of bed. The curtains aren't open, and all the lights are on. Because he can't live without telly, his new carer, Gillian, has found him a small upstairs one. It's sat with a glass of water on a wooden table that has wheels, so he can move it where he wants it. There's also a notepad and a pen, in case he wants to make up a new poem. His room smells strange, a bit sweet, like pineapple cottage cheese or gone-off rice. Mum says he's very tired and we're not to pester him too much. She hasn't brought him any leftovers today, because last night's dinner was too spicy. Instead, she cooks him cornmeal porridge with a blob of raspberry jam in the middle.

Cyril pats the duvet, but I don't want to sit too close. There are yellow stains on it and I'm not sure what made them. Sonny's not fussed. He sits right up near Cyril's pillow.

'So, what have you . . . ?' he says, but it turns into a cough, which makes spit lumps fly out of his mouth and land on his pyjamas making wet spots. Some of the buttons are open and long white hairs poke out. His skin is pink and wrinkled like a baby blackbird's. It's ages before he gets his breath back.

'We haven't got time to go through the whole book. Just get to the good bits,' says Sonny. He pulls a grey hanky out from underneath Cyril's pillow. Cyril picks it up and wipes his chin.

'Ah, blasted handkerchief, I was wondering where it had got to. Now what was I saying?' Me and Sonny show him the pages of animal tracks. There are paw prints we recognise – badgers, otters, foxes, minks, voles, even weasels.

'None of them match the tracks we found on the river-bank,' we tell him.

'Do they not?' Cyril leans forward so he can see the pages better. 'Still think it's that big cat of yours?'

'What else can it be? But no one believes me. They all think I'm seeing things.'

Cyril sits back against his pillow and looks at me for so long I feel uncomfortable. 'Go and get those figurines you covet so much from off the dresser,' he tells me eventually. I run down to the kitchen, snatch the golden figures and race back up to the bedroom. Cyril makes space for them on the duvet. 'Have I told you how I got these?' His voice crackles like a badly tuned radio and his breath wheezes between each word. We've heard the story loads of times, but like hearing it again. 'A very dear friend gave these to me while we were shooting a film in Bogotá. I was playing a lieutenant on the run from the Brazilian militia. They are made from tumbaga.

Do you see? A harmonious mixture of gold and copper. Artefacts. Very old. Made by the Quimbaya people. Where is the one I wanted to show you?' He pushes the figures about with his finger. 'Ah. Here it is. Go on, pick it up. We've not got all day.' I reach for the one that's shaped like a cat. It's got cat ears, but lots of pointy teeth like an alligator.

'Is it a panther?' I ask, turning it around.

'Close. Close. A jaguar. A black jaguar to be precise. Have you . . .' He stops to cough up more spit. This time there are flecks of blood in it.

'Maybe we should let him rest,' says Sonny. He climbs down from the bed and moves the glass of water closer.

'But I want to hear the story,' I tell him.

'And you will. Do not worry, I am fine,' replies Cyril. 'Although I am sick to the back teeth of being confined to this blasted bed.' He gobs into his hanky and takes a sip of water before continuing. 'Have you ever heard of a spirit guide?'

Sonny nods, but I've never heard of one so he must be lying.

'The South Americans believe there are two planes of existence. One that you and I inhabit, and another belonging to the spirits. This jaguar here.' Cyril points to the figure curled up in my hand. 'He is an important link between the spirit and the physical.'

'Physical? What does that mean?'

'What it means is unimportant. All you need to know is that the black jaguar represents courage, which you will need in order to face the dark times in your life.'

'Dark times? Do you think it's a jaguar then, not a panther?'

159

'Panther. Jaguar. It doesn't really matter.' Cyril lays his head back into his pillow and closes his eyes. 'Did you know that in ancient Rome, the black panther was also thought to bring courage? So much so that its likeness was carved as a talisman on houses and tombstones.' The rattling in his chest sounds much louder. 'Pop those back downstairs. There's a good lad.'

Richard

'Fucking hell!' Richard aims a frustrated kick at the wheel-barrow, which tips precariously, pouring gravel to the ground. Nothing is working. No matter what method he employs – meticulously following the expert advice in his many books and taking a careful, long-handed approach rather than his usual shortcuts – it ends in failure. Could be the batch of seeds got too old or had spoiled, having not been sealed away properly and allowed to get damp during the floods. They should have been good for two more years at least, but he will have to start from scratch and order in a new load or see if there are enough pennies to scrape together for some pre-grown seedlings, an excessive expense he fundamentally disagrees with. Normally, when things are not working, he instantly knows how to go about fixing them, is usually the first one on the scene in a crisis, always ready with a foolproof solution, but with his own life, he is bloody useless. Without bothering to pick up the wheelbarrow, Richard forsakes the polytunnel and heads over to the shed, where he grabs a bottle of cider from a carrier bag stashed under the worktop. It is gone in a few gulps, barely touching the sides.

'Fuck it,' he yells again, lobbing the empty bottle at the shed wall where it rebounds loudly and, unbroken, rolls through the metal filings on the floor. There are marks down there, as though someone has been drawing pictures in the dirt. Reaching for the carrier bag once more, Richard is dismayed to see there is only one bottle left. He wonders if he should screw it all and walk to the pub, but the once-white clock on the wall warns him that it is only quarter past ten in the morning.

Max

'You shouldn't believe everything Cyril tells you,' says Dad.
He's stuck with us this afternoon because Mum says she's
feeling under the weather and has gone back to bed. We can
tell he's super-cross about it, like he has more important
things he wants to do. But there's not a lot he can do as the
veggie patches are completely iced over and the ground's as
hard as concrete. Plus, he finished his deliveries early this
morning. I guess there might be stuff he has to do inside the
polytunnel, but nothing grows this time of year.

'Well, he knows more than you do,' I reply. He's deliber-
ately trying to ruin everything.

'Look, Max, I haven't got time for this. Just get in the van,
will you. I've got to get bread.'

'I am getting in the van!' I shout. Dad slams his door, starts
the engine and drives onto the road before me and Sonny
have time to fasten our seatbelts. 'Hang on!'

'Well, hurry up then.' He slows down but doesn't stop. I
don't know why he's so angry all the time. He's not the only
one with stuff to do. We planned to sneak out while Mum
was resting. Now, we're stuck with him. It's never just *get
bread*. We always have to stop somewhere or go to somebody's house and wait for ages while he fixes something or
talks about gardening. Our whole afternoon will be wasted.

When we get to the shop, Dad parks the van next to Les
Pollard's truck, which has a pile of rusty metal hurdles

balanced on the back of it. Janet's outside in her stripy blue apron, sticking up a poster on the noticeboard about the village pantomime. It's Rumpelstiltskin again. Janet takes drawing pins out of her mouth.

'Alright, Richard.'

'Alright, Janet,' Dad replies. Crunchy brown salt has been sprinkled from the kerb up to the shop steps to make them less slippy. Outside, there are sacks of coal and wood briquettes, and some old person's busted mobility scooter that has a peeling Union Jack sticker on it. Large boxes filled with bottles of Happy Shopper tomato ketchup are stacked up inside the shop doorway, blocking the door. Dad shoves his shoulder against it until it opens wide enough for us to squeeze through.

'Be right with you,' Ted calls out. The shiny bald spot on the top of his head moves behind the till and then all of him appears. 'Sorry 'bout that, Richard, bit behind with the unloading today.'

Les waits by the till with Trevor, the churchwarden. Before him on the counter is a packet of Hobnobs and six cans of beer. Even though it's warm in here, Les has got a woolly balaclava on under his hat, so we can't see his long grey rat's tail. 'And get us some baccy while you're at it, Ted,' he says.

'Right you are, Les,' replies Ted, and lays a large green bag on top of the cans. On the shiny plastic counter are bottles of homemade ginger ale and a plate of cupcakes with yellow icing. They look tasty, but the label says they're made from courgettes. Behind them is a box of toy windmills that little kids like to blow. Everything in here is really boring, just the usual stuff, eggs, flour, sugar, and lots of tins and jars. Sometimes there are nice biscuits, like the chocolate Florentines Janet got in at Christmas time. She's got a Requests book where customers can write down fancy things they want that the shop doesn't normally stock, like filo pastry, French coffee, hummus or chorizo sausages. Cyril always gets us to ask for pitted green olives. Once, me and Sonny asked for light-up yo-yos, but we never got them.

'What can I do you for, Richard?' Janet comes up behind us with a crate of our butternut squashes.

Dad leans his elbows on the counter. 'A cottage please, Janet, if you've any.' He and Janet both went to our school when they were younger.

'Only got one granary left, I'm afraid, will that do?' She reaches up and takes down the last loaf of bread on the shelf.

'Can we buy something?' I ask Dad.

'No more than 50p,' he replies.

'50p! That's not enough. 'Ere, make it up to two quid.' Les pushes the extra coins into my hand.

'Thanks,' I shout as me and Sonny sprint over to the sweet aisle before Dad has a chance to make us be polite and give them back. The coins are warm and covered in dirt. I scan the packets on the shelves, but there's not much to choose from. The best sweets are in the One Stop Shop in Combe Leigh. 'What about fruit pastilles?'

'Nah. We can get them off Marge. Aero?' suggests Sonny.

'Won't last long enough. What about . . .' My eyes skip over the Animal Bars – last time we bought them they were so old the brown chocolate had turned white.

'Minstrels?' says Sonny, and he points to the bottom shelf.

'Minstrels,' I agree. We've got enough money for two packets.

Back at the till, Janet puts a large steak and kidney pie into a plastic bag. 'Having this for your tea are you, Trev?' she asks.

'Not tonight. Missus says she fancies a chinky from that new place in Meare,' says Trevor. Me and Sonny look up at Dad to see if he heard. We're sure Trevor means Chinese food. You're not allowed to call it a *chinky*, are you? Dad looks down at us but doesn't say anything.

'Oh, that sounds nice,' says Janet. 'Wonder if it's any good. Ted and I usually go to the Jade Palace in Branstock, but it's such a long drive, the sweet and sour balls are cold by the time we get home. Well, let me know what it's like.'

'Will do, Janet. Will do,' replies Trevor as he goes out the door.

When we get home, Dad says he's got to pop out, so drops us at the gate with the bread. He doesn't even bother to turn the van engine off. Mum's still upstairs, but it's nearly four, so we know she'll be down soon to get tea on. We dump the bread in the porch and slip round the back of the house where dirty old snow has piled up. It was only white for a few days, and we missed most of it because we were trapped in school and Mrs Haycock made everyone stay inside at break time so we didn't ruin our school shoes. Me and Sonny squish the brown mush with our wellies. Down on the bank, nettles are the only things left alive. They've taken over the reeds, blocking our usual path down to the river. But they've lost most of their sting and can't get us through our jeans. Pulling off our gloves, we squat down to drag aside tangles of dead grass. It looks like a heron's been here, scratching about. Probably looking for one of the bumpy brown toads that hide under the rocks, or the tiny yellow snails stuck to bits of wet wood. Past the weeds, the dark river moves slow and thick like Mum's treacle.

We head over to the wall running between our house and Barbara's. Mum says Barbara had it put up a few days after she and Dad moved in. It's not very tall, so if we stand on tiptoes we can see over into her garden. Dad's new polytunnel reaches way higher and Barbara complained to Mum that it's an eyesore and blocks out the light into her conservatory. She's threatened to report Dad to the council. Her wall ends at the start of the riverbank. After that, there's nothing sealing off her garden. Sonny wanders over and I know straight away what he means to do. That's the best part of being twins; we don't need to explain everything to each other, there's a magic bridge our thoughts can travel across.

'She might not catch us if we're quick,' he says. My heart beats faster and the taste of chocolate comes back into my mouth.

'What if Mum finds out?' We both look up at the landing window to check she's not watching us. Out on the moor, redwings shimmer like a swarm of giant insects. We pretend to be ninjas and sneak over the invisible line from our side onto Barbara's. Even the grass here seems different. Spikier. It pokes up out of the icy mud. Fewer nettles grow here and vole tracks twist and turn along the river's edge. But before we have a chance to take a closer look, there's tapping on a downstairs window, which then opens. Barbara's wrinkled bird face pokes out.

'Hey! Who's there? Don't think I can't see you.'

'*Run,*' Sonny shouts.

We race back to the house, sliding through the slush, and fling off our boots in the porch. In the kitchen, we pant so hard we can't talk.

Sonny

White feathers float downy boats downstream. A swan has died upriver. Maybe a fox got it, or it hit the power lines. Sheets of ice bump at the water's edge. Overhead, a new moon drags the tide and pierces the cold black sky with stars. Look – there's Andromeda. Snowdrops appear like magic during the night. Push! The ground's hard with frost. It's nearly Candlemas. Melted snow drips secrets into the rhynes. On the bird feeder, starlings fight over the peanuts. We've eaten the last of the pink coconut ice. All that's left of the mint balls is a tiny pile of sugar. Come on, let's press our licked fingers into it. Dad's busy. The door of the polytunnel is always shut.

Bent before the mirror in her bedroom, Mum puts on her mask, pats her face with brown liquid from a small glass bottle until her skin is quiet. She lightens the dark under her tired eyes. Her tubs of shea butter have nearly run out. But it's okay, there's always olive oil to smooth down any ashy flakes. There's Vaseline to hide the peeling and make her lips look soft and shiny. She doesn't take as long over it as she used to. There are other things that have changed. Max can't see, but I'm watching. Look how her nails are bitten away. Sleepiness follows her, but at night she still creeps around the house filling the kitchen with chocolate brownies and scones dotted with raisins.

Nana calls, but for once the phone isn't answered. This scares me the most. It's as though Mum's too worn out to speak. *Ping, ping, ping* her phone goes with text messages. I wish Nana and Aunty Peaches would get on a train and come and find us. Even Nathan. Though I know he hates getting mud on his white trainers. But I could show him how easy it is to spot where the grass grows higher, where the ground's firmer, so we can leap and hop and jump from place to place without getting our feet dirty. I wish someone would come. Anyone. It won't be Dad. He's lost in the garden. It's turned into a maze and he can't find his way out.

Tess

The playground is lively with chat even though all the children have gone in. I squeeze past in the hope I can get away unnoticed, but there's a barricade of loitering mothers in front of the gate. None of them seems to mind the cold. They all stand idle in little more than jeans or leggings topped with thin jackets.

'God, Tess. You look awful.' Diane blocks my path as I try to escape. Her face is a larger version of her daughter's, with Ruby's snub nose decorated with dark brown freckles. She stands so close I can smell coffee on her breath.

'Do I? Oh . . . I'm not really sleeping.' My mistake. It's like waving a red flag. In an instant, several of the mums in earshot close in on us.

'Aren't you? Oh. That's how I was when Ian got laid off. Couldn't sleep a wink,' says Lorraine. The wind has fluffed her frizzy hair into a more substantial afro than mine.

'What you need is a few glasses of wine before bed,' Diane offers. She smiles, pleased to be the initiator of what's promising to be an entertaining conversation. I twist the buttons on my coat and pull my scarf tighter.

'Tell me about it. I can't sleep unless I've had at least half a bottle,' answers Sarah Winslow, who is blonde and petite, and the appointed leader of this particular clique. Her hangers-on nod in agreement, each excited to add their own accounts of sleep deprivation and the benefits of alcohol. Around us, the

171

playground empties, until it's only our small group left. As yet, not one of them has actually asked me how I am.

'Have you tried lemon balm or valerian?' says another. She's new. I don't yet know her name – perhaps Cathy, Carol or could be Karen – only that she moved here a few weeks ago, from Sussex I think, to be closer to her in-laws. Already, she's a bona fide member of the gang, indistinguishable from the village-born veterans, and instantly absorbed into PTA mornings and cake sales. I still feel like a newcomer.

On that first day of school, we walked through the gate straight into a crowd of watchful parents. How differently people behave when it's only one-on-one to when there's the power of the pack behind them. Richard was oblivious to the stares. There were friends for him to greet, some he'd spent his own childhood with at the very same school. One of the teachers even recognised him and wanted to say hello. They were clowning around and there was banter and mock sur-prise at the sight of the boys, imperfectly matched in their brand-new uniforms. It was all an act. *As if they didn't know we were coming.* We couldn't step outside our house without setting off the feverish village drums. I knelt down out of the intrusive eye line and fussed with collars, kissed small, nervous foreheads and made feeble promises that they'd love it. Before moving here, nothing could have prepared me for being the only black person in a completely white environ-ment, for being looked at in such a penetrative way. They were so intent on their inspection that at no point did any one of them stop for a moment to wonder how it felt to be alone in such sharp contrast. My heart felt like it was going to explode, both with the fear of leaving my boys at the mercy of this mob and with the unwelcome comprehension that this really was my life. Afterwards, Richard was astonished that our recollections of the morning were so different. He was sure I was exaggerating.

'Valerian? Urgh. No. That herbal rubbish doesn't work. You're better off taking sleeping pills,' says Sarah. She taps my arm to make sure I'm paying attention.

'Or there's always an orgasm,' adds Amy, who's late and throws in her comment as she rushes past towards the office with a sullen Mason. Delighted, all the women cackle.

'Goodbye. Enjoy your morning, ladies.' Mrs Haycock appears from nowhere. Her neat mauve anorak flows cape-style over her cardiganed shoulders. Anyone would think it was September, not the coldest February on record. She herds us out, her hands flapping like we're a flock of stubborn sheep, and locks the school gate behind us.

'Tess. Wait up.' Breathless, Amy runs to catch up with me. Together, we walk to her car, which she's left with the back end jutting out into the road. Towering above us, a teenager in an enormous blue tractor shouts for her to hurry up and move it.

'What a dreadful morning. I swear that child's trying to turn my hair grey. He made such a fuss, just because . . .' Amy notices my face. 'Tess, what's wrong?'

'God knows,' I answer, too weary to pretend otherwise. 'I don't know what's wrong with me.' Unexpected tears prick my eyes and I scrub them away with my scarf. Impatient, the tractor squeezes past so that its monster truck wheels pulverise the verge, shooting mud and grit halfway up the Meades' front garden wall.

Amy links her arm through mine. 'Oh, love. Come on. Let's go back to mine for a cuppa.'

'It's fine. Really. I'm just tired.'

'Look, come back anyway. I want to show you the amazing dress I bought for Saturday. It's got a plunging neckline. Thought I'd get my tits out and give all those boring farmers something to look at,' she says, trying to make me smile, but my nostrils flare and drag in cold air as an apple I had for breakfast climbs back up my throat. I swallow it down hard.

'Thanks, Amy, but another time perhaps.'

'You sure? Well at least let me run you back.' I don't argue, relieved I won't need to make the long walk home.

The inside of Amy's car reeks of new leather. It's pristine, like its exterior, and not a single crumb litters the seats. It's hard to believe she has children.

'Tess, I hate to say it, but you do look a bit crap.' Amy takes her eyes off the road to peer at me over the top of her sunglasses. 'Have you thought about seeing Frencher?'

'Dr Frencher? God, no. I'll be fine.' I try and reassure her, fully aware the only thing I'm suffering from is misery at how my life is playing out and paralysing indecision.

'Go and see him. Don't worry about school pickup. I can easily do it if Richard's not about.' She lets me out at my gate with a hug and I realise, not for the first time, that despite all of her faults, I'm grateful to have her.

I sit by the kitchen window for the rest of the morning sobbing after my 'World's Best Mum' mug that Sonny brought me for Mother's Day two years ago slips between my clammy hands and shatters on the stone floor. I'm too distraught to eat lunch and can't bear to look at last night's batch of brownies. Perhaps I should see Frencher. No doubt he'll say it's grief, but what if he says it's depression? Mama's voice, loud inside my head, reminds me – *we* haven't got time for that kind of nonsense.

Sonny

Wild ducks race across the sky. Listen – can you hear the thunderclap of gunshot? Turlough Woods are hidden in mist. Deer split soft gums in search of new grass. Apple trees waiting for leaves jerk and sway in the wind. In the Scots pine, jackdaws tease the barn owl. See the light darken over the Woodholt viaduct. Cold water freezes the back of my throat. Overnight, the world is painted white. Let's hide behind closed doors and build up the fire. There's the small glow of Max's night light through the landing window. Nightmares crawl like earwigs underneath the duvet. In my bed, I dream of ice and fog. The house bricks tremble as Dad snores.

There are no more arguments, no more muffled shouts floating up the stairs and keeping us awake at bedtime, definitely no more singing and dancing around the kitchen or anywhere else, no more sleeping in or goodbye kisses over the garden gate. I don't know what's worse, them fighting or them being silent. Frozen tongues disappear behind frozen teeth and lips.

Mum's phone pings again.

'Why won't you answer it?' I want to ask. She sighs and goes out to see the chickens, staring down at the path as though she can't bear to see what winter has done to her garden. Inside the chicken house, black eyes watch as we cup the feed. Then they run, sharp beaks darting. While their backs are turned, Mum collects the few eggs. It's wintertime so there aren't many. She rolls each one in her hand like a fortune teller trying to guess what lies beneath its shell. We clear away dank sawdust, top up the water, block the rat holes with stones. In the cold they come to steal the eggs, sometimes so big they carry off the traps, leaving only a trail of blood behind them. When it's dark, they run over my feet in a hurry. We don't like rats. They chew holes in Dad's potato sacks, drag old dry maize husks in under the floorboards, slip through the gaps between the walls and skirting, and hide their babies in the roof insulation. Sometimes I'm quicker than they are. I cut them off as they sneak up the drainpipes. 'Go next door instead,' I tell them, and I point the way to Barbara's. She can have the rats. They leave their cosy nests underneath the chicken house and let me lead them nose to tail through the orchard. One by one, they scamper along the riverbank. I know Barbara hears them, scratching along her gutters. I watch through the conservatory windows as she sits in her pink armchair, gently tapping her orange talons on the armrests. Sometimes she calls Dad late in the evening, worried someone's prowling around her garden. Dad always goes over to look, but there's never anyone there.

Max

Barbara likes thin white bread, toasted until it's nearly black. Then she smears it with an inch-thick layer of Lurpak. 'Lots of spread, lots of spread,' she shouts to Mum from the conservatory. Mum does as she's told, but it's not good enough for Barbara. 'Next time just bring the bloody spread,' she says when Mum gives her the plate. Today, Barbara's long fake nails are bright orange. The Lurpak gets all caught up under them. It's disgusting.

'Do you want anything else?' Mum asks.

'Get me a piece of kitchen roll and you can leave me to it,' Barbara replies. She flicks Mum away and leans back into her pink armchair. Barbara doesn't want us here, but it was her that called us over as her nurse, Sue, is running late. Barbara's the same as Marge; she won't ever go upstairs again. Next to her armchair is a hospital bed that can move up and down when she presses a button. But I don't feel sorry for her like I do for Marge. Everything in the conservatory is pink, even the rugs and curtains. First-prize rosettes, like the ones Dad wins at the Flower and Produce Show, are pinned up on the wall and there's a shelf filled with silver cups and photos of show dogs. Barbara also likes paintings of fox hunters and has a freaky stuffed fox with black glass eyes that she keeps on the fireplace in the sitting room. Whenever the hunt rides across the moor, she stands on the riverbank to watch. Mum likes to see them too in their fancy red coats, but Dad says we're not to look because they're a bunch of overprivileged dickheads.

Even though we're going to be here a while, me and Sonny don't sit down. All the chairs are full of fluffy toys, mainly rabbits, that smell perfumy, like they've been sprayed with air freshener. Sonny says it's creepy. As soon as Mum's gone, Barbara twists her crooked head sideways so she can look at us.

'I know it was you on my riverbank the other day,' she says. Bits of toast are stuck on her lips and there's spread caught between her teeth.

'We haven't been on your riverbank,' I tell her. 'Really!' Sonny throws a look at me. Barbara squints her tiny pink eyes at us.

'What rot. I saw your blue anorak. Course, it was you. You know you're not allowed out there. It's private. If I see you out there again, I'll shoot you.' She jabs her horrible nails at my face.

'But it wasn't us,' I reply.

'Bloody peeping Tom, that's what you are.'

Sonny steps forward like he's not afraid of her, but Mum comes back with a tissue before Barbara can say anything else. Leaning by the door that leads out into the garden is an air rifle, bigger than the one Dad has at home. A lumpy wodge of Blu Tack waits next to it on the floor.

Even though we don't like her, Mum says we have to be polite. Every year, she buys me and Sonny Easter eggs and gives us both a five-pound note at Christmas time. Mum tells us we shouldn't judge a book by its cover. But I'm not sure. Barbara's not friends with anyone else on our road, not even John and Edith, who are really nice and friendly with everyone. She said they stole her washing line.

Barbara has cancer as well as the scoliosis, but we're not sure where because she won't go to hospital to get it checked out.

'But surely you want to know?' asks Mum as she sits down between more fluffy rabbits in another pink armchair.

'Never. Those fucking doctors have got no sense. They're all foreign and can't talk proper. The whole lot of them should be . . .' Barbara stops and points one of her horrible fingers towards the window at the oak tree opposite her house. 'Just look at those bloody birds shitting on my car!' Me and Sonny try hard not to laugh. Barbara's white car never gets used anymore, so it's spotty with starling poo. We remember when she used to come out banging a tin with a spoon to scare them away. Now she can't get up from her armchair easily by herself. Mum gives us a look that means *behave yourselves*.

'This is so boring. Please can we go next door and see Marge?' I ask. We're expecting her to say no, but she nods as though she's too tired to argue with us. She doesn't look like Mum today; under her eyes is dark and swollen.

'There and nowhere else,' she warns us.

Outside's freezing. There's no more snow, but everything's glittery with ice. It makes the road slick and shiny. If we skid on it, we can make patterns with our boots. We take turns racing and sliding along the verge, grabbing at the hedge so we don't fall. It's really quiet. Even the sparrows have disappeared under the edges of the roofs. A car passes and slows down when it sees us, and Oliver sticks his head out of the open window.

He shouts, 'Aren't you coming?'

'Coming where?' I shout back. Oliver shakes a present wrapped in robot wrapping paper.

'Evan's party. It's already started,' he says, but then his mum makes him close the window and drives away.

We knew it was Evan's birthday yesterday – he brought in a big bag of Haribo to share with the class. I didn't know he was having a party. Usually, invitations are handed out by Mr Reid at the end of school. There's only twelve of us in our year, so everyone's supposed to be included. But I definitely didn't get one, neither did Sonny, and I know Evan's mum hasn't spoken to ours.

'Bet it's going to be rubbish,' says Sonny. 'They'll have to play stupid baby games like musical chairs and pass the parcel.'

I can hear the cry of curlews out on the moor.

Why wouldn't Evan invite us? I thought we were friends. But then I remember when Laura didn't invite me to her party, even though she promised she would. She came to ours in the village hall when we were eight – they all did. And, in Year 3, there used to be a boy called Liam, who asked everyone to his barbecue party except Sonny. Mum wouldn't let me go even though I had an invitation and there was going to be an epic water fight with Super Soakers. In the end, Liam moved away because his dad said there were too many pikeys round here.

I don't want to slide on the ice anymore.

'I'm going home,' I tell Sonny. I walk back towards our house without waiting for him.

'But we're supposed to be at Marge's,' he calls after me.

'I don't care!'

Dad's in the garden loading heavy bags of compost, one by one, into the wheelbarrow. His nose is bright red from the cold, and he's pulled the furry flaps of his trapper hat all the way down.

'Thought you were with your mum?' he asks as I come through the gate.

'Leave me alone!' I yell, running past him, through the back door into the kitchen and up the stairs. He doesn't follow me, and neither does Sonny.

I hate Evan. I hope his birthday party is rubbish. My face feels hot. I kick my bedroom wall hard until small chunks of plaster crumble onto the floor. It's not until I stretch out on my bed with my feathers that I feel okay again.

Mum comes home shouting. I guess she went to Marge's and found out I wasn't there. I creep out of my room and wait at the top of the stairs. She's crying really loudly. There's the sound of Dad coming into the kitchen to see what all the fuss is about.

'Calm down, Tess, he's upstairs,' he's saying.

'Max . . . Max!' Mum calls. But I don't answer. 'Richard, where the fuck is he?'

'Here, Tess! He's here,' Dad shouts at her. 'But how come he's not with you? I thought he was on your watch?'

'*My watch?*' Mum's voice shrieks out, which is a sign that an argument is about to start.

'Oh, you know that's not what I mean! He was with *you*. So how the hell am I supposed to know what's going on?'

'Well, maybe you would if you ever bothered to take your head out of the ground!' Mum's feet stamp up the stairs and I leap back onto my bed. But she doesn't come to tell me off; she goes into their room and slams the door. Sonny comes up straight after.

'Max. Why didn't you answer her?' he asks.

'I dunno,' I reply, scooping up my feathers and stuffing them back into their jar. 'Why's she so angry anyway? It's not like I wandered off somewhere.' But I do feel guilty. The rock that sometimes lives in my stomach comes back again. I look up at Sonny. 'Is she still crying?' I ask him.

He goes out onto the landing. Without stepping on a single creaky floorboard, he presses his ear against Mum and Dad's bedroom door.

Mum's eyes are wet when she comes down to start dinner. Her hair's flat on one side like she slept on it funny. She takes a plantain from the vegetable rack. There are only two left. They've gone completely black but they're still good inside.

'Do you want to help?' she asks.

Sonny nods at me from the table.

Mum passes me the knife and moves my hand under hers

until the plantain turns into a pile of n
me how to drop a small piece into the
enough. Then we spear each slice with a
in the frying pan. Sizzling fills the kitcl
sweetness in the air. It makes me think of
Nana's house. Is that why Mum's so ar
comb my hair back away from my face.

'You need a haircut,' she tells me. I shake

'I know. So does Sonny.' His curls have gr
Mum nods but starts to cry again. There's no
only wetness on her cheeks. It frightens me. \
come in and made her feel okay? Instead, i
comes. He puts his arms around Mum's waist
hug, but it only makes her cry even harder. Ta
he leads her over to the table.

'Maybe we should put the kettle on,' he tell
shoulder. Grandma Hembry says a cup o
everything. Quickly, I take one of Mum's chamo
out of the cupboard. Dried yellow flowers in:
square. I remember to put a drop of cold water i
just like she does, otherwise it'll burn her tongu
spilling any, I take the mug over to her and Sonn
up so I can sit down.

'Are you alright, Mum?' The fear inside me coi
my voice. She tries to smile, but her mouth doesn
work.

'Don't worry, Mum,' says Sonny. 'Everything wil
On the stove, the plantain's burning.

Spring

Richard

Stark, early morning sunlight hammers on Richard's retinas as he drags a large sheet of black plastic over to warm the asparagus beds. Progress is slow and painful today, but he must carry on because the endless list of jobs to be completed in the garden is the only thing keeping him out of the pub. He had not planned to stay out so late but was caught out by the easy atmosphere inside the Swan, six miles away in Heycott, where no one knew him and he was not required to do or say anything, but could simply sit inert with his crossword, letting the bar hold him up. The relief of forgetting everything for a while had been intoxicating – free from thoughts of Tess and the ticking time bomb of his marriage imploding. Really, he should not have driven home, but this past year he has had plenty of practice, careering through the lanes in the van blind drunk.

The base of his spine throbs. There is coffee waiting in the shed, but Richard cannot stop yet, cloches are needed, just a few, ready for the early carrots – Scarlet Horn and maybe a couple of rows of Pioneer if any of last year's seeds are still usable. In the shelter of the fence, the hard ground has already been worked and sown with parsnips, onion sets and clusters of elephant garlic. Fussy cauliflower seedlings are protected in the warmth of the greenhouse, while in the cold frames, lettuce and radish seeds split and sprout. On the gate hangs a brace of pheasants, no doubt from Les, two drab hens this time, their brown speckled feathers camouflaged against the perished fence post. Richard pockets a few long ones from the tail to add to Max's collection.

'Looks like you've got your hands full,' says Marge when Richard stops in after lunch to drop off a small crate packed with cavolo nero and an assortment of root vegetables. Her rheumy eyes are partly obscured by soft folds of skin, but their keen brightness is unmistakable. With her gaze on him, her fingers tear apart a roast chicken that still steams from the oven. Oil splatters darken the front of her shirt. 'You sure you're going to get it all in the ground in time?'

'Probably not,' Richard replies, head bent low to avoid smacking himself on the wooden lintel above the door frame. 'But I have to try.'

'Ah well. It won't be easy, but don't fret . . . you'll figure it out eventually,' Marge says, tipping the stripped chicken carcass onto a sheet of newspaper. Ignoring Angus's hopeful whining, she folds up the paper's edges to prevent the bones from escaping. 'At the very least, this gives you summat else to think about.' Richard manages a tired smile and rubs his hand through his hair. Marge thrusts the newspaper parcel in his direction. 'You couldn't take this with you and chuck it in the hedge for the badgers?'

Out in the front yard, half a dozen marans scratch in the thin grass sprouting up through the concrete. Richard crosses over the road and tosses the chicken remains under a bank of blackthorns, kicking in stray bones with his boot. The jobs waiting for him at home beckon; there are seed tables to construct, the arranging of topsoil and, most urgently, the polytunnel needs another layer of insulation. A second great roll of polythene sheeting has sat waiting since he picked it up from the post office in Branstock not long after Christmas.

Richard hurries back to his shed, grabs a stained notebook from the cluttered worktop and jots down a few ideas. He needs more fertiliser and must give some serious thought to pest control, and, of course, there is the difficult question of what to put where, seeing as his rotation method has gone to pot this year. The whole thing is all-consuming, but maybe that is a good thing. Out here, only the wind rushing over the river troubles him.

'What you doing?' Max watches from the shed door, anoraked and hatted even though the day promises to be unseasonably sunny. Richard stuffs the notebook in his pocket. His guilt returns. Winter has left Max looking fragile.

'Getting organised. Can't sit around expecting seeds to plant themselves,' he tells his son, who comes in and perches on a moth-eaten deckchair that has partially collapsed under a stack of seed catalogues. 'So how come you're here?' Richard continues. 'Thought you were going with Mum to see Cyril?' Max pokes with a gloved finger at the packets of seeds lining the worktop that wait to be sorted into piles based on sowing dates. There is a system; customers like to know in advance what they will be getting, although sometimes there are mix-ups – the packet says cucumbers but instead, melons appear. Richard used to suspect it was the kids having a laugh, but now fears his own muddled brain is the culprit.

'She's not going. Says she's got a headache.' Max fidgets, dislodging the catalogues, which slide noisily from the chair to the floor. 'What's wrong with her?'

'Oh, nothing for you to worry about. Tired, I expect. You know how she gets in cold weather.' But as Richard reaches down to gather up the fallen papers, he makes a mental note to chop up a few more logs from the stack of willow heaped in front of the woodshed – they will not burn well but will keep the temperature in the house from dropping lower than Tess can tolerate. 'So, fancy helping me out today?' The expression on Max's face shifts from worry to boredom.

'Do I have to?' His gaze slides towards the shed door.

'No, you don't *have* to. I thought you might *like* to, seeing as you're at a loose end.'

Richard used to console himself that at least one of his children was a keen gardener in the making. As soon as they could walk, he had encouraged them both to give it a go, supervising the growing of margarine tubs of cress on the kitchen windowsill, and giant sunflowers, first in pots and then outside to stretch over the fence into the road. Sonny's small brown hands had been as green as his, but it was never Max's thing – his eyes were tuned to a different frequency, alert only for things with fur or feathers, or tiny critters that crawled, slithered or buzzed. Nature mad, that one, almost to the point of obsession. 'What are you going to do with yourself then?'

Max, already out of the door, turns to look back at his father. 'Not sure yet, it's up to Sonny.' Richard returns to his notebook but can no longer concentrate.

Sonny

Come. Let's race across the moor and clamber over felled ash, brittle and grey with dieback. Look – there are soft buds appearing on the field maple. Careful not to crush the colts-foot or the tiny purple cyclamen. Thick brambles snag our wellies. I drag my brother over grassy ant hummocks, where the ground is soft with moss. Horses' hooves have churned up the track. Don't scare the twitchers lurking in the hedge. Shall we show them the nightjar's bed of fallen leaves or where herons clean out their nests? Don't stray too close to Marsh Farm or the barking collie will come after us.

Happiness comes in the smell of freshly mowed grass, the aniseed of early cow parsley thrusting through the hedge-row, the sweet hay scent of the first marsh marigolds. The house enjoys it too. Bricks contract and revive their strength. At last, after spreading for all these cold, wet months, the mould fades away. Pleased house spiders venture downstairs again and settle back inside the bookcase. I stay in the garden in case Dad needs my help. It's a race to get everything done before dinner. There's never enough time, despite Dad's thorough planning, the hours he spends each day figuring out his next steps. Together, we work our way along the rows. Dock leaves grow deep, and we must remove the taproot. If he leaves even a tiny sliver, they will be back, hardier than before. Same with thistles and hemlock.

When I was little, old people walking up our road would stop, relax their tired legs against our fence and watch me dig. They thought I was cute, the way leaves and dandelion fluff stuck to my hair as though it was Velcro. Dad said they found the sight of me amusing. When I asked him why, he thought about it for a long time, but couldn't give me an answer. I can't see what was so strange or so funny. He gardens all the time, and no one finds that surprising. Nana loves to grow flowers and Mum told me when she was young, Grandad grew Jamaican vegetables in his tiny London garden – callaloo, okra, sweetcorn and chilli peppers. So really, I'm no different from most of my family.

When I see Dad's had enough and the blisters on his hands are aching, I pull him into the house. Never mind Mum at the stove, I tell him. Let's go upstairs to my room and look at all my fossils like we used to.

Tess

Wash the saltfish for the third time. It's my last pack – I'll need to stock up again. Soft translucent flakes fall into hot pork fat. Above my head, the ceiling makes known the heavy tread of Richard's footsteps. Add thyme, fresh now it's growing back, crushed pimentos, the emptied-out quarter of a yellow scotch bonnet. What is he doing up there? His loitering unnerves me. Add tender ribbons of boiled cabbage. Condensation fogs up the kitchen window. I'll open it a crack ... *There he is again.* From between the spiny naked branches of the apple trees, my own dark eyes reflect back at me. It's easier when I think of other things. Stops me panicking. Stops the walls closing in and the constant influx of heartbreaking reminders of everything I've lost. Where's the pepper mill? Must mix this lightly, so as not to crush the saltfish. Can I get away with rice again? Probably not, they're always happier with slices of granary bread.

I manage to fob Mama off and blame bad phone reception for all her missed calls. When we finally do speak, I try to be cheerful and convince her there's nothing wrong, but I needn't have bothered; she's far too preoccupied with herself to pester me. She doesn't even ask if I've sorted things out with David yet. She talks about *our* home that she's selling, about the land she's buying in Ocho Rios, a half-acre, semi-urban plot only fifteen minutes' drive from the sea. She asks for my advice about timelines, materials, building contractor rates. Since I *nearly* became an architect, I must be an expert. She wants my full attention, but my mind fizzes, jammed with unspoken words. Excitement spills out of her and rushes down the phone – she's *going home* after all these hard years and will stay with one of our many aunts in Claremont until the building work is done. Her flight to Kingston is booked for the Tuesday after the Easter bank holiday – she's confident our house will have sold by then. An estate agent is coming next week to take photos – it's expected to be snapped up, even though it's unmodernised and still has a 1940s walk-in pantry complete with a wire-mesh meat safe. Mama insists I come up to London within the month and clear out my bedroom. Peaches has already started to box up and throw away our things.

Not once does Mama ask if I want to come with her to Jamaica. It hasn't even occurred to her that I might need to get away from this place too. What if I need to bathe my chilblained toes in that warm blue sea and be among my own kind for a change? No doubt she thinks Jamaica's not for me and though it galls me to admit it, she's right. The last time I visited, people saw me coming from a mile off, looked upon me with laughter and heckled 'Hey, foreigner' or 'England'. They don't have to hear my accent; everything about me screams *English*. I can't figure out how they can tell, there's nothing about my clothes or appearance to give me away. To them I'm as English as Richard.

Peaches isn't so easy to evade. She rings me non-stop leaving countless messages demanding to know why I'm being so flaky. Eventually, I call her and struggle to apologise, although she doesn't buy my excuses. Her concern makes me feel wretched. Tears, which arrive too readily these days, start up again and Peaches freaks out completely, telling me I've been through enough and need to put myself first for a change. She's sure it will only take a month or two for me to be back on my feet. I can stay with her, if need be, until I find a place of my own. I mustn't worry about Max, he'll be fine, this move will help us both restart our lives, we'll be able to leave all this pain and grief behind. She doesn't explain how she sees Richard fitting into these plans.

. . . *and what about Sonny?*

Busyness is my only comfort. I use it to blot out the decisions that must be made. Cupboards are cleaned from top to bottom, old receipts, emptied seed sachets, elastic bands that no longer stretch are thrown away. I scrape hunks of ice from around sandwich bags of frozen runner beans in the freezer, polish the radiator pipes with Brasso and root through the wardrobe intent on filling up bin bags with clothes for charity, until my frenzy is derailed by a pile of Max and Sonny's old baby clothes. They still smell of sweet milk and soap. *What am I saving them for?* Seeing them brings back so much – my disbelief at the sight of *two* ghostly creatures during the ultrasound scan, but how within days, despite my mounting apprehension, I rushed out to buy duplicate, irresistibly tiny, sage green dungarees with matching stripy jumpers. How

Mama fretted, reading me statistics about slashed maternity budgets in rural hospitals. I told her to stop being ridiculous, it wasn't the Dark Ages, the hospital here was as good as those in London. She kissed her teeth loudly to let me know that nothing here could be considered good. The truth is, I was as nervous as she was, with too many worries of my own to take on hers. So I didn't tell her about my lonely trips around Mothercare, where I picked out pastel striped towels, onesies, cute embroidered sleep bags and fluffy blankets, envious of the other pregnant women shopping arm in arm with their mothers, whereas I had only a suspicious security guard trailing after me for company. Didn't dare mention the elderly man with the kind, grandfatherly face standing at the bus stop where I waited with my precious shopping bags, how he spat on the ground, swore under his breath and called me that dreaded word.

Beneath the bed, my old suitcase sits in dust. Inside are skirts, too tight and too short, leather trousers, bodycon dresses and ridiculously low-cut tops I used to wear clubbing in Leicester Square. Laughably, there's also a pair of tan suede boots with four-inch heels. For some stupid reason, I packed them all those years ago. What was I thinking? That I'd be whining my waist to ragga in the village pub. When empty, the suitcase makes me think of possibilities – London, the refuge of the city, anonymity, freedom from this accursed landscape.

Downstairs, wood inside the Rayburn's firebox hisses.
But what about Richard?

For weeks, we've danced the solitary dance of two people who've forgotten how it feels to be together. We're never in the same room; come to think of it, he's rarely in the house when I'm here. He must wait for me to go out, because whenever I return there are signs he's been in the kitchen, made a sandwich, left bits of cheese on the chopping board, dirty coffee cups and teaspoons in the sink, a pair of gardening gloves caked in dirt on the table. The radio station has changed from my Capital Xtra to his Planet Rock. Like migrant workers on rotating shifts, we take turns to eat.

When there's nothing left to clean, doubt, fear and guilt creep in, so I wrap myself in my coat and take the empty midday bus into Combe Leigh. There, I walk the entire length of the high street, stopping to window shop, drop off Max's library books and grab a few bits from the supermarket, where I get ogled by wide-eyed preschoolers whose parents have failed to teach them it's rude to stare.

Sonny

Deer hide frightened eyes inside the withy beds. Be careful of
the fairy rings rising on the lawn. Inside a gall is a parasitic
wasp. On the hills, there's secret snowfall. The wood's so
hard, Dad needs his splitting maul. But it's okay; the sun
comes closer every day. Look – the tips of the willows are
turning orange. Spring softens the earth under my fingernails. The peacock butterflies inside the shed shake off their
winter sleep. School shirts dazzle white on the washing line.
Listen – can you hear pygmy shrews fighting? Mum cooks
toad-in-the-hole with onion gravy. Behind the ketchup and
mustard, there's an unopened jar of jerk paste.

Wherever we went, people always asked us if it was strange to
be a twin, not a normal twin, but a mismatched one, as though
they thought there must be something unnatural about us,
like we were freaks or some weird fairy-tale creatures: *He the
sun and I, the moon.* To me and Max, it feels like the realest
thing in the world. We're the Chinese yin-yang picture Cyril
once showed us. Each side has a bit of the other in it. He called
us a 'harmonious contradiction', whatever that means. All I
know is we've both been here since the beginning, when the
two of us spun in a dark, hidden pool. It's hard for us to be
apart. Listen – he hears my laughter ringing out between the
crack willows.

Dad used to say we were two peas in a pod, especially when

we wore our green hoodies and tracksuit bottoms. But I was always the one who got in trouble, whether it was my fault or not, my name remembered over whoever else was there. It was fine for them to hang out with me in the playground, but not inside their house. Sometimes I was the lucky one, who everyone thought was funnier, cooler, cuter, the first to be picked when we played Capture the Flag because I must be faster. Max gets the worst names – *weirdo, ghost, albino*. I only got *fluff head* and *sheep*, sometimes, on a good day, *Fresh Prince*, and at least I never had to explain who my mum was. Other people think Max doesn't belong to her the way I did. Like that time he got lost in Combe Leigh library. When we found him, he was crying so much he couldn't talk, but the librarian refused to give him back, making Mum first prove she knew who he was. Old photos on her phone were her only proof: the three of us, jumping the stones at Tarr Steps, under a mackerel sky at Kilve searching for fossils with our hammers and chisels, me and Max riding in Les's trailer when we helped with the apple picking and sneaked our first taste of cider, a littler Max, his hair still fluffy baby-blond, cuddled up in Mum's lap. No amount of sorrys could make it alright.

Max

Outside our bedroom window, the birds are going crazy. It's the breeding season. They sing louder and louder each day and wake us even though it's still dark outside. Inside my head, I try to recognise as many birdsongs as possible. I'm getting really good and can pick out about eleven. Blackbirds are the loudest and normally start first. As well as singing, they make other noises, a bit like a warbler, but with more trilling and squeaking. If I listen carefully, I can hear a woodpecker drumming on the telephone pole and, far off, a chiffchaff, *chiff-chaffing*. Mum loves the robins best because they sound the happiest. She remembers listening to them outside her bedroom window when she was little. When I tell her the birds here are way better than the ones in London, she says I'd be surprised and that she'll show me next time we visit. The thrush's voice is pretty too. But then the house sparrows under the roof wake up and their squabbles take over. The birds carry about bits of sheep wool or fibreglass and strands of orange baler twine. Me and Sonny watch them pull tufts of insulation out from the loft through a hole made by a squirrel last year. Dad keeps meaning to block it up. Soon there'll be blue dunnock eggs to find, buried under downy feathers in the hedge. Tiny white speckled wren eggs are always in the nest round the back of the woodshed. Added to the birds is the *clang, clang* of machinery up at the farm. I wiggle deeper into Sonny's bed. His feet are freezing, like he's been outside during the night without shoes on.

'Why are your feet so cold?'

'I snuck out to go and check on Barbara's. To make sure she's definitely gone,' he tells me. He looks very pleased; his eyes are extra black and sparkly, which makes me think of a photo I saw of Mum in Nana's album. She was smiling really big because someone had given her an ice cream with a Flake in it.

It's weird Barbara doesn't live in the Gables anymore. She's gone to stay in a hospice in somewhere called Crawley. Marge says they found rat droppings all over her conservatory floor. She must've had an infestation. The best news is now we can walk all over her side of the riverbank without using stealth mode. Dad said 'Good riddance' and that it won't be long before the estate agents put a For Sale sign up. I wonder who'll move in. It would be fun to have someone our age to play with. Cyril is too poorly even for Go Fish.

We're late for school, even though we were up in loads of time. First, Dad keeps us waiting. He's on his phone in his shed talking to someone. Mum gets cross and makes us go and tap on his window.

'We have to go,' I shout.

'Okay, okay,' he mouths back. But he's got to unload more bags of compost from the van before we can get inside. Then we have to wait for the cows from Winslow Farm. If we'd left earlier, we'd have missed them. Eric Winslow, who's taller and hairier than Roger, and two other farmhands on bikes try to herd them on, but the cows' hooves slip about on the road. Plus, they keep slowing down to chomp at the hedge. Dad stops the van but leaves the engine running making empty beer and cider bottles roll about in the footwell. We've not seen the cows all winter. They've been locked inside the giant barn opposite Mr Brewer's bungalow. Now, they're going to the milking parlour at the top of our road. They must be busting. Some have really gross udders that look like they might burst at any minute. There's one cow whose udders are so big they almost get dragged through the gravel. I can't bear to look. At the back are the ones that can't walk very well, the zombie cows, all skinny and bony with puffed-up bellies.

'When I was a kid, they used to put shackles, metal ones, on their legs to stop them from splaying out,' Dad tells us. 'They've had to stop doing it. People think it's too barbaric.' The cows turn back to look at us, as though they can hear what Dad's saying. I can see faces in their black and white patterns, and strange animals, like you can with clouds. Only the black makes a shape, the white is just background. Eric slaps the cows with a piece of blue pipe to make them hurry up.

Miss Simmonds is inside the office when we arrive at school. She must've left her class with Joanne the teaching assistant. Dad doesn't come in with us. Lately he drops us off outside the gate, so me and Sonny have to cross the empty playground by ourselves.

'Late again?' Miss Simmonds says as she writes something down on a piece of paper.

'We couldn't get past the cows,' I tell her.

'Everyone else manages to get here on time,' she replies. That's not true. Mason's late more often than we are, but he never gets in trouble. 'Does your mum understand that you need to be in school by nine o'clock?' she asks.

Miss Simmonds doesn't like us. I can tell by the way she talks and how her eyes stare at us without blinking. Seeing us makes her mouth curl up as though she's tasted something sour. She doesn't speak this way to anyone else. When she's with her Reception children her voice is soft and silly like she's a children's TV presenter. Me and Sonny wait for her to press the big button that opens the main door, so we can get to our classroom. Mr Reid will be worried that we haven't turned up yet. But instead she takes her paper and puts it away inside a large metal cabinet. After that, she starts to tidy up a pile of lunch slips waiting on the desk. It's obvious she's ignoring us. Luckily, Mrs Welsh, who's normally in charge of the office, comes in through the side door with tea and a plate with custard creams on.

'Thanks for manning the fort,' she says.

'No problem, Liz. Give me a shout if you need me. Right, let's see how Joanne's coping with my lot,' Miss Simmonds replies before disappearing through the door. Mrs Welsh puts down her tea and starts munching on a biscuit.

'Excuse me,' I ask, which makes her spin round as though she's been doing something naughty.

'Max. What are you doing here? You're very late.' She presses the button with her elbow. 'Go on, in you go. Hurry up. Mr Reid will be wondering where you are. Think he's got something exciting planned for you this morning. It'd be a shame to miss out.'

Our classroom is on the top floor, so I have to run up the stairs. Mr Reid's talking, but he nods once, which means come in quickly and sit down. He's holding sheets of card and showing everyone how to paint spring scenes in the style of some painter called Monet. But it turns out not to be that exciting, just Mother's Day cards, which we make every year. Only the girls are excited, but they get excited about everything. Like a few weeks ago on Valentine's. They spent all day whispering and passing each other cards they made with red hearts drawn on them. Megan gave one to Daniel, with lots of crosses for kisses, but the other boys laughed about it at break time, so he tore it up and chucked it round the playground. Mrs Welsh made him pick up the pieces and put them in the bin. When Megan found out, she hid in the girls' toilet until the bell rang. I've never had a Valentine's card. But one year, Sonny had three. *Three!* And he never tore up any of them. One was from Ellie and two didn't have names on. He took them home to show Mum. She said they were sweet and stuck them up on the fridge next to my painting of an osprey.

Maybe this year, a Mother's Day card will cheer Mum up. I hope so, even if it's only for a little while. Maybe she'll put it on the kitchen table next to a vase of daffodils, which we'll pick for her on Saturday. Maybe they'll make her happy and she won't need to go into her bedroom to cry anymore. Now I've started thinking about Mum I can't concentrate. Paint splodges everywhere. My card's ruined and Mr Reid says there isn't enough time to start over. There's so much paint it still hasn't dried by the end of the day. On the way downstairs to the playground, I scrunch it into a soggy mess and throw it away.

Tess

All eyes in the surgery waiting room turn towards me. They look startled, as though I've blundered in here by mistake. It's busy but silent, bar the slow flick of outdated magazines, and the squeak of the plastic chair as I sit down. I try to occupy as little space as possible. There's no one here I recognise, although the old lady seated next to me leans in, rests her delicate hand on my thigh, smiles and asks quietly how Richard is getting on. Every ear is strained for my answer, a few unable to hide their wonder that someone here actually knows who I am. Pricked by embarrassment, I tell her in a tight voice that he's fine. She deserves more. I don't mean to be curt, but self-consciousness fills my mouth and makes it hard to talk. She pats my leg, then returns to her *Reader's Digest*. On the wall are posters for the next flu vaccination clinic, reminders about eating five a day and one of a little crying black boy with snot smeared under his nose advertising a need for more local foster carers. A cardboard collection box for a charity sending reusable sanitary towels to a village in Mozambique has been placed by the door.

I'm not sure why I'm here. I know it's just tiredness, but after seeing me looking more haggard by the day, Amy insists I get some sleeping pills. I'd like to think I don't need them, but my brain is so fogged I can't think straight. I forget to feed the chickens until they come and demand my attention at the back door, forget to take out the bins, misplace the caster sugar inside the fridge. *Why can't I sleep?* During the day, I struggle to stay warm and drag on layers of thick jumpers, even tights under my jeans, but at night, sweat sticks the sheets to my skin. I try to nap for a few minutes during school hours, but instead end up biting my nails. Shouldering for space in my tired head are thoughts of David that shift erratically between dim girlish memories of him to more practical considerations of what his job offer could entail. *Oh God, why am I hesitating?*

Dr Frencher's on leave, so a new locum raises his head as I enter the consultation room.

'Tessa Hembry? Yes. How can I help you today?' His eyes fail to make contact, so I tell the space above his head that it's nothing really, just a bit of trouble sleeping, that I've not been very hungry – stress, probably. He makes no response but taps out a few words on Dr Frencher's keyboard. 'So . . . insomnia, loss of appetite . . . Let me see.' He looks at me for the first time. 'Ever been tested for diabetes? Let me check your notes. No, that doesn't seem to have been done. What about HIV? Any reason for concern there? I'm assuming you've been consistent with your sexual partners. Any family members with sickle cell?'

'I don't think so,' I reply, flustered by the stream of questions. Alarmed, I wonder if he's noticed my gold wedding band. I shift in my seat and place my left hand over my right one.

'Well, we can't rule anything out without a blood test. I'll see if the nurse can get a sample today.' I put his bluntness down to the fact he's a stand-in and return to the crowded waiting room, where some of the faces have changed. Nearly twenty minutes go past before I'm called again, this time into the examination room, with its wipe-clean laminated charts and rubber weighing scales. Anne, the surgery's nurse, greets me warmly. She knows us well. The boys came to her for their preschool jabs, a series of cotton wool balls pressed onto their chubby arms while I tried to pacify them with toffees. She was the one who took Sonny's stitches out after he slashed open his palm falling from a tree onto barbed wire. I remember his crying, how he hid his face in my chest, too afraid to watch. My notes flash up on the computer screen.

'Apparently, I need to take some blood,' Anne says with an apologetic furrowing of her eyebrows. She locates several small sample bottles on her trolley and gathers them together on a metal tray. 'So, how are you keeping? Haven't seen you in a while.'

I summon up a smile. 'I'm okay. Just tired. Not sleeping much. I tried telling that new doctor there really isn't any need for a blood test. I think I probably need some sleeping pills or something . . .' Anne switches her attention from my exposed arm to my face, and I know she's analysing my puffy eyes, whites marbled red and eclipsed by permanent dark circles. I'm sure I look years older than I should.

'Well, it's not surprising really. You mustn't underestimate what you've been through.' Her ready sympathy cracks my defences. 'Help yourself to a tissue if you need it,' she says, rolling her chair up behind her and sitting down with the unhurried composure of someone who's seen people break down before. She lets me cry for a while before speaking. 'It never helps to let things bottle up. There's no shame in saying you're not coping. Is there someone you can talk to? Your husband perhaps . . .' My face must betray something at the mention of Richard because she adds, 'Or maybe a family member or close friend? Or I could see if we can get you a referral for counselling if you prefer. You would be eligible.'

There's that word again, as though counselling is some miracle that will solve all my problems. I don't need goddamn counselling, I need to escape – escape from these glimpses of my son, his bare feet running alongside the hedgerow, sunlight lightening the thick darkness of his hair, from the way he moves, shadowy and indistinct, between the rows of seedlings growing in the greenhouse, from the way I feel the weight of him easing down beside me on the sofa every evening. Sometimes I feel his hand in mine, small and warm, his arms wrapped tight around my waist. Worst still is the laughter that echoes down to me from where he sits high in the branches of the alder.

I take the fast train, desperate to get back to London as quickly as possible. Richard doesn't say a word about the expense, just drives me to Combe Leigh Station in silence, with a dejected Max squeezed between the two of us in some warped imitation of a happy family.

'But why can't we all go?' he asks for the third time.

'Max, please stop asking. I've told you. This isn't a pleasure trip. I'm going to be really busy. It won't be any fun and you can't miss school.'

'But why d'you have to go today? It'll be Easter holidays in a few weeks, then we can come with you,' he pleads, yanking on my hand. 'Aunty Peaches won't really chuck your stuff in a skip if you don't clear your room out right away. Will she?'

If only I could reassure him, tell him not to worry, that I'll be back to collect him as soon as everything's organised. For now, I have to leave him standing there alone at the station's entrance. Richard waits outside in the van – he doesn't even try to kiss me goodbye this time.

As the train speeds past Swindon, I don't look out of the windows at the world streaming by but stare unseeing at the back of the blue upholstered seat in front of mine. The next moment, there's the announcement for Paddington and my tear-blurred sight shows me a haze of cow parsley springing up from between cracks in the graffitied embankment.

Max

Fat bumblebees crawl out of tiny holes in the house bricks. They rest for a bit, then set off to find the comfrey in the orchard. Soon their legs are floury with pollen. If we move really slowly, we can stroke their furry backs with our fingers. There are hoverflies too that flit round the daffodils, which the bees aren't keen on. Me and Sonny pinch off primrose petals and rest them on our tongues until they melt away to nothing. It's Saturday afternoon, so everyone on our road is busy in their gardens. All we can hear are lawnmowers and hedge trimmers. Tractors charge up and down, shaking the petals off magnolias. The frost has gone, and it's time to plant the maize. The smell of cow muck will be soaking into everyone's drying laundry. If Mum were here, she'd put ours back in the washing machine again. From up on Barbara's wall, we look down at the riverbank. The reeds are finally growing back. Means the river won't be able to spy on us so easily.

Inside the house feels wrong. There are no cooking sounds or smells, or cupboard doors and pot lids banging. I miss her quiet humming as she irons our school trousers. Even the chickens miss her. They sulk on their nest boxes and won't come to me when I shake their food at them. Dad tries to make the best of it, but we're stuck eating his horrible vegetable omelettes that have big bits of tomato in them.

'Go on. Dig in,' he tells us, although he covers his in hot pepper sauce, which means he doesn't like it either. Sonny sits next to me, but I miss Mum so much I can't eat. 'Will she be back by the time we break up for Easter?' I ask. 'She'll be back soon. Come on, cheer up.' Dad nods at our plates. 'Get that down you.'

Left to ourselves, me and Sonny run across the fields to where bird watchers are setting up expensive gear underneath the heronry. Even though Sonny says he prefers fish to birds, he still loves coming with me. It's tradition. Dad used to bring us every spring, and Mum too. We'd make a day of it, with sandwiches and banana bread with chocolate chips in. Afterwards, we'd walk to the top of Turlough Woods to look out at the view.

Large grey-blue wings flap like kites above our heads. The herons croak and cackle to each other, and leap about in their giant nests, reminding me of pterodactyls. If we're lucky, we'll catch sight of one of the fledglings. I wish I'd brought my binoculars with me. We could watch them for a while in the new hide built last summer, but it's full of twitchers who won't want kids in there. Last time we went inside, they tutted and wouldn't make room for us. Between the trees, we pick starry white wood anemones and purple dog violets for Mum, but we know they'll have withered by the time she comes back. If she were here, she'd kiss us and put them in an empty jam jar. We know we're not supposed to pick wild flowers, but we don't care. We'll get her soft pink apple blossom too when it's ready and, maybe, a few bluebells.

On Monday morning, it's harder than normal going off to school. Mum's left plenty of clean uniforms, but Dad's packed lunches are rubbish. All we get are boring cheese sandwiches and one of our own bruised apples. At least he makes an effort to get us in before nine o'clock, so Miss Simmonds has nothing to grumble about, but it means we have to wait in the playground with all the other parents. Dad's chicken. He sits in the parked van by the Meades' house with his window rolled down.

'You going to be alright?' he calls as we force ourselves through the school gate. 'Don't forget, Oliver's mum is bringing you home.' Me and Sonny feel worse than ever.

'So, you're coming to ours for tea then?' Oliver's mum asks. It's not really a question because already she drives fast past the shop and church, past Salter Close, up Puttford Lane towards their house.

'Isn't our dad at home?' I don't want to go to her house, and I know Sonny doesn't want to go either.

'Your dad's got quite a bit on,' she replies. 'He'll pick you up later. But it's fine. We'll have a lovely time, won't we, Oliver?'

Oliver doesn't like the idea any more than we do. He throws his head back and thumps his fist on his seat. 'Uh, Mum. Really? I wanted you to take me to Evan's so we can play his new FIFA game.'

'Shut it, Oliver,' says his mum. She glares at him through the rear-view mirror.

Branches poking out into the lane shatter as we hurtle past. Lots of kids live out this way, so there's a line of cars following us.

'I don't know how your mum copes without a car.' I'm not sure if Oliver's mum is talking to us or to herself. Stone lions roar above the gateposts outside their house. When Oliver's mum presses her car key, the large metal gates open electronically. The garden here is super-tidy, all the flower beds are arranged in neat rows and the hedges have been snipped into giant pom-poms. Inside their house is really tidy too. It's the same size as ours, but new. All the colours match, like in one of those home makeover programmes, and the walls and floor meet without any gaps, so there aren't any spiders or woodlice. But their tea isn't proper dinner. All we have is toast with butter and marmalade on. While we're eating, Oliver's older brother Mark comes in and goes straight upstairs to his bedroom without bothering to say hello. He doesn't go to Combe Hill Secondary, but to Barrington's out by the hospital. Oliver will be going there too in September. At first, he moaned about it because he wanted to come to Combe Hill with the rest of our year, but now he's happy as he'll get to ride horses and join the army cadets and shoot machine guns. Plus, they've got their own swimming pool and tennis courts, and they get longer summer holidays than we do.

'So, how's your mum and dad doing?' Oliver's mum asks. She gets up from the table to pour herself a drink from a big glass bottle. It smells like sugared almonds. Mum says she's a gossip, so we don't answer her. 'And the veg business? Doing well?'

'Yes,' me and Sonny reply together.

After tea, we follow Oliver up to his room. He's got even more stuff than Daniel. We know not to touch anything that might break, definitely not the Lego *Star Wars* models or any of his Warhammer collection. If anything goes wrong, we always get blamed, Sonny more often than me, even though he's the careful one. For a while, we dig through his gigantic box of K'nex.

'Let's see who can build the best quad bike,' Oliver says. He grabs lots of different-sized wheels. 'Bet you can't make one with shock absorbers.'

I don't know what shock absorbers are, but I don't let on. He'll think I'm stupid. Maybe Sonny knows and we can work together. We never make quad bikes with our K'nex, or cars, only animals and sometimes weird monsters or pretend rods that Dad fits out with real fishing line.

Oliver's soon bored with us and gives up.

'I would let you play, but I've only got one controller,' he tells us as he stares, with massive headphones on, at his large TV screen. Being at his house is rubbish.

Me and Sonny are still here, waiting at the dining table with our coats on, when Oliver's dad gets home from work. He travels all the way to Exeter on the train every day. I can't remember the last time we saw him. He's one of those dads who only turn up at school for the Christmas concert and, sometimes, sports day. Bit like ours, lately. He looks at us, then over at Oliver's mum, who shakes her head. By our legs are two bright blue Ikea bags filled with Mark's old primary school trousers and what looks like his outgrown winter things. Oliver's mum said she would've kept them, but Oliver insists on having everything new. We thanked her but know that Mum will take them straight to the charity shop without even looking at them. Oliver's mum whispers to his dad while she fries him a steak.

'So, it's been a long time,' he says to us, taking off his jacket and hanging it on the back of a chair. 'Where's your mum this evening then?'

We tell him about Nana, the old house in Lewisham and the new one being built in Jamaica.

'Jamaica, eh? Lovely. So is that where your mum's from originally? I thought it was Africa.'

'No, she's from London.'

He laughs. 'Jeez, I still can't get over how different you all look from each other.'

'Patrick. Here, stop talking,' says Oliver's mum as she puts his dinner down in front of him. He's got chips too and mushrooms.

Tess

David sits opposite me at the table. He wears a suit, a smart nondescript grey and not in the least bit showy. Clean-shaven and freshly barbered, he's a businessman now, not the gawky teenager who used to hang out with me under the climbing frame in the park. I struggle to look directly at him, afraid he'll see my nervousness. *Why did I let Mama and Peaches talk me into this?* He's on his second coffee, milky with a sprinkling of sugar. Nonetheless, I can tell he's tense – his buttered teacake remains untouched. There's more at stake here than either of us is willing to acknowledge. Whenever he leans towards me, I catch a hint of his aftershave, something woody, reminiscent of resin in split kindling. Being with him makes me feel treacherous. There's an undercurrent of tension I wish I wasn't feeling. I shut out Mama piping up in the back of my mind telling me he's single now and, it seems, still has a thing for me. *Oh God, do I still have a thing for him?*

Keen for this not to look like a date, I chose the last greasy spoon left on the high street, where the chalked blackboard offers pie and mash alongside breakfast burritos, Portuguese custard tarts and Jamaican patties. The whole place smells of burnt bacon. I can't stomach anything but a mug of weak tea. Across the street, the fruit and veg market vibrates with its usual busyness. All these years have passed but it's still the same as when Mama used to drag us here every Saturday

223

morning before ballet lessons. Peaches and I would stand bored, but too well trained to fidget, while she nattered with the other women and argued with the halal butcher over the price of oxtail.

'You okay?' David asks, his manner gentler than I remember. I stare at his hands, at the ivory crescents of his trimmed fingernails. As much as I don't want to admit it, being with him feels good – dare I say comforting. 'I know this can't be easy for you.' As he speaks, the built-up pressure inside me slowly diminishes.

'I'm fine,' I tell him, surprised by my own quiet surety. Here's a man I once knew intimately; the boyhood face I loved peeks out at me from inside this unfamiliar grown-up one. To avoid the pull of his eyes, I concentrate on my teaspoon.

'Still can't understand why you upped and left like that,' he says with a wry smile. His words hang in the air, unanswered. At the next table, a young woman with shiny Bantu knots spoons baked beans into her toddler's open mouth. She catches me staring and grins contentedly.

David drains his coffee. 'Tess. Man. It's cool. Don't stress.'

When I smile back at him, he gets that hopeful look I saw the first time I met him.

'So, what do you think?' he asks, mock businesslike, back to the real purpose of our meeting. 'I know it's not much, just an admin role really.'

'Oh no, it's more than enough,' I answer truthfully. 'Really. More than I could have hoped for after . . . well, you know . . .

everything. And the fact it's part-time. Means I can think about studying again, or maybe retraining.' I listen to what my mouth is saying, while the rest of me grapples with the enormity of this situation. David bites into his teacake and moves a hand across the table closer to mine.

'It's gonna be so good to have you back. Typical, though, you'll be coming home right when your mum's leaving.'

'Yeah, bloody typical,' I reply, turning away to watch through the café window, old ladies with their wheeled shopping trolleys congregating at the pedestrian crossing as they wait for the lights to change.

Richard

'So, how far back shall we take this?' Richard waves his loppers in the direction of the shrouded living-room window. Twists of clematis wind their way up the sides of the house, enclosing the drainpipes and guttering in dense, heavy knots. Many of the deep pink lantern-shaped flowers are already limp and faded. 'Would be nice to have a bit more light in there.' From underneath his swaddling of blankets, Cyril gestures with a skeletal hand to indicate his assent. Gillian was the first carer to listen to his repeated plea to be allowed to leave the confines of his bed for the comfort of his reclining chair, which Richard moved from its usual place behind the table to a sunny spot in front of the open patio doors. From here, Cyril can watch him work and enjoy the view of the garden and the light breeze flowing in from the riverbank. Although there is not much for Richard to do, the garden being of the self-sufficient sort, with rambling self-seeding perennials that look best untended, mostly cornflowers, poppies, buddleia, brunnera and columbine. Apparently it was Cyril's idea, relayed to Richard via Marge, who stated with no room for argument that Cyril's garden wanted looking over, £30 an hour – no negotiation. Richard is not to think of it as payment, but rather that he is doing the old man a favour seeing as his time is short and it would be nice to see the garden restored to its former glory before he popped off, so to speak. Seemed innocent enough, although

Richard can feel some sort of conspiracy going on seeing as Cyril has never asked for his help before, saying he prefers a natural, more uncultivated look.

Richard prises apart tangles of clematis with his hands to give his loppers better access. Exhaustion makes his arms feel heavy. It had been another late and disappointing night. Most of the seeds planted a few weeks ago had failed or been picked off by slugs despite all of his deterrents, and a branch, ripped from one of the apple trees in a sudden gale, had torn a large vent in the polytunnel wall that will need patching. There is so much for him to stay on top of, but the opportunity to earn a few pennies here at Cyril's is too tempting to pass up. Richard will earn more in a couple of days than from a whole week of delivering veg and, as Marge said, Cyril has pots of money and nothing to spend it on. Really, Richard worries, he should have picked up Max from school, but surely he will have a better time at his mate's house than stuck hanging out with his dad. Richard would have when he was a boy. And now, without his brother for company, any time Max spends with another kid his age must be beneficial.

There is a tapping and Gillian waits by the patio door with a glass of cold water, which Richard gratefully accepts. 'Starting to look better already,' he says, easing himself down to sit at the foot of Cyril's chair.

'Ah yes,' whispers Cyril, leaning forward as far as he is able. 'Sometimes you get so used to seeing things a certain way, it is hard to believe it can be improved upon.' Richard laughs out loud at the irony. Ignoring the outburst, Cyril continues, 'I've missed seeing Tess these past few Saturdays.'

'Yeah,' admits Richard, scratching at his head so crushed clematis petals are caught up in his hair. 'It's better she's in London really.'

'Yes. I can understand. Although . . .' Cyril gestures again towards the living-room window. 'See what time has done to my clematis. It's become so convoluted one can no longer appreciate the simple beauty of the flowers.' A spasm of coughing overtakes him and forces him back into his chair. On cue, Gillian reappears with a clean hanky and an inhaler.

'Water?' she asks, but Cyril declines with an impatient shake of his head.

'I believe reconciliation is always the best approach, no matter how quixotic.' He smiles at Richard the smile of a man sharing a secret. 'As my dear old mother always used to say, seems you cannot help who you fall in love with.'

Richard remembers his own mother saying something similar, but with different underlying sentiments.

Daylight has faded by the time Richard packs up his tools. He hurries home to first wash his hands, then grab the keys to the van so he can pick up Max. As he enters the dark kitchen, the beam running the length of the room *cracks*, lifting the hairs on his neck. Fumbling, Richard switches on the light in time to see woodlice fleeing underneath an empty log basket. The cold Rayburn silently accuses him – there will not be time to relight it before he leaves. But what about tea? Richard sags against the table. What useless excuse for a father is he? There is no guarantee Max will have already eaten. Over one of the dining chairs lies Tess's fluffy green scarf. So soft in his hands, Richard gathers it over his face and inhales deeply.

Sonny

Mist rises above the river. The water's warmer than the air. I skim with pond skaters through clouds of shadowy algae. Graylings nibble at my toes. Look – the first swallows are black clothes pegs perched on telephone wires. Shall we return to our old nest in the roof of Dad's shed? Gather up the straw, it's time to mulch the trees in the orchard. Fed up with feeling cold, the house leans back to catch the sun's far-off heat. Easter waits around the corner. Without Mum, who will fry our Good Friday escovitch fish and slice our bun and cheese? We'll have to make do with poor man's hawthorn leaves. Let's wait together by the village signpost. Don't leave your seeds behind in exchange for city tarmac or stroll on pavements in mud-covered clothes. Stay home and press a four-leaf clover inside Max's animal encyclopedia. Can you smell the soil perfume sweetening the wind?

Max

Dad says today we can have pizza – he wants to say sorry for picking us up late again. Out of the freezer of course as we can't get pizza delivered out here. And he's taking us fishing early tomorrow morning as a treat. I'm excited until Mum calls to check on us and then everything feels horrible again. She promises to be back soon, only has one more thing she needs to take care of. What can be so important?

'She is coming back. Isn't she?' I ask Sonny, who sits cross-legged on our bedroom floor looking through his fossil collection. He's pulled out the boxes Mum shoved under his bed. His trilobites are covered in dust.

'Course. It's like she says, she's got stuff to take care of,' he replies. If he's not bothered, then I'll try not to be either. Wrapped inside tissue paper is a fossilised coelacanth Cyril gave him instead of the megalodon tooth. Its smooth surface is criss-crossed with webs of tiny bones. 'This one's special,' Sonny tells me, 'I don't want to keep it hidden under here.' He hands me the fish and I push aside books and one of his school photos and lean it at the front of his shelf. 'That's better. Now I can see it properly.'

'Let's go!' Dad shouts from downstairs. No Mum means he must bring us with him on his veggie rounds. Marge is first because she's the closest. We walk over and, as usual, Angus is outside and the path to the front door is covered in dog poo. While Dad chats, me and Sonny leap along Angus's rubber mats, pretending they're stepping stones and the rest of the floor is molten lava. As well as fruit pastilles, Marge gives us a jar of pickled cucumbers she made last year. They swim about in murky liquid and taste revolting, but Dad likes them in sandwiches when he's run out of chutney.

Next is John and Edith's. We drive this time as they've ordered an extra-large crate. They're not regular customers, just ones that Dad calls 'top-ups'. Their two yellowy green budgies, Ginger and Fred, cheep at us from their cage in the sitting room. Old TVs and radios are stacked behind the sofa where Edith sits knitting.

'How you keeping, Richard?' she asks. 'Go on, love,' she says to me and Sonny, pointing with her knitting needle at the fruit bowl on the coffee table. For some reason, she always gives us an orange when we come to visit, and a homemade jumper on our birthday. They're much too itchy to wear, so we stash them at the back of our wardrobe.

'Can't complain,' Dad replies loudly. Edith's going deaf and can't hear unless we shout. 'How are you getting on?'

'Oh, don't get me started. Everything seems to be aching. Must be the change in the season. Still waiting for the hospital to give me a date for my hip.'

'Sorry to hear that,' says Dad. 'But once you've got that sorted, you'll feel like a spring chicken again.'

'What's that? You're doing chickens now? 'Ere, John, do we want a chicken?'

'No, I said *spring chicken*,' Dad shouts.

'I don't think we want no chickens,' John calls from the

kitchen. 'We prefer ornamentals, songbirds and the like. Keep chickens and you get rats.'

'On second thoughts,' says Edith, who hasn't heard anything John said, 'I can't really eat meat at the moment, dear, on account of my reflux. Did I tell you about that, my reflux? Oh, it's awful, like my guts are on fire. That, on top of my hip and poor old knees. They'll both need replacing before the year's out. Worst of all is there's a fluttering in my chest, like a bird. You know? Right inside my ribcage. Though Frencher did a few tests and said he couldn't find anything.'

John comes in carrying a newish-looking radio under his arm. 'This any good to you, Richard?' he asks, handing it over to Dad.

'Thanks, John. Very kind of you. Perfect timing too. My old one's nearly had it.'

'Don't chuck it away, mind. Drop it in next time you're passing. I'll see what I can do with it,' John replies. Inside his silvery beard, his lips smile.

'Stop interrupting,' snaps Edith, shooing John away with her knitting. It looks like a blanket, pink and white, like the ones babies get, or it could be the back of a gigantic cardigan. 'What was I saying?'

'You were telling me about your chest, Edith, about Dr Frencher's tests,' Dad shouts at her.

'Oh yes. Frencher. That's it. I wanted to ask if Tess is doing alright now. I heard from Valerie. You know? Valerie, from up at Hillside. She said she saw Tess in the surgery not long ago. She looked ever so pale, well pale for her sort. Don't get me wrong, I think your wife's lovely, I'd kill for her skin. Used to sunbathe for hours covered in baby oil, but only ever went red. I wanted to pop down and ask after you all, but I've been so busy with everything, this knitting and whatnot.'

She waves the blanket again.

Dad looks surprised. 'Tess?'

'Well, yes. There isn't anyone else round here who looks like Tess. Well, apart from that coloured chap in Thorney. Surely even Valerie would know the difference.'

'I . . . I'm not sure. But I know she's fine. In London at the moment, spending some time with her mother.'

'That's good then. I won't worry anymore. Nice that she gets to see her mum. Must be lonely for her living so far from her family. Especially after what she's been through. Poor thing, can't even stop for a cuppa with them when the mood takes her.'

Dad nods, but his eyes seem confused. 'No, definitely no need for you to worry. We're all fine. Aren't we?' he shouts, looking across to me and Sonny. 'Right, best be off.'

'Don't forget to bring me that radio,' calls John from the kitchen.

Sonny

Max creeps into my bed. Listen – there are strange sounds on the wind. They stir up the river water and frighten the fish. Wet, grey worms live underneath the compost heap. Don't forget to prick the lid with a knife. It's time to make an offering to the River Mumma. Black braids stream behind her as she counts her rudd like gold pennies. Moorhens wade through duckweed. Dad's empty vegetable crates rest in the yarrow. Let's make an eel trap with chicken wire and rancid bacon. Or shall we make plastic-bottle boats and send some beetles downstream? There's the *crack, crack, crack* of a pheasant strutting behind the hedge and the smell of wild garlic flowing through the trees.

Above the sluice gates, the water's still and dark. It's nothing like the slow, brackish river heading downstream past our house that breathes in and out with the tide. At the gates, two worlds meet. In the deep pool below, fish and other creatures lurk. Listen – that's the rush of the weir stream. It's a sparkling thing that races down to join the deep water below. Here, the water is crystal clear and beautiful with reeds. This part of the river isn't muddy or sluggish or filled with silt. Clouds float away to let sunlight shimmer golden on the stony riverbed. Midges hover and long green stems bend with the current. Up here is the only place we can see the fish. They shine like silver leaves.

Wait – is that an otter or just a big mink?

The water's so cold it shoots icy needles into my feet, but not for long; soon they're as numb as stone. Horseradish grows thick. It's wild now, but a hundred years ago it was an outsider that escaped from a garden on the bank. Yellow wagtails pluck insects from between the rocks, and we push the rushes over so we can sit down without getting our bottoms wet.

The rapids are where we catch chub. Around us, the air smells warm with fish. Dad tells us that when he was a boy, he would walk across the sluice gates to the tiny island, a good place to camp for the night with friends under a fishing umbrella. If they got hungry, they would eat the bait – luncheon meat, soft, white bread and sweetcorn. Now the island's hidden in nettles and has worn away to nearly nothing. Under stones in the weir stream are bullheads and spotty stony loach. The float's there bobbing, bobbing ... then, suddenly ... it's gone. A river carp would be the top prize. We never want to catch an eel that's hard to unhook and puts slime all up the line. Although maybe secretly we do – they fight hard and swallow the bait whole. Dad calls them the totem of the river, £4 a pound back in the day. We cast again and again, pausing while Dad untangles bird's nests in the reel. Snagged up on trees is a graveyard of tackle – hooks on twisted line, spinners, red and white floats and jelly lures scarred by pike teeth.

We're quiet, patient. I listen to the sound of water and Dad's thoughts rushing past as the sun climbs higher and turns up the colour. Greens brighten and the blues blend into the hills. Our breakfast of muesli feels far away, so Dad takes cheese and onion crisps from his rucksack, ham sandwiches, an old lemonade bottle filled with orange squash and a surprise bag of chewy coconut drops. We thought there were none left, but he secreted these away for a special day. Max sits high up the bank with his back pushed against the trunk of a willow. The water scares him. His eyes follow the bubbles as they churn over the edge. One of his hands grips the rod, while the other grasps tightly to the reeds beneath him. I go and dangle my feet in where the froth foams to show him it's safe. I tease him, pull at his stiff fingers and call him a wuss. Dad's too busy with his own thoughts to tell me to behave. The wind shifts and through the fish smell comes something rotten that catches on our noses. Max is the first to investigate. There, caught in the overflow is a dead calf, but it's got no head so it could have been a deer. Round and round it spins, bloated with gas and bald because its hair's all gone. More often it's sheep and if we throw stones at them, it's like shooting a leather drum that plays a tribal rhythm. We've never managed to burst one, but we know once it goes bang it will sink quickly.

'Food for the fish,' Dad says.

Tess

Spring arrives earlier here and already fallen blossom from municipal cherry trees blankets the pavement. It makes me think of apple blossom in the orchard and how the wind likes to tousle the pink-white petals. In the corners of my windowsill is something I never noticed before – moss growing. Minuscule beads of water glisten like on the thick moss coating the stones along the riverbank at home. Sonny's voice inside my head tells me moss isn't lots of individual plants clustered together as I always thought, but one plant, fully self-contained with no need for any others. I peer closer. According to Max, there'll be microscopic creatures living all over it. When I reach out under the window to push my fingertips into the soft greenness, it springs back undamaged. No doubt the new owners will scrape it away so the windows can be repainted or, more likely, ripped out and completely replaced.

As predicted, offers for the house come flying in, but Mama, not wanting to dally, accepts the first one seeing as it's well over the asking price – seems I'm not the only one who thinks this house is valuable. Lucky for her, it's a cash buyer and there's no chain on either side, so contracts followed by house keys are to be exchanged sooner than expected. Relieved, she breaks open a bottle of Baileys left over from Christmas.

'So, how tings with David?' she asks, straight to the point.

I put down my drink. Peaches won't be back until tomorrow evening, so for a rare moment it's just us and I can speak without my sister's interference. Mama heaves a sigh and sits down at the dining table, which is hidden under half-filled bags and boxes. 'Tessa. Before I leave, I need to know you're gonna be alright.'

'I'm going to be fine, Mama,' I tell her. 'Really. He's managed to find me some part-time work. Not much, but it's a start. I am really grateful, but—'

'But Tessa, dis means you can finally finish your training.'

'Hmm.' I nod. 'It does. But I'm not sure if that's what I want anymore. I thought maybe . . . I could go back to college. Do something different. I don't know what yet. I've always liked cooking. Oh, I don't know. I've got to find somewhere to live first. I don't even have enough for a deposit.'

Mama clasps my hand with palms that are dry and stiff. 'Don't worry. I can help with dat.'

'Mama. No. I can't take your—'

She laughs me away. 'Tessa, stop your nonsense. Don't you know it's a parent's job to make sacrifices for their children?'

Outside on the driveway, a dirty yellow skip spills rubbish and from among the debris, I recognise the lacquered sitting-room side table, its battered legs poking up past my dad's worn leather armchair and a broken hobby horse from Woolworths that used to belong to Peaches and then to me.

Cardboard boxes, sealed shut with gaffer tape, stretch along the hallway back towards the kitchen, blocking off the cupboard under the stairs. On the dining table, like a coffin laid out for viewing, sits Mama's old black trunk, waiting to return home, this time filled with British contraband: floral cotton sheets from Petticoat Lane, lace-trimmed Marks and Spencer's nighties, Fenjal bubble bath, Old Spice and bars of Imperial Leather. Between packing and cleaning, Mama scours the shops with Peaches in tow, who's taken a week off work, in search of suitable *take-home* presents.

I, on the other hand, take a bus to New Cross to visit a secondary school. It's huge, more than twice the size of Combe Hill Secondary and very modern-looking. Earlier, over the phone, my garbled request for a quick meeting was granted and the headmaster greets me personally in the lobby. As he walks me past the library and music rooms, he listens without interruption as I attempt to fill him in on our particular situation. When I finish, he takes pains to assure me that not only will Max be very welcome, he will also be very well looked after – they have their own on-site Family Support Adviser. In the corridors, paint has been splashed across large white sheets hung up to protect the walls. 'We've been celebrating Holi,' the headmaster tells me proudly. He invites me to peep through windows into busy classrooms and I'm in awe of the colourful mix of faces arrayed before me. So, when the tour is over and the headmaster is called away to attend to a dispute that's broken out in the dining hall, I follow the receptionist into her office and sign all the necessary paperwork for a place in September. All that's left for me to do is register Max's name with the local authority.

Packing away a whole lifetime is not easy – it takes us two days just to clear out the loft. Saying goodbye might take longer than I anticipated. I should ring Richard to make sure he's managing and to let Max know I haven't forgotten him, but I already called twice today, hoping Richard would answer, and both times his phone was engaged. Rather than call again, I sit on the carpet in my room with a glass of cold sarsaparilla and try to assign my old possessions into 'charity', 'rubbish' and 'keep' piles. The last time I sat here like this was on my return from university, only back for a few days to introduce my latest boyfriend and drop the news that I was pregnant and that I'd be leaving home for what was basically the other side of the country. Then, it only took me a few hours to pack – so impatient to start a different life with a man I barely knew. I still can't explain what it was about him that made me so willing to give up everything. His quiet way, maybe, his kind hands, how he kissed my neck when he was tired. He seemed to ground me somehow, stop me floating. I know, Cyril would say it was providence or something confusing about the incandescent nature of belonging.

Despite all the chaos, Mama still finds time to cook. Nothing elaborate, just corned beef with sweetcorn and onions, and fluffy white rice, my favourite after-school dinner from back when she worked two jobs and there was only enough time to toss something in a frying pan before rushing us off to Brownies or swimming lessons. Afterwards, while I help Peaches wash dishes and pack away the plates, Mama hums gospel hymns as she carefully seals her china ornaments in bubble wrap. Around her is a sea of paper: bank statements, expired premium bonds and credit-card bills, tea-marked letters from the tax man.

'Look at all dis rubbish,' she says, sweeping her hands over them. Birthday and Christmas cards Peaches and I made as kids end up in the recycling. From everything rises the worn scent of talcum powder and bay rum. To get some air, I retreat to the garden, but the plant pots and their riotous colour have vanished, leaving only a stained, empty stretch of grey concrete.

That night, I sleep alone in my stripped room. Police sirens wail and, in my dreams, tawny owls call from the orchard.

Max

Instead of going straight home after school, Dad stops outside the park. He tells us to play for a while as he has a final job to do. I know he's lying because when we got inside the van there were no crates in the back, so all the deliveries had been done. His phone, which was on my seat, said he'd missed three calls, but he snatched it up real quick as though he didn't want me to see.

'I won't be long,' he shouts to us as he zooms away. Flocks of seagulls on their way home from the rubbish tip squeal above our heads. Caleb and his little sister Evie are playing on the swings. We don't want to get caught hanging out with them, so me and Sonny stand on the field and watch the older boys play football. Henry Taylor's in goal. He's looped his red and black Combe Hill tie around his head like a bandana. They used to ask Sonny to play when they were a man short, until they figured out he was rubbish.

'Who are you again?' asks George Marshall, looking over at me. He rests the ball under his foot so the other boys can't play until he's finished talking.

'Max. Max Hembry,' I reply. I'm surprised he's noticed me. George used to go to our school, but he left for secondary school when we started Year 2. Now he's had one of his ears pierced and has got really tall. 'Max,' I say again when he frowns at me. 'You know. Sonny's brother.' I glance at Sonny, hoping he'll back me up.

'Sonny Hembry? Oh yeah,' he says, rolling the ball back and forwards.

'Get on with it, George!' shouts Henry from inside the goalposts.

'You can't be brothers. You're not black,' says George.

'We're twins,' I reply.

'Twins? You sure 'bout that? You can't be twins.'

'We are,' I shout. He grins and kicks the ball high into the air.

'Yeah, right. Sure you're not the pink afterbirth that followed him home?' The others laugh like it's the funniest thing they've ever heard.

'Come on, Max,' says Sonny. He pulls my arm. 'Don't listen to him. He's an idiot.'

We go and sit on the dirty step of the tennis pavilion, but I can still hear them laughing and making jokes from here. They're all staring in our direction. Dad always tells us 'Words are just words', but George's words make me feel hot and prickly like I was in an actual fight.

I am black. I think. I must be because everyone says Sonny is and we're twins. Plus, Nathan told us that if one of your parents is black, it automatically makes you black too, even if you're half white or half Indian or half whatever. I wanted to ask him, what if everyone says you look white? But I didn't because he'd have given me a stupid answer or said something mean.

Dark clouds fly in and cover up the sun. Suddenly, it gets really cold. It's going to rain. Henry and his mates pick up their rucksacks, blazers, mobile phones and half-drunk energy drinks, and head off. George sticks his middle finger up at me as he walks past. Me and Sonny stay on the step until Dad finally turns up.

'Hurry up then,' he calls from the park entrance. He sounds cross, but I don't want to hurry. To annoy him I drag my feet slowly through the grass, so mud smears up the sides of my school shoes. Today's been *shit*. Mum would tell me off for swearing, but Daniel swears all the time, so I don't see why I can't. Anyway, Mum's not here to stop me.

There's no dinner waiting for us when we get home, no rice or roast potatoes, just an empty house that's too quiet. I tell Dad we're starving, and he makes us peanut butter sand-wiches but doesn't have any himself. Then he's gone, saying he won't be a minute. But he's hours. Eventually, me and Sonny put ourselves to bed. Through the landing window, the light from Dad's head torch bounces about as he pushes the wheelbarrow along the garden path to the polytunnel. He doesn't seem to notice that rain is pouring down.

Richard

Thunder shudders against the shed's tin roof. Overcome by the din, Richard collapses into the broken deckchair so that it creaks dangerously. He takes a long swig from his second bottle of ale. According to the clock, it has gone midnight and he really should go to bed, but he cannot seem to switch off, not quite yet. The whole day was a complete washout, not just because of the rain, which always made working outside more challenging. Richard drove like a maniac, going as far as deserting Max at the park, thinking he would prefer to play with his friends rather than tag along, but still did not make it to the garden centre in time and was met by shuttered doors and a closed sign. There would be no time to go again tomorrow, not with all the deliveries backed up and customers waiting. The French beans, calabrese and purple sprouting need planting, the asparagus cutting, and he had promised to pop over to Cyril's for an hour or so and finish pruning back the gunnera. He cannot muck about wasting time like this. Bills and notices pile up on the worktop, including one from the county council questioning the purpose of his new polytunnel – is it commercial or recreational? Richard shoves the letter behind the radio with the others to be dealt with later – better to keep them here than left in the house for Tess to find. If only he could focus. Even with Cyril's handouts, he will have to do the sums again. He still needs to buy more heat lamps. The one in the greenhouse is on its last legs, so a priority if he plans to get the bell peppers, celeriac, lettuce and aubergines started.

'Dammit!' he shouts, flinging the empty bottle down on the shed floor to join the first and reaching for a third. Anger at his own incompetence flows through him like a tidal bore. He drains the bottle and lobs it at the floor where it breaks, sending thick chunks of brown glass spinning under the worktop. It is not until his fourth bottle that the sharp edges start to blur with that addictive rush that slows Richard's brain to a steady, warm pulse. Pacified, he staggers to his feet and heads back through the rain to the polytunnel.

Sonny

Electric forks are thrown across the sky. Yellow snails disappear inside their sugar-glass shells. Dad's anger bounces off the polytunnel walls and fizzes like white lightning in a tightly corked bottle. Listen – drenched lambs are yelling for their mothers. Plans fail and seeds die. He's still out there at midnight. Wet spider webs sway like fairy hammocks between the angelica. All the birds have disappeared. Shouldn't we cover the mirrors and telly with sheets like Mum did when she was a little girl? Let's hide under our pillows and count elephants. Cracks in the brickwork widen as the mortar crumbles. Through the soles of my feet, I feel the damp earth sigh.

It's just a spring storm, an April shower, that rages through the night but blows itself away by morning. The house breathes out dust up through the floorboards. I leave Max sleeping and go outside to run my fingers over shining wet stones. Broken red bricks have been pounded clean. Pink streaks the sky, and tiny bubbles *pop, pop, pop* in the sunlight. Look – can you see all the little rainbows dancing? Overnight the hedgerow explodes, everything arrives all at once and the May tree blooms early with the blackthorns. There's so much blossom, the leaves vanish. Grass grows faster than the mowers can manage, and escaped fluorescent oil seed rape narrows the lanes. Cowslips drip gold all over the meadows. Everything is washed bright and fresh and green. Inside the polytunnel, I follow behind Dad's footsteps, whispering to the seeds and begging them to grow.

Tess

'Girl. You sure you're gonna manage this thing?' Peaches asks, testing my suitcase's weight with one hand. 'Why are you taking all these bags with you anyway? Let me take them home with me until you get yourself sorted.'

Get myself sorted . . .

Who will be there to visit the churchyard every week? What about Cyril and my chickens? The thought of leaving Richard hurts as though a part of me is being destroyed.

'So? What do you think?' Peaches demands impatiently.

'You're probably right,' I mutter as I collect up the last of the bulging rubbish bags and drag them out the front door to be dumped on the kerb next to the overflowing wheelie bin. From over the neighbour's fence, what I know to be a yellow brimstone drifts towards me like a drop of sunshine.

'Tessa! Your phone's ringing!' Peaches shouts from inside the house.

It must be Richard. I dash upstairs to where the phone lies on my bed, but it isn't him. It's Anne at the surgery with the results of my blood test.

Time stops.

Heat rushes to my head, making the room spin. My breath quickens as nausea rises like a tide, and I finally recognise the distinct taste of metal.

Oh God, how has this happened? My panicked thoughts

stampede and throw me forwards until my face hits my hands. My brain fights to think. Richard and I haven't been near each other in months. Our bed has become a place of segregation; he has his side, I have mine, where the strict control of my elbows and knees adds to my insomnia. But then . . . memory trickles back to me . . . moments on the edge of sleep, dreamlike almost, the fault of too much alcohol on both our parts and my suppressed yet desperate longing to be near him.

Peaches drops her cleaning rag when I appear in the kitchen doorway. 'What's wrong? Have you been crying? Was that Richard on the phone?'

My mouth won't open.

'Tessa? What's happened?' She seizes my arm. 'Why aren't you saying anything?' She shakes me gently, then stops in abrupt alarm. 'It's not Max, is it?'

'No, no . . .' The realisation that I'm scaring her loosens my tongue. 'It's me . . .'

'You? What do you mean?'

'Oh, Peaches . . . I'm pregnant.'

'Pregnant?' She lets me go and lowers her face so she can peer with anxious eyes into mine. 'Tessa – are you sure? How did this happen?'

Worn out, I lean against the counter. 'I don't know. We weren't talking, still aren't, but . . .'

'Bloody hell, Tessa. You really *do* know how to complicate your life.'

I bark out a laugh, sounding like a mad woman.

My sister steers me into the living room, where we sit close together on the sofa, which feels out of place now there's no other furniture to keep it company. 'How far gone are you?' she asks.

I bow my head. 'I must be nearing thirteen weeks by now.'

'*Thirteen weeks.* Bloody hell, Tessa! How did you not notice?'

'I . . . I've been so caught up with everything.'

'What are you going to do?' she whispers.

'I don't know,' I moan into my hands. We listen to the grumble of an approaching bin lorry. Through the net curtains, the bin men are making their way haphazardly along the road. They stop outside the house and gather up the discarded contents of our former lives.

Max

It's not just Dad that's acting weird. This morning, while he's next door fixing Marge's boiler, I spy John sneaking through our garden along the path to the polytunnel. His white beard looks even whiter in the sunshine. Maybe he's come to get Dad's broken radio. But I'm sure Dad took it over a couple of days ago. He was there for ages, probably because Edith kept him talking. John can't see me up here in the window. I hide against the landing wall and watch him through my binoculars. He's only in the polytunnel for a few minutes, then he hurries away without knocking on our back door.

'John was in our garden,' I tell Sonny, who's sitting at the top of the stairs eating a satsuma. 'What do you reckon he was doing out there?'

'Must be helping Dad with something.' Sonny peels the stringy bits off each satsuma piece the same way Mum does.

Later, we forget to tell Dad about John. When he gets home from Marge's, he's in a rush and yells for us to stick our shoes on. We've got to go to the supermarket, even though Dad hates shopping in town. He much prefers to buy everything we need from the village shop. It's good to keep things local, he says.

Mum's not here to get groceries, so we've been living off bread, the boring tins of soup at the back of the cupboard, and whatever mystery meat Dad can find in the freezer. There must be a reason he's in such a hurry to get the shopping done. Whatever it is, he doesn't tell us.

Inside the supermarket is chilly. Dad sends us to find basmati rice, which is better than regular rice, while he looks for chicken in the meat aisle. Me and Sonny stop to inspect all the different types of yogurts they have here. The village shop only has plain or strawberry.

'Hello, Max.' Mason's mum stands next to a trolley filled with wine bottles. She's still got her sunglasses on even though we're inside a building. 'Any news yet from your mum? She's been gone so long I've forgotten what she looks like. Hope she comes back soon – I've got no one decent to talk to.' She laughs and nudges Mason, who's holding a giant Easter egg, one of the ones that have extra chocolate bars inside them. 'Aren't you going to say hello to Max?'

'Hi, Max.'

'Alright, Mason,' I say to him.

'Max! There you are.' Dad's face is red and he's panting like he's been running. 'I've been looking everywhere for you. This place is a flipping labyrinth. I told you to get rice, not yogurt. You can't just wander off by yourself. Christ! How could I tell your mum I lost . . . Amy . . . Mason. Sorry. I didn't see you standing there.'

Sonny

A red fox slips along the hedge. Inside the badgers' sett, the earth is crumbly and soft. Do you remember when we used to eat hot-cross buns split and toasted? Take my yew branch and come and sing hosanna. Never mind the green man watching us through the stained-glass window or the rooks fussing outside in the churchyard. My roots are tangled up with bittercress. Let's swing on Hector's gate and watch the lambs headbutt each other. Young bullocks lick our hands with rough pink tongues. Forget about the farmer on Holly Lane who got trampled by his own cows. Listen – there's the faint tapping of a deathwatch beetle. A metallic rose chafer has fallen in the bird bath. Look out for eddies stirring underneath the loosestrife.

Along the river, pipistrelles are catching mayflies. I wait on the bank late into the evening, with my toes plunged into hungry mud, until I see the last slice of sunlight. After that there are no street lights to show us where the cracks are. Hares leave the withy beds to sniff at wild mustard. Wind falls and rises. There are no stars and it becomes so dark it's hard to tell if my eyes are open. Max goes up to bed early. Sometimes it's easier to be asleep, but I remember to switch the night light on for him. Around us, the house gets comfy on its loamy mattress. Dad can't sleep so takes his turn to talk to the darkness and hear creaking in the walls. Listen – is that a hand turning the door handle? Lately, he's been pretending it's not night at all and carries on with his work in the garden, but tonight he sits at the table, alone like me. No part of him moves except the arm that lifts a bottle to his mouth. Night-time noises skim past – badgers grunting underneath the washing line, a nightingale somewhere out on the moor, there's the low hum of lorries on the main road – but Dad doesn't hear them. Sly draughts squeeze between roof tiles and shimmy down past the rafters to mix with the warm air around the chimney breast. They tease us with Mum's sandalwood and vanilla so when we dream our dreams, we see her coming through the door.

Max

Mum's home. She arrived last night. I heard a car door close and her moving about inside the porch. I wasn't asleep, but for some reason I didn't want to see her or speak to her. I stayed dead still and listened to her tiptoeing up the stairs. I thought she'd go straight to bed, but after getting something from the airing cupboard she came into our room. Next thing, there was light at the window, and I could hear a robin singing.

'Did Mum really come home, or did I dream it?' I ask Sonny. He's in his own bed for a change. Only his hair pokes out from the duvet. I know he's not sleeping, but he doesn't move until I chuck my pillow at his head.

'What?' He comes up for air.

'Mum? Is she here?'

Sonny just smiles at me.

When we get downstairs, she's in the kitchen making scrambled eggs. It's like she's been here all along, but we didn't notice.

'Mum!' I try to bury myself inside her soft jumper, but I must've grown because now I'm as tall as her. She asks me how I've been, whether I've been good for Dad, how school has gone. Did I eat properly and get to bed on time? Have I been to check on Cyril? She hopes he hasn't been too poorly. We both talk at the same time, and I tell her I don't want to go to school today. She calls Mrs Welsh and tells her I'm unwell.

'Just this once,' Mum says to me.

Instead of school, we take the bus to the high street, and I'm allowed to look inside the bookshop for a new bird-spotting guide. We have lunch in a café that's full of old people and crying babies. Mum has a decaf coffee and a piece of fruit cake, and I have a cheese and ham toasted sandwich, a square of caramel shortbread and a big glass of Coke. Then Mum buys me a huge Easter egg that has two packets of Minstrels inside it. The whole day is perfect, even though Dad's nowhere to be seen. Mum doesn't seem bothered. We have bangers and mash for tea, and afterwards she comes and sits on the sofa with me, and we watch David Attenborough playing with meerkats on telly.

Tess

Outside in the garden, a wren feeds its hungry fledgling underneath my peach rose bush. Better use the whole tin of coconut milk; half is never enough. Finally, I've got some gungo peas – they're so much nicer than kidney beans. Black pepper, two pinches of salt . . . maybe a third for . . . my eyes settle on electric blue forget-me-nots.

It's strange to be back in my own kitchen, pouring cooking oil into my own blackened Dutch pot. Discomfiting, but somehow calmed by Mary J's 'Not Gon Cry' on the radio. Where's my spatula? I need to scrape off this marinade. Did I add too much jerk paste? I should've cut more onions. Sunlight quivers through the window showing me faint pencil scratches beside the back door made to measure the boys' growth each year. For the first time, Max is taller.

Richard was not out in his garden or inside his shed when I arrived home that night but slumped like a dead man at the kitchen table, trussed up in his coat with an empty bottle of wine under his arm as a pillow. Thank goodness I'd sent him a text the day before saying there was no need for him to pick me up from the train station, a taxi would do just fine, thanks to the money Mama pressed into my hands as I was leaving. I leant over him and tracked the marks of age, the grey at his temples and streaking through his beard, the surprising looseness of his skin, even his colour, wan now, so pale. A muscle in the hollow of his exposed cheek twitched. I gently removed the bottle and fetched a blanket from the airing cupboard to cover him. Lightly, I stroked back the hair sticking to his face. He looked so fragile, like a child sleeping.

But today is another day and though I've wanted to tell him how much I've missed him, he's shown no sign of being pleased I'm home. If anything, he's even more distant, never staying in for dinner, but instead taking his plate out to the shed, claiming he's too busy to stop.

Oh God, at what point will he say it's all over?

I know I can't stay – it was naïve of me to think life here would ever be easy. But, if I'm being honest with myself, I'm still here, despite this, still floating through this house, bewitched by sunlight falling on old limed walls, letting the heavy spell of this place continue to bind me.

I watch him as he passes the kitchen window with renewed resentment as well as worry. *What will I do?* Peaches agrees, I can't tell Mama, not yet, as the news will derail her plans, and though I want to call Amy, anything I say will likely be round the village by morning. Muck spreaders hurtle past, and the house shakes me out of my downward spiral. I must get the cooking done if I'm to make it in time for the maypole dancing. We've never missed a year, well, apart from last year, and this will be Max's final one. He'll be looking for me in the crowd.

Cars are parked in every available space, making it difficult for the bus to drive its midday loop around the village square. Red and white bunting flutters on the school fence and the sound of fiddles crackles loudly from the PA system. On the sports field, parents fight for chairs, rearranging the rows so they can squeeze in one more relative or sit with friends. It's only May, but already there's an excess of floral summer dresses and pastel-painted toenails – dads casual in chinos and polo shirts. They gossip and chatter while collecting homemade fairy cakes or slices of Victoria sponge on paper plates and cups of tea from the table manned by Sarah Winslow and the rest of the PTA brigade. I manage a small wave to Amy, who sits looking pretty with new blonde hair beside her husband Graham, before hiding at the back, where hopefully no one will notice me or the fact I'm wearing my heavy winter coat on such a warm day.

Little ones come first, skipping awkwardly and out of step, nervous of all the eyes watching. Parents reposition phones and cameras, while their teacher, Miss Simmonds, claps in time encouragingly. Inside my mind, I see Sonny, only five and still in Reception, in his grey shorts, his short brown legs running to keep up with the rhythm. The youngest finish, and there's applause and a welcome break from the music as the older children come to unwind the ribbons. We wait patiently until a sudden wave of movement ripples through the crowd and heads turn to watch a family of latecomers pick their way through the rows to where seats have been reserved. *There's a black woman with them.* My heart speeds up. It's like catching my own reflection in a shop window but then realising . . . it isn't me. There's a nearly indiscernible hush as parents crane their necks towards her as subtly as they can manage. I'm no better than everyone else, desperate to take a closer look and bursting with questions. *Who is she? Why is she here? Is she staying or only visiting?* I'm flooded with mixed emotions, but my delight at not being the only one here is soured by acute discomfort – in noticing her, everyone will remember me.

The music restarts and heads turn back to watch the next class take their turn around the maypole, but I can't pull my eyes away. She must feel me looking as her face turns in my direction, but she doesn't allow herself to see me. I know this game. If our eyes meet, we'll feel compelled to show some sign of acknowledgement, a slight smile or nod, an act of mutual recognition. Like the time I bumped into a black man outside the chemist on Combe Leigh High Street, and we stared grinning at one another as though we'd each found a long-lost relative. Is it better to feign ignorance? I mean, who smiles and nods at strangers? I force myself to pay attention as the next class gets ready to begin but can't help listening in to the snatches of hushed conversation flitting between the groups of parents. Seems *she* is the new fiancée of Darren Bulmer, who has a daughter in Year 2 with his ex, Andrea; *she's* visiting from Birmingham, but no one's sure yet if she'll stay or if she'll convince him to move to somewhere more cosmopolitan. Must have come as a shock to old Mrs Bulmer, seeing as she's such a stickler for tradition.

Max

It's hot enough that we can take our school jumpers off for the first time this year. The slow-worms living under Dad's log pile might be out sunning themselves. There are so many other things I would rather do today than skip around a stupid maypole. Cyril said we're skipping around a giant penis, but Mum says I'm not to repeat that. It's so embarrassing. All the girls take it seriously, and haven't stopped skipping everywhere all week, even though the jingly music on the CD player is awful. It's not even May Day anymore, we're nearly in June. Loads of people have turned up to watch, more than last year.

It takes ages for each class to take their turn. While we wait, Mr Reid makes us sit quietly on the grass, so we can think through our steps. As we're the oldest, we're expected to make a much more complicated ribbon pattern than the other classes. For two weeks, we've practised every day after lunch. Mr Reid says he wants us to do him proud. But I'm not thinking about the steps, I'm looking for Mum. She promised to come. Last year, I was the only one in my class who didn't have anybody. There she is . . . I spot her standing way at the back even though there's still one empty chair left at the front. I wave, but she's not looking.

'So, your mum came back from London then,' whispers Daniel, who's sitting next to me. 'My mum thought she'd be gone for good.'

269

'Gone for good?' I whisper back and shift my bum over, so we're closer. 'No. She had to help our nana move out. Though . . . it might be cos her and my dad keep on arguing.'

Daniel leans in so our heads are nearly touching. 'My mum and dad were always arguing. They were at it non-stop, shouting and swearing and everything. She called him a *wanker* and then they split up.'

The rock in my stomach comes back and I forget to whisper. 'Split up? My mum and dad aren't . . .' Somebody makes a dark shadow over us.

Miss Simmonds, with her hands on her hips. 'Stop talking and *con-cen-trate.*'

Behind us, Mason and Oliver start laughing.

It's our turn. Miss Simmonds runs back to manage the CD player, while Mr Reid hurries us into position. Then the music starts, and he counts us in . . . *one, two, three* . . . we begin skipping. Mum sees me, so I wave again. She waves back this time and I daren't take my eyes off her in case I lose her attention. I'm so busy keeping her in sight, I stumble over my own feet, miss my in-and-out steps and get my ribbon tangled up with Ruby's. The music stops. Mr Reid rushes in to sort out the mess and gets us all to return to our original places so we can start again. Some of the parents are yawning.

Evan prods me in the back. 'Idiot,' he mumbles.

'I can hear you, you know,' I tell him.

He prods me again. 'So, it's no secret you're an idiot.'

'I'm not an idiot!' I turn round to shout at him.

'Yeah, you are. You're an idiot and a *weirdo*. It's your fault. You ruin everything.'

'It's *not* my fault,' I yell, and I shove him so that he falls backwards and whacks his head. But it's not enough. I leap on him and let my fists *thump, thump* into his face until I see blood. Someone's crying, but I don't know if it's him or me. My fists aren't mine anymore. 'It's not *my fault!*' I shout, but then I'm being pulled away. Miss Simmonds grips my arm and starts dragging me across the field towards the main school building. 'Sonny!' I call, but Sonny's not here. I start screaming. '*Sonny!*' I twist my arm and try to break free. 'It's *not my fault!*'

'Enough of this!' snaps Miss Simmonds. Her fingernails dig deeper into my skin.

Summer

Sonny

Underneath a brilliant blue sky, our dreams are stained by colours so much brighter than before. Tears get tangled up in pink dog roses. Day by day, the maize grows taller. Ants in the garden stock up their summer larder. I sit among the water mint and feel the day's heat fade, while the river turns slow somersaults and the cooling house clicks and twists. Listen – doesn't it sound like bare feet tiptoeing along the beams? Beneath the murk, the old barge waits. An evening sun falls behind the willows and turns the house bricks from brown to blood red. They glow and all the cracks disappear.

I died on a summer's day when the air was full of liquid skylark song and the constant *thrum* of tractors, and the fields around our house were dotted with rows of golden hay bales. We went out hunting grasshoppers and those small brown bush crickets that hide under dock leaves. Max took his bug viewing pot, the one with the magnifying glass in the lid, and I took my net that I used for catching butterflies and for pond dipping. We ran through the meadow, letting spittle-bug foam streak our shins. It was hot and thick, and barely any water trickled in the rhynes. We played in the long grass, colourful with knapweed, marsh buttercups, purply-blue cornflowers and red campions. Fluffy white thistledown settled on my hair. We stayed for hours, letting the sun turn me a darker brown and Max the colour of eggshells.

Eventually, the fiery tips of the aspens told us it was time to go home.

We made a plan to take out *Bernadette* and have a quick dip, only for a few minutes before dinner. The smell of frying garlic wafted over the orchard. Mum was cooking spag bol. She didn't like us going, but Dad said it would be okay, boys will be boys, it's what he used to do *back in the day*. We'd be fine, as long as we went together, never alone. Dad promised he'd come and check on us as soon as he finished hosing down the runner beans.

Me and Max rushed along the riverbank through nettles and honey-scented meadowsweet, sneaking past Barbara's, past Angus at Marge's, who came out to bark at us, and onto Cyril's jetty. Clouds of midges hummed. We floated *Bernadette* out across the water, our oars pushing apart the wide lily pads, to the middle of the river. Huge and silent, a great white egret lifted out of the reeds and sailed slowly over us. Max suggested a game – who could dive down to the riverbed, probe their fingers into the deep mud and find something, treasure maybe, but most likely an old belt buckle or a piece of broken chain harrow. After such a hot day, we both longed for the cool sweetness of the water. I dived first, as brown and quick as an otter, with barely a splash, but it wasn't deep enough – my fingers felt nothing in the dark. Above me, *Bernadette* tipped and rocked. Even though it was his idea, Max was nervous and flung himself in feet first, with arms raised and no hope of reaching the bottom. Again and again we dived, leapt, jumped; our laughs echoed to the other side of the green moor and bounced back to us. We could hear Mum shout that dinner was on the table. Sunset on the house bricks turned the whole world red. One last dive. I leapt off harder this time, determined to be the one to make it all the way down. Silver poured past my eyes. I couldn't see, only feel the solid metal of the old barge strike the side of my head. Then darkness came. The river wrapped itself around me and carried me home.

Tess

That first time, we waited for magical lines to appear in the window of a pregnancy test. The two of us paced the small room in my student flat. Well, I paced. Richard sat smiling to himself with that unruffled calmness of his. There was something magnetic that drew us towards each other at the expense of everything and everyone else. Something in those unexpected eyes and capable hands of his seemed to see me more clearly than anyone else ever had. He was the first white guy I ever dated. Not that I had much experience with men; until then there'd only really been David, who I thought was enough until . . . he wasn't.

First came the shock – *we were having a baby* then we found out it was twins. Richard wasn't fazed. But me? Fear crept in. *Twins.* We could barely afford one, what with the new house, a crumbling dank cottage in dire need of a structural survey, mortgage payments, council tax and astronomical flood risk insurance. Mama begged me to come home, offered to help so I could still have a shot at a career. But Richard wasn't made for London. And the thought of those babies made it all okay.

They arrived early, by fourteen days. My waters broke as I sat at the kitchen table shelling peas. Only enough time to grab my bag, which I'd packed and repacked at least twice a day for the last month, laying out each tiny item on the bed so I could stroke them and breathe in their softness. Sonny was first. Through the epidural fog, the midwife's rosy face loomed as she presented me with my chestnut-brown infant. Then, seven minutes later, came Max, pale, pink, as slippery as a fish, and her face transformed into confusion. Other midwives and nurses on duty hurried in to look. The on-call paediatrician said they were *one in a million*. I cried, too elated to care. But even then, something sang inside me to see Sonny. I couldn't get enough of him. My nose continually pressed into the sweet-smelling curls at the nape of his neck. With Max, it took much longer. The paleness of his small body beside mine alarmed me and brought back Mama's horror stories of her years as a midwife, having her hands slapped away by mothers not wanting her to touch their babies. It felt like he would be taken from me at any moment.

For a while we were famous. The local paper ran a short story and came to take our photo – a grainy colour print of the boys, perfect in their newborn innocence, and me, caught off guard, looking dazed in one of Richard's jumpers. People stopped us as we walked through the village, eager to take a peek. Then came the comments, snide and hurtful, jokey suggestions that I'd been playing the field.

What if it happens again?

Sonny

Listen – there's the sound of water. Hear it running as fast as light over shingle and shale. Withered petals wash away to swirl through the house and out into the biodigester underneath the garden. I wait by the bathroom door, smelling the mintiness of her toothpaste. Don't be fooled by the stillness of the river. Danger lingers below the slipstream. Did you know that hogweed leaves taste like camphor or that the pike eats ducklings? Ripe elderberries splatter and stain. Let's sprinkle blood and bone underneath the raspberry canes. See the red wave of marsh orchids rolling through the grass. Steam gushes from the iron. Soon it will be time for haymaking. Stacks of drying withies are tied up with baler twine, while high in the alder, the cuckoo sings his song.

Tess

For once, there's no heavy tread of hikers traipsing the length of our road hunting for footpath signs, no cars breaking the twenty-mile-an-hour speed limit or the incessant to-ing and fro-ing of farm vehicles, only a gentle quiet, agitated in intervals by air easing down through the air vent spinning slowly on the bathroom ceiling. I fill the bath and let the water consume me inch by inch until my legs are submerged, leaving only my kneecaps and distended belly button sticking out into the cool bathroom. I'm safe in here, protected from those tongues wagging at the playground gate and on the step of the village shop, everyone eager to add their two pennies' worth. Eventually, I'll have to face them. I scoop up handfuls of water and let the droplets run over and down my stomach. Steam rises from the bath distorting the angles of the room as the horror of that dreadful day flashes back to me.

It's uncomfortable to think about my child, the one next door in his room, most probably with his face at the window and binoculars fixed in front of his eyes as he searches the fields for birds, who will have to be coaxed back to school once this exclusion period is over. It was for his own good, they said, not to mark him out as a troublemaker but to give him, and *us*, some time to mend.

Oh, Sonny, none of this would be happening if you were here.

As though eager to fill the void, the house begins to speak to me, much more talkative than any city house could be. Up in the roof, eaves groan as though someone has woken them from sleep, windows tick in reply to the day's heat, somewhere ivy rasps against bricks. There's something small, a beetle or its grub perhaps, chewing inside the wall. Minute sounds vibrate into my ears, a soothing pulse.

Max

Angus lies under Marge's tiny kitchen table and slurps on a dirty beef bone. He was supposed to eat it out in the yard, but it's too hot out there and the flies won't leave him alone. Marge tells him he can stay as long as he doesn't make a mess. According to the weatherman on the radio, today's going to be a scorcher. The kitchen window is already propped wide open. Flies try to come in, but the swinging strips of extra-sticky paper catch most of them. Marge still has her boiler lit and her rigger boots on. Sweat glistens on her forehead and makes a wet moustache under her nose. She's cleared a space at the table for me and Sonny, so we can watch her make elderflower champagne. She sniffs each bunch of blossoms to make sure it doesn't smell of cat wee before adding it to the bowl.

''Ere,' she says. 'Don't just sit there gawping, pass us that fork.' It's one of those old ones that's got three prongs instead of four and is made of real silver. Marge uses it to scrape the elderflowers off their stalks. A small black spider escapes up the side of the bowl.

It's already Friday. Means I've only got the weekend and then I have to go back to school. None of them like me, not really. Whenever I think about Evan, I feel sick. Although Sonny's pleased I punched him in the face, he reckons Evan's been asking for it for ages. Marge adds the elderflowers to a bucket of sugar water, throws in some sliced-up lemons and covers it over with a cloth.

'There, that's done. Now. How's about we find ourselves summat to eat and pop the telly on? Must be time for *Cash in the Attic*.' Marge finds us two apple turnovers with cream in, then we help her shuffle her walker into the living room. On the telly, there's a man who's found a painting of a pig. Sonny laughs and says it looks like Angus.

'Expect you're looking forward to getting back to school and seeing your friends again,' Marge says through a mouthful of cream.

I look at my fingers. 'Haven't got any friends,' I tell her. 'Nobody likes me. I'm broken or something.'

Marge turns the telly off. 'Look.' She takes hold of my face with her soft hands and makes me look at her. 'Ain't nothing wrong with being broken. Nothing at all. You hear? You're like these houses, not a whole brick in 'em and look how strong they are. Been 'ere hundreds of years and nothing's destroyed them, not floods, not war, not people, *nothing*.' She lets go, and me and Sonny snuggle down next to her on the sofa. 'Did you know you live in a house made of broken bricks?'

'No,' I tell her, shaking my head, but Sonny doesn't say anything.

'Has your dad not told you about 'em? What's he thinking?' Marge gobbles down the last bite of her apple turnover. 'Let's see. These bricks were fired in a giant kiln, not far from 'ere, where the river spills out into the Bristol Channel, but sometimes they came out broken, so were only good for ballast. You understand?' We nod to show her that we do.

286

'Well, some of 'em went off to weigh down them clipper ships sent to collect sugar from the Caribbean. Could've been Jamaica . . . yes, where your nana and grandad came from. The others, well the bargemen took 'em, so they could squeeze under low bridges and head upstream. Once they reached 'ere they most likely swapped 'em for barrels of cider, bundles of withies and, in the summer, sedge grass for those poor Welsh pit ponies, and those basket weavers and cider makers, some of 'em Hembrys no doubt, your great-great-great-grandparents, they used those broken bricks to build their riverbank houses. These houses, yours and mine.' Marge ruffles my hair then puts the telly on again. Turns out the pig painting is worth ten thousand pounds. 'Ten grand! A load of rubbish. Don't even look like a pig, s'more like a dog,' she says, reaching into her handbag for a packet of Murray Mints.

Sonny

Listen – can you hear the voices? They've been calling. See the men with their horses pulling their barges against the tide? I'm one of them now. *They see me and smile.* Here beneath the river, I search for fossils, bones of expired water creatures, brachiopods, belemnites, devil's toenails. Minnows flow like blessings over me. I could leave with them, get carried past the pumping station, the weir and sluice gates downstream to where dabchicks spuddle in the watercress, under Pike Bridge to follow the tide northwards into the estuary and out to sea. There I could tumble, unclaimed, belonging nowhere forever, but it seems I've become one of those broken bricks, trapped between lime and ash in our crooked walls. The river clings to my skin as though I'm too heavy to move and the land ties me down with honeysuckle. I belong to them now, even if I don't look like I should. Worries about looking different wash away with the current.

Grandad Hembry said men don't cry, but that's not true. I sit on the broken deckchair and watch tears run down through the dirt on Dad's cheeks to shine in his beard. Like dew on a teasel. It's much bushier than it used to be and nearly all grey now. He's been too busy to shave or cut his hair and hasn't noticed he's been wearing the same clothes for a fortnight. He wipes his wet face with the inside of his T-shirt. Above us, the swallows flit in and out through a gap in the tin roof, bringing new bedding for their nest. It's time to raise a second batch. Their *peeps* rain down and make Dad forget his sadness, just for a moment. He rests his forehead on the worktop. Sunshine heats the thin glass in the shed's window, which has grown filthier too, but the warm light can still get in and dance along the wooden slats. Outside on the road, there's the clopping of ponies and girls laughing. Before the tears can come again, I go and stand before him, take hold of both his hands and help him to his feet. Dad takes in a huge breath, so his chest grows large and wide; he holds it – I silently count the seconds – then blows it out so that dust blasts through the air. He takes an unopened envelope from behind the radio but puts it back again without opening it, then reaches for his phone to make yet another plant order, his seventh this week. Seeds cosy in their warm beds are finally settled, with their roots drilling deep and their long green arms reaching . . . reaching. When they hear the sound of my feet, they turn their heads towards me. Dad should be able to relax a little now. I told him I would take care of it, but as always, there's still too much for him to do.

Richard

Things keep appearing. A month or so back, four beers in and unsteady in the dark, Richard tripped over a set of solar panels leant up outside the polytunnel door. There were five of them and, although he could not fathom how they came to be there, they were exactly what he needed to power the new heating pump with enough watts to push warm water round the entire perimeter. All he needs are a couple of leisure batteries and, mercifully, now he will not have to faff around trying to connect to the house's electrics, which would possibly have invalidated their home insurance policy and meant one more piece of paperwork to procrastinate over. There have been other things – a bucket of brass munsen rings, a large coil of blue alkathene pipe, several old galvanised pipes of shorter lengths that looked to have once belonged in a milking parlour and, most surprising, perched on top of the compost heap, an old green plastic bunded oil tank that someone had scrubbed clean. When questioned, none of the neighbours had any clue, though during Richard's last visit, Cyril managed a faint but mischievous smile, saying it must be pixies. The shame in Richard's tight chest rises to his face at the thought of everyone knowing the extent of his failure. Since Christmas, only two new customers have joined his meagre list – Judith, the new minister at the Baptist chapel, wanting an extra-large crate, but only once a month for the church suppers, and Brian over at the Bird in Hand, who has fallen out with his regular veg supplier.

Richard takes his empty coffee flask over to the kitchen sink to give it a quick swill. Time is too short for a proper lunch, so he settles for the hard end of the bread and one of last year's pickled eggs. No time even to chew, just to gulp the food down and get back to work, with his body hiccuping in protest. Now the seedlings in the polytunnel are finally established, Richard hoped to spend the day in the greenhouse training the cherry tomatoes and cucumbers and staking out the aubergines till it was time to pick up Max, but now, after an unexpected call from his mother, he will have to scrap his plans and go over to Withy Grove instead to check on the state of the place before the new tenant arrives. Setting the flask aside, Richard pours himself a glass of cold water and turns to find Tess standing by the kitchen table. They both stop, startled by the sight of each other. Inside Richard's brain, words scramble and fall over themselves to try and get into a sensible order. It was almost easier when they were arguing.

'Would you like a drink?' He shows her the half-empty glass in his hand. 'It's so hot.' Only her eyes move, darting around the room as though looking for an escape route. Her 'No, thank you' is no more or less than he expected, but in that brief second he sees the weariness in her face and the beauty, the sunlight glowing behind her hair. 'You sure? Won't take me a minute . . .' He spins back to the sink and refills the glass. 'Here . . .' But he is too late. Her footsteps retreat back up to the bedroom. Cursing, Richard strides after her, determined to make her say something. He will take whatever she gives him as long as she looks into his eyes and makes contact with him. As he follows her up the stairs, which complain as he bounds up them in his work boots, suspicion begins to seep through his frustration – why is she being like this? He reaches the bedroom door seconds after it closes. Afraid of what might be waiting on the other side, Richard feels his courage desert him.

Inside the van is sweltering. Dead flies bake on top of the hot dashboard. For a long time, Richard sits staring at the young acorns, green and bright, that have appeared in the oak tree opposite. Regretfully, he starts the engine. The lanes are quiet as he makes his way to Withy Grove. It is just like his mother to not give him any notice, expecting him to stop whatever he is doing at the drop of a hat. Richard wishes his parents could, just for once, consider someone other than themselves. Do they even remember he has a wife and children? No, Richard corrects himself . . . a wife and *child*. As he drives past the corner house, Janice Fisher is out arranging bedding plants for sale on a small trestle table beside her gate. Her blue rinse reminds Richard of hydrangeas. She waves, flagging him down.

'Everything alright, Janice? Not your internet playing up again?' he calls, trying to keep impatience out of his voice.

'Oh no, Richard,' she says and puts down a bright pink geranium so she can wipe her hands on her canvas apron.

'It's not veg you're after, is it, Janice? If it is, I'll have to pop back with a delivery tomorrow. 'Fraid I'm a bit pushed today.' Sprightly for a woman in her nineties, Janice totters in plastic clogs to the van and places her sturdy hands on Richard's opened window.

'No, no, Richard, nothing like that. I only wanted to say I heard about what happened to your boy at school.'

'Oh,' is all Richard can manage.

'You do know we're all here for you,' she says, reaching in through the window to pat him on the shoulder.

Tess

Heatwaves shimmer, making the road look liquid. The bus should've appeared over half an hour ago, but I've been standing here in the burning sun, shuffling to keep step with the mottled shade underneath the oak tree, for so long my legs tremble. The air's syrupy, too thick to breathe, but I know I can't complain – heat was what I wanted, after all. My fingers bloat with it and my wedding ring cuts a painful groove into my skin. Usually, the bus runs like clockwork. Its timetable is etched into my brain – I'm a true local – so I know instinctively when I'll hear it rumble by as it leaves for Combe Leigh. No one ever waits here on this road except me. My heartbeat throbs in my eyelids. I feel faint and so damn tired. To make things worse, my empty stomach is painful with heartburn because I didn't eat this morning.

What was Richard doing in the kitchen? He's rarely been inside the house that time of day, so I can move about freely. I wince as I think of him thundering up the stairs behind me. I should have faced him and whatever it was he wanted to tell me. But I hadn't finished getting ready; my dressing gown was in danger of flapping open and I'd only a thin T-shirt underneath. *What if he'd noticed?*

Now it's been acknowledged, my stomach swells slowly like a small ripe melon. I don't think of how to hide it, I just do, mechanically replacing jumper with jumper daily, despite the warming weather. My breasts ache from being

295

squeezed into my too-small bras. Each night, I make sure to keep myself secluded on my side of the bed, pulling a pillow down to act as a barrier between us. If Richard thinks anything of this rejection, he doesn't say. Not that he sleeps much these days.

Sweat trickles down my back making me glad I wore a flowy skirt and sandals. I ditched my coat – it was getting ridiculous – and now only have my waterproof jacket for a cover-up, which isn't much cooler and not nearly long enough. If anyone sees me at close range, there'll be no mistaking the state I'm in. *It will be fine, it will be fine.* A sudden wave of giddiness reels me back against the tree's broad trunk. Maybe I should head back to the house and see if I can reschedule for another day? *No*, I tell myself, better to get it over and done with. Although I told Anne I won't be living here for the birth, a letter still arrived from the hospital booking me in for an overdue ultrasound scan. Soon the proof will be here in black and white, and I won't be able to pretend this is not really happening. I'll be forced to tell Mama and endure her disappointment for a second time. And what about David? *Oh God, I can't do it. Peaches will have to tell him for me.* I think of the emails she sent me about flats for rent, in particular one – ground floor with two minuscule bedrooms – in Ladywell that has a tiny private backyard, which the landlord states the occupant can do what they want with. I glance across the road through the gaps in the fence at my own garden. My dahlias are flowering. I wonder if he'll dig them up and use the space for something sensible. As I worry about the hopelessness of my life, I'm jerked out of my thoughts by what appears to be Amy's car speeding down the centre of the road towards me.

'Tess, love! You're not waiting for the bus, are you?' she shouts through the open passenger window while she swerves, stopping inches from my toes. 'It's stuck! Our new boy, Peter, the idiot, jackknifed the trailer, got it jammed in Puttford Lane. Now the bloody silage harvester is caught up its arse. Nothing's getting through any time soon. I've rung Graham to come and sort it out, but he's with the steers at the cattle market.' She leans across, flings the car door open and looks up at me over her sunglasses. 'Come on then. Jump in!' There'll be no refusing her, so I get in as quickly as I can while trying to wrap my jacket around me. Preoccupied with a three-point turn, which on this road needs more like seven points, Amy continues talking over the racket of the Pussycat Dolls about the nuisance of finding decent staff who don't need their hands holding. I let her rant, relieved she hasn't noticed my discomfort.

We take a different route to town, racing along quiet, picturesque lanes that see so few cars grass can grow undisturbed down the middle of them. Honeysuckle hedges overhang and graceful hollyhocks and foxgloves frame soft-focus cottages that look as though they've been constructed from icing sugar and rose petals. There's something so dreamlike about it, so perfect . . . this is what I've learnt to be wary of, to not let the beauty rose-tint my perception. I know on closer inspection, the truth will emerge: 'Keep Out', 'Private

Property', 'No Trespassers'. Amy drives so fast that as we pass the willow works her slipstream pummels the towers of wicker baskets. She grips the steering wheel with hands and arms that have obviously been topped up with tanning lotion. They're so brown they're not far off from mine.

'Where to? Food shopping?' she asks as we leave the quiet villages behind and enter the built-up monoculture of housing estates.

'No. Just chuck me out any . . .' My eyes flick down to the clock on the dashboard. I'm late. 'Er . . . actually, anywhere near the hospital would be great.'

'The hospital? What for? Nothing wrong is there?'

'No, nothing's wrong. Got to pick something up from the pharmacy for Cyril,' I reply quickly, which is partly true.

Amy frowns. 'Couldn't Frencher get it ordered to the surgery? Seems a big ask making you come all this way.'

'Oh, it's fine, I don't mind. Cyril's in such a bad way, I'm glad to help him out.' The palms of my hands are slippery with sweat. To avoid getting caught in the hospital's dreaded one-way system, Amy parks on a nearby residential street, where the houses look surprisingly like the one I left behind in Lewisham.

'You're a bloody saint if you ask me. Well, I'll only be getting my nails done so call me if the bus doesn't turn up to take you back and I'll come and get you,' she says, twisting towards me.

'Thanks,' I tell her, and I try to leave the car as quickly as I entered it, but it's harder than I expect. My jacket swings open just as Amy's mouth frames the word 'bye'. She stares, takes off her sunglasses, and stares again at my stomach with eyes so wide I can see the intricate greens and browns of her irises.

'Tess, what the fuck?' she shouts.

This photograph is much less grainy than that of the boys. Though the image is still no bigger than a very small avocado, I'm able to pick out the head, a delicate jaw, the shadow of minuscule teeth, ghostly bones of the legs and what I guess will be feet. Tiny hands splay outwards like one of Max's plankton creatures. My relief at being told it wasn't twins was much greater than I anticipated – only one amniotic sac, one placenta, one fragile heart beating – and I cried then, at first confusing the sonographer who assumed they must be tears of joy until she realised, no doubt by the raw extent of my bawling, they were due to something else entirely. Maybe she wondered where the father was and why he wasn't there to support me. Thank goodness there was Amy who insisted on coming to enfold my hand in hers and pass me tissues. How stupid I was to think I could get through it alone.

My tea grows cold as I sit mesmerised by the flimsy photograph trembling in my grasp. I'm supposed to be cooking dinner, something from a tatty cookbook Mama once gave me. Seasoned lamb chops grow lukewarm on the kitchen counter. A bumblebee trapped inside the house bumps persistently on the window, asking to be let out. I bring the photo closer, hoping to see some detail in the scan that will let me know what trials this child will face. *Will it look black or white or somewhere in between?* Such a simple choice, but such a vast difference in what its life will hold.

'Mum?' Max's voice from inside the porch shocks me awake. He's home from school. Already! *Oh God, what time is it?* I didn't hear the van arrive. Max swings open the back door. I tuck the scan photograph between the pages of the cookbook spread open on the table.

Sonny

Secrets clamber over the house bricks. Soon we're going to suffocate. The air is stifling. In parched wheat fields, there's still no rain. Blanket weed blooms at the sluice gates. It's time to take our shears and trim the overgrowth away. On the kitchen counter, flies gather on vegetable peelings. Look – there's a grass snake lying dead in the road. Can you hear the *knock, knock, knock* of wooden skittles up at the pub? Days are stretched so thin the stars can blink only once. Hawk moths search for darker shade, while high on the hill, men crowned in antlers *bang* their gongs. Ribbon wishes flutter in the hawthorn. Shake off your cardi. Sunlight flickers through the leaves of the alder. I lie in the rushes and twist daises through my curls. Between the small white flowers of the water plantain, the shrinking river shows me my own face.

Max

Inside Cyril's kitchen feels colder than usual. It's always much colder than ours, but after roasting outside, it's like we've walked into a freezer. Goosebumps ping up on our arms and legs. Mum's fine though because she still has her jacket on, which is zipped all the way up. Gillian, the nice carer, yanks the blinds higher to see if the sun can warm things up a bit, sending the dusty parrot mobiles spinning. She whispers to Mum as they stand by the kettle that Cyril's quite upset this morning. He's not been able to hold a pen. Means he can't write any more poetry. Little fruit flies hover over the powdery grapes and peaches in the fruit bowl on the dresser. They only live for a few weeks. Sonny blows at them, and they scatter and go and hide inside a mouldy plant pot. While Gillian lines up pills on a saucer, Mum gets on with making tea. She makes a cup for Cyril, even though Gillian says he won't drink it. He won't drink or eat anything now, only sip water. Still, Mum unpacks yesterday's dinner of stew peas and rice, in case she can tempt him with some proper cooking.

'Grab a biscuit,' she tells us, but me and Sonny don't want to eat either.

'Can't we see Cyril?' I ask.

Mum looks at Gillian, who nods and says, 'Go on then, love. But he's had a hard morning, so try not to overtax him.'

As me and Sonny climb the stairs, we can hear buzzards outside screaming like lammergeiers as they ride the thermals.

Cyril looks worse than we expected. His eyes have gotten smaller, like they're being swallowed up by his face. He's much thinner too. Sharp bones poke out behind his cheeks.

'Ahh,' he says as we get closer to his bed. I think he's saying something else, but his voice is too quiet. We bend our heads nearer to his mouth, which smells awful like blocked drains. 'Do *you* know what day it is?' he asks. His hand, which is covered in strange brown splotches, pats the duvet. Sonny sits down, but I think I want to stay standing.

'When will they let you out of bed?' I ask. Seeing him like this upsets me.

'I remember your first visit here. You were both so young. Barely out of nappies.' His eyes shift upwards to me, then down to Sonny sat next to him. 'All those questions, questions, questions. Two conquistadors searching for answers. You with your feathers and *you* with your fossils. Two halves of the same coin.' He closes his eyelids. It's like he's sleeping.

'Cyril?' Sonny whispers, leaning in a tiny bit closer. Cyril wakes up and looks at us properly.

'Max. At last. I wondered where you'd got to. Come to see me off?'

I know he means he's going to die. The rock in my stomach feels very heavy. I sit down on the bed near his feet. It's hard to breathe. Sonny watches me.

Eventually I ask, 'Aren't you afraid?'

304

'Afraid?' Cyril answers. 'Of what? I was dead for billions of years before I was alive.'

'But . . . but it means you won't be here anymore.'

'You won't get rid of me so easily, lad. Haven't you heard what people say? We're made of stardust. We'll all be hanging around for eternity.' Cyril closes his eyes. Me and Sonny stare at each other. We wait for a long time, but it doesn't look like he's going to wake up again. But as we get off the bed, Cyril lifts his hand and shakes a bony finger.

'Bring that here.' He's pointing at a large parcel wrapped in newspaper that sits on his wheelie table. I quickly fetch it and hold it out to him. Cyril taps the parcel with a cracked yellow fingernail and tells me, 'You're not to open it yet. It's for your birthday.' I thank him but feel miserable. Sonny waits for me by the door.

'We better go. Gillian said not to overtax you.'

'That woman. Overtax me! Who are you, the bloody inland revenue?' Cyril tries to laugh, but coughs and splutters. Blood turns the inside of his lips bright red.

Mum puts her arm around my shoulders as we walk home.

'Everything's changing again,' she tells me. Her eyes stare down at the road where the tarmac's melting into black shiny puddles. In the verge, the dry grass is turning yellow and there are clouds of flies on the gone-over elderflowers. But there's tons of willowherb, so there might be elephant hawk-moth caterpillars. The last time me and Sonny found one, we kept it on the kitchen windowsill in one of Mum's pickle jars, half filled with earth. We waited while it buried itself and turned into a chrysalis, but no beautiful pink and brown moth ever appeared. We didn't know the caterpillar could only transform after living through a cold winter.

When we get to our house, Les is parked by the gate and honking his horn to get Dad's attention.

'Where's that husband o' yours?' he calls to Mum. Now it's summer, he's got rid of his woolly balaclava and instead wears an old leather cowboy hat. Underneath it, his rat's tail curls over his shoulder.

'Not sure, Les,' Mum replies as she steps round his truck. Les shakes a carrier bag at her filled with something wet.

''Ere. Mackerel. Redford caught 'em. Down at Lyme. Couldn't leave 'em on the gate and let the sun spoil 'em.'

'Goodness – how kind. Thank you.' Mum smiles and takes the bag from him.

'Bugger me, ain't you hot in that get-up?' Les nods towards Mum's jacket, which is still zipped up. 'Reminds me of when I used to play cricket. 'Twas this West Indian chap, always wore his sweater no matter how hot it got. Oh, how we used to play tricks on 'e.' Les laughs and his few rotten teeth flash in the sunlight. 'Took it well though, 'e was a good chap.'

'Aw, that's nice,' Mum replies, but her smile has faded away. 'Well, I best get this lot in the fridge.' She holds up the carrier bag.

Les starts his truck. 'Tell that husband o' yours I'll need a hand with the cattle end o' next month.' He drives off without bothering to wait for Dad, who I'm sure is inside the poly-tunnel because I can hear the muffled sound of his radio from across the garden.

While Mum gets tea ready, I take Cyril's present upstairs and put it on my shelf. It'll be Sonny's and my birthday at the end of August, but I'm not looking forward to it. Apparently, I'm growing like a weed, which must be true, because when I stretch out on my bed, my feet nearly reach the end and they never used to. In September, I'll be going to Combe Hill Secondary. Mum's right, everything is changing again, even though I don't want it to.

'Come on, Max! It's too nice to stay indoors,' Sonny calls to me. He's standing at the top of the stairs in my jeans and C-3PO T-shirt. We run downstairs, through the kitchen, ignoring Mum when she shouts for us to slow down, and out to where the trees are heavy with baby apples. They're still too sour to eat, but we try anyway, crunching hard with our teeth and spitting out most of it. Hornets roam up in the leaves on the lookout for dragonflies. They've built a paper nest inside an old dead Bramley.

'Race you to the top,' I shout, and me and Sonny climb, though the branches are spiky and it's easy to slip and catch our clothes on pointed twigs. We grip on like tamarins with our rubber-soled trainers. Long-tailed tits dip in and out to see if we've disturbed any spiders. It's been so dry, leaves crackle under our fingers. From up here, we should be able to peer over the tall reeds and rushes to the river, but it's so low and still, we can barely see it. Sunlight catches Sonny's eyes and they don't look black but brown, flecked with golden lines like a pheasant feather.

'Listen,' he tells me. There are voices drifting along the riverbank. People are next door in the Gables. They've opened up the conservatory so we can hear them talking. Me and Sonny climb down out of the tree and creep through the orchard onto the riverbank to spy on them from our side of the wall. Red mason bees leave their tiny holes in the stones to buzz in our ears. They much prefer living here than in the bug hotel me and Sonny once made with Dad. On the other side of the wall, the grass has grown waist high and is choked by ox-eye daisies. Since Barbara left, no one has bothered to take care of her part of the bank, though Dad did take the mower to it back in early spring. Wild poppies have appeared from nowhere. There's a man in a pink shirt and a stripy pink and purple tie standing by the conservatory door.

'. . . as you can see, the view of the moor is breathtaking and, of course, being a flood plain, there's no danger of it ever being developed, so there's no worry of being overlooked by a housing estate or a supermarket,' he's saying.

'Hmm . . . I'm still concerned about the proximity of the river,' a lady replies. We can't see who she is, but she sounds posh. 'It must be a nightmare to get insurance. What do you think, Charles? The insurance? Won't it be extortionate?'

Another man inside the house answers her. 'Can't be too steep or everyone else on this stretch wouldn't be able to manage it. Although . . . we are further away from the centre of the village than I would've liked, but I do agree, the view *is* cracking and . . .' He comes out into the garden and wanders over to the cubby hole where Barbara used to keep her wheelie bin. His knees are red and knobbly under his shorts. '. . . this would be a great spot for a hot tub.'

The man in the pink shirt hurries over to him. 'A hot tub. Yes, that would massively increase your rental potential. I think, with a bit of clever remodelling, the house would probably sleep six at a push. Really, it will need some modernising throughout, but it's undoubtedly a worthwhile investment. You should expect back-to-back bookings over the summer and probably quite a few takers for the Christmas period. The living room has a working open fire. It might also be worth considering converting the conservatory into . . .'

They're so busy talking they don't notice a kingfisher streak past and perch right there next to them on a willow branch. Inside its beak is a tiny silver fish.

Sonny

Listen – I hear a new voice calling my name that's sweeter than the others and makes me want to stay a little longer. She lives inside my mother, her honey smell mixing with that sandalwood and vanilla. In my mind I see her, a small bud on an apple tree blossoming, skin stretching as her fruit ripens in the heat of summer. I whisper riddles into the soft shell of her ear, link my fingers into her small hands, webbed like mine, follow the thin river of hot red blood through delicate veins as we swim beneath that warm skin bathed in sunlight. I blow my kisses over her, coat her face with rich dark earth and the mud of my beautiful river. Look – she's turning brown. I paint her hair with golden moonshine, place rowan leaves inside her eyes. Together we fill our mother's dreams with great crested newts and caddisflies.

Shadows of other summers draw patterns round me as beautiful as a freshwater limpet shell. There's the smell of ozone mingled with Mum's nag champa, and smoke winds through an open back door. I remember the taste of spareribs cooking on the barbecue, homemade salad dressing made with apple cider vinegar, shrieks of laughter as we ran naked through the garden sprinkler, sitting with Dad when he showed us how to gently pull out the tender end of a grass stem, bees hard at work on the salvia. Dreams float dandelion fluff over the trees.

Mum sits on my bed and cradles a pair of torn jeans in her lap. The rip in the knee is so big now they're only fit for the bin. Hot, dry wind puffs in through the open window and, around her sagged shoulders, the curtains swell, curl and twist like arrowhead teased by the current. I hear her thinking, *Are these Max's or were they Sonny's?* Our clothes are the same, so it's hard to tell who things belong to – identical shorts with grass-stained backsides, pullovers knitted by one of the neighbours, T-shirts with logos of aliens and skateboarding animals. Mum holds them to her nose, but the only scent left is washing powder. Her thoughts boomerang between the wardrobe and the bookshelves like swifts bouncing against an empty sky.

Oh, Sonny, how will I bear leaving you?

With my hands fastened tight over hers we pull out drawers, fold away jumpers, tuck sock inside sock, slip hangers into the shoulders of school shirts. Dust specks glitter. Mum takes her cloth and wipes down the bedside table, lifting my silver cup, my notebook of scribbles, my glasses, which she cleans on her skirt.

'Mum,' I whisper. 'Maybe it's time to pack these things away.' But she ignores me, takes down my coelacanth fossil from the bookshelf and holds it against her heart. When she's done tidying, I follow her downstairs, help grate the carrots and cabbage for coleslaw, stop the potatoes from boiling over, keep an eye on the mackerel crisping in the pan, while she goes to take another look at her photograph. Me and the house watch as she hides it inside the cookbook, the safest place, *she thinks*, as she's the only one who cooks.

Richard

Dust rises in great clouds as cows stampede into the barn. Richard whacks at the behind of one as it tries to jump the railings, sidestepping just in time to avoid being swiped by its horns. Holding up his piece of plastic pipe for protection, he herds them on – knows not to go straight at them, but to coax them in, his hands waving left then right then left like an orchestra conductor – while Les's son separates off the mothers with calves and rounds up the stragglers. If only everything in life was as straightforward as herding cattle, Richard muses. The cows, spooked, shove and panic, circling, snorting and mounting each other with frenzy. Horns reach down and under to hook and topple their companions. Richard's boots slip and slide in piss and shit. Despite the barn having no walls, the heat inside ramps up the stench. Redford, stocky and ginger like his mother with none of his father's swarthiness, weaves through the heaving bodies towards him.

'Right, that's the last of them,' he yells over the din of desperate lowing.

'Is the crush here?' Richard shouts back.

'Dad's bringing it now.'

Relieved, Richard escapes out into the muggy air. He hopes the weather breaks soon; it has been weeks since it last rained, and the pressure is palpable. Sweat soaks his chest and back, turning his grey T-shirt black. He and

Redford lean against the gate and watch as Les reverses the tractor to manoeuvre the crush into place. Although he has plenty to be getting on with at home, Richard is glad of the summons to lend a hand with the TB testing. This is the only way he can pay Les back for all the game that appears on the gate and is one of the few things that make Richard feel like he truly belongs, that he is no different from the other men who are village born and bred – a farmer, like his father and grandfather, and his father before that, though he owns only a handful of chickens and a loft full of rats. Being here also helps to keep his mind off the second letter to arrive from the county council, demanding Richard respond with the requested information at his earliest convenience or else face an inspection. Tess collected the post that morning and he had needed to grab it quickly from the table before she saw who it was from. Richard's fury surges back – bloody busybodies, the lot of them. Did they think he had not noticed them sneaking around, prying over next door's wall, searching for something incriminating? What business is it of theirs what he does inside his polytunnel?

'Where's that vet to?' asks Les as he joins them at the gate. 'Hope 'tisn't that there Polish chap again. Got nothing against 'e but can't understand a bloody word 'e says.' Richard swallows a laugh as he remembers when Tess, who speaks better than most, first met Les and how she later asked if he was actually speaking English. Les did have the broadest accent, after all, especially when the drink took him.

'Redford,' Les orders his son, who jumps to attention. 'Go

up the shed and get 'e some cider.' Behind them, the cows settle into a big cluster with only the occasional mournful bellow. 'Good show at the church last Thursday,' says Les, shielding his eyes against the sun.

'I know. Can't believe so many turned up, must have been nearly the whole village,' Richard replies, trying to ignore the knot forming in his throat. Cyril's funeral had been hard, being back in the church and forced to sing hymns when all he wanted to do was wail. He had held it together for the most part, only cracking inside when they stood around the open grave for the committal. The sound of earth hitting wood will haunt him forever. He and Tess had gone together, wordlessly complicit in their need to put on a united front for both Cyril's and Max's benefit, but Tess, even more reticent than usual, had avoided the crowd in the church, choosing to wait alone outside in the churchyard, tight-faced and sweltering in her black coat with a bunch of blue cornflowers, Cyril's favourites, in her arms. After the service, Richard joined her, wanting to say something of comfort, but unable to open his mouth for fear of disintegrating into tears. Tess, somehow aware, reached out to touch his arm. Richard watched her leave the cornflowers nestled with the other wreaths and bouquets near the yew tree, only yards from Sonny, who had been left a small posy of forget-me-nots. He wanted to go after her, knowing she couldn't have made it far along the road home, but he got roped into pouring tea and handing out plates of sausages rolls and cheese and cucumber sandwiches in the church rooms.

317

Les spits a glob of phlegm onto the dry ground. 'Who were all 'em foreigners? I thought Cyril's people was from Salisbury? Funny how they weren't here to wipe his arse but turn up the second 'e's in the ground.'

Richard has to laugh at that. 'Foreigners? You mean the northerners. From Sheffield, I think it was. His mother's family, cousins or some such.'

Redford returns with a filled plastic bottle just as the vet's Land Rover screeches into the yard, churning up the dust.

'Quick, get some o' that down 'e, afore teacher confiscates it.' Les laughs, passing the bottle. Then it is back to business, and Richard must concentrate if he is to be helpful and not get himself trampled to death.

Tess

'Shit! What did he say?'

'He just said, "Whose is it?" The scan photo was *right there* in front of him on the table. I don't know how the hell it got there. I'd hidden it inside that cookbook Mama gave me.' Gripping the phone between my ear and neck, I try to hoist my body over the unsteady stile into the meadow. 'God, Peaches, it was awful. I didn't know what to tell him ... I mean, what does he mean ... *Whose is it?* He's the one getting phone calls all hours of the day, dashing here and there, and coming home late.' My heart pounds like it's trying to split my body in half. 'I'm ... I'm the one that sleeps in bed alone most nights, while he's off *galivanting*! I'm the one who should be asking *what the fuck's going on* ...' My shaking hands fail to grip the fence and I slip from the stile, crying out as I roll over my ankle and fall, twisting, so I sprawl among nettles with a leg bent under me. Blood blossoms red on the knee of my trousers where something sharp has torn the thin fabric. Stinging blisters cover my hands. Then there's fear. Pain sears deep inside as my stomach cramps and pushes my breath from me in hard, fast pants and I'm engulfed by wave after wave of panic. *Oh God, please, please, please ...*

'Calm yourself.' I say it out loud and it's my mother's voice. I picture that look of hers telling me to pull myself together. *Yes, Mama*. I slow my breathing – in then out – and take stock of what's happening inside me. The pain, piercing at first, slowly subsides and there's no warm gush of liquid, no dull ache, no telltale signs of my pregnancy ending, but it's a long time before I dare to move, robotic, as though I'm a reanimated puppet. Using matted weeds as leverage, I tug myself to my feet and rub my tingling hands against my thighs. Sheep, which fled to the other side of the field, amble back to bleat at me. I remember Peaches and my phone. Her distant, tiny voice screams from a nearby patch of clover.

'I'm fine, I'm fine. I just slipped . . . but I'm okay. Yeah . . . I'm okay. Gave myself a fright, that's all,' I tell both her and my beating heart, though my hand continues to press hard against my stomach.

'Gave you a fright? You gave *me* a bloody fright is what you did.' She stops and takes a slow breath. 'Girl! You're in no fit state. Go home. *Please.*'

'I can't!'

Peaches sighs, but I don't care what she's going to say, because I'm not going home, not yet. I can't face him. My knee throbs and my arms feel weak and incapable. Still, I reattempt the stile, successfully this time, and head across the field, extra careful now not to trip over wide, low-growing thistles or get my feet snagged in hidden rabbit holes.

'Look, Tessa. Maybe this is a good thing,' reasons my sister. 'It all had to come out sooner or later, and . . . well, now it's done. I don't know how you kept it from him for so long anyway. If it's really over between the two of you then you'll have to face facts – won't you?'

She's right, I should, but . . . it seems *I can't*. Of course, I don't tell her that. I just mumble agreeing noises as I find myself on the drove, where the hawthorns grow thicker and there's shade to protect me from the sun. I walk, sandals slapping against mud baked so hard it feels and looks like concrete. Here and there, animal footprints have dried into contorted hieroglyphics – if Max were here, he'd be able to translate them for me. I'm not thinking of where I'm going, but soon I stray too far from the phone mast, wherever it is, and it's a relief when I start to lose reception and have to promise Peaches I'll head home now and call her back when I get there. But instead of home, my feet take me along a familiar footpath, skirting round the far side of the village, past the tidy allotments, where scarecrows swing their scratched CDs, then upwards through parallel lines of pear trees and out by the small wooden gate leading to the bottom corner of the churchyard.

Now I'm here, I sit on my usual bench below the large yew tree to recover my strength – *everything's fine* my body reassures me. Squares of lurid plastic grass, almost fluorescent, like the stuff that used to sit under the veg in the greengrocers back in Lewisham, have been placed over the huge mound of earth on Cyril's grave to make it look less unsightly while it settles. Bouquets of flowers wilt in the heat, including my cornflowers, which I picked from Cyril's own garden. I miss him so much more than I thought possible, though some part of me is glad he's now here, among all these strangers, to be a friend to my son.

Max

Dad drenches dusty squash leaves with an overflowing bucket. Now he's not allowed to use the hosepipe, watering the vegetable beds takes longer. He hasn't changed his clothes since helping Les this morning and still stinks of cows. Mum should be here making tea, but she's disappeared off somewhere. When I got back from school, the house felt strange, all quiet, like something bad happened. Dad hasn't said anything about it and won't answer when I ask if he knows where she is. He's even grumpier than usual. When he barges along the rows, his legs snap off the squash's papery yellow flowers. Me and Sonny stay out of the way and watch him collect the ripening beefsteak tomatoes before their ruby skins split. Usually, Mum cuts and layers them into bowls of salad or turns them into pasta sauce or jars of chutney. But I doubt she's going to bother this year so Dad's customers will get a bumper load. Around the carrots, the dry earth's cracking and flying ants crawl out from their underground nests and rise up to where a green woodpecker's waiting.

'Max! Aren't you going to help him?' Sonny asks as he searches for cabbage white caterpillars on the brassicas. They must be squished until green blood oozes from them. Long fingers of runner beans dangle above our heads. Hiding in between them are black and yellow garden spiders. There are hardly any cars on the road and even the tractors up at Winslow Farm are quiet. The only sound is honeybees swarming the lavender by the front fence. It's so hot, the sparrows have given up squabbling and gone to hide in the hedge. Soon it will be the summer holidays.

I know I ought to help, but I don't want to. They think they're the only ones who are upset, but they're not. And I know they're keeping things from me, even Mum. Her mouth opens but nothing comes out. I want her to come home so I can ask about the village fete tomorrow afternoon. I'm not sure if I want to go, but everyone else from school will be there even though it's the same every year. There's always splat the rat, guess the weight of the lamb or how many jelly babies are inside the large glass jar. There's throwing crickets balls at shelves of crockery and queues for rides round the playing field on Ernie Pollard's vintage tractor. Janice from the corner house sells pot plants and the church ladies barbecue burgers and hot-dog sausages. All the men stand around drinking flat cider out of plastic cups. Ellie and Daniel say that if I go, I can be on their team for the tug of war. But Evan will be there too and his parents. He hasn't stopped calling me names, but now he only does it when he thinks Mr Reid can't hear him.

Dad's furious at dinner, chomping too loudly at his celery and throwing his knife down. Mum got home too late to cook so we're having tinned tuna with bits from the garden. I don't know where she's been. Her hair has grown into a big black cloud that hides her face when she tips her head forward. It should be nice, all of us sat together, but it isn't. I don't think they've argued because Mum keeps sneaking looks at Dad

324

through her hair as though she's waiting for him to say something. Sonny's bare feet *tap tap tap* under the kitchen table. It's unbearable. I drag him out into the garden as soon as we've finished eating.

'What's wrong with them?'

'I think it's something to do with a photograph,' he says, grinning.

'What photograph?' I wish he'd speak normally and stop being so secretive. Lately, I can't hear what he's thinking. It's like our magical twin bridge isn't working.

Next door, the estate agent's sign has changed from For Sale to Under Offer. This seems to make Dad angrier.

'Bloody nimbys,' he shouts at Barbara's wall before disappearing into the polytunnel and dragging the flimsy door shut behind him.

Sonny kneels on his bed and stares out of our open window. It's harder to fall asleep now there's so much daylight. The moon's a thin white semicircle in the pale sky, but the sun's still shining. We're too hot for pyjamas, so only keep our underpants on. Mosquitoes sing around our ears. Eventually, we'll have to close the curtains, or we'll wake up covered in itchy bites, which Mum'll have to dab with stinky tea tree oil.

'Aren't you getting into bed?'

'Not tired,' Sonny replies with a shrug, but his voice sounds sleepy. I leave my bed and climb up beside him. He's statue still. He looks different somehow, older, even though that's impossible as there are only seven minutes between us. His face reminds me of the photo of Grandad that used to be on Nana's mantlepiece. I follow his gaze to the fields and withy beds opposite.

'What is it?' I ask, looking out. Over in Hector's field, a little owl is perched on a fence post. Sonny points and my eyes catch a large streak of black sprinting along the hedge.

Sonny

Memories are pictures in a book that flash then disappear like wild strawberries winking in the verge. See how the kestrel hovers over the maize field? The river sulks and strains to lift its heavy arms. Brown sugar drips from Mum's wooden spoon. The other mums try to catch her, to find out her secrets, but she's too quick for them. Let's hide from the heat where eels coil in darkness with sludge worms. Dragonfly nymphs climb upwards, while green leaves wilt. Dad – try not to worry about the hosepipe ban. Did you know secrets evaporate in sunlight like tears on sunflowers? Bees search for nectar in the willow blossoms.

Me and Mum offer up our faces to the sun, and I remember warmth, redness lapping against my eyelids. We're both darker and enjoy our summer coats of deepest chestnut. All around us is pretty. Rooks high in the yew branches shout to us, while here on our bench, heat splits the wood into deep gashes. Look – there are ladybirds tucked into shady crevices. Mum's secret is out. I can feel her weight lift until it's so light, the dry wind can carry it away to make room for the seed growing inside. 'It will be easier,' I tell her. Mum takes off her jacket.

Don't forget, eyes are always watching.

Hazy summer pink roses tumble over the churchyard walls. Mum's tired of sitting, so we walk hand in hand on

327

paths worn smooth by other English feet, past older headstones that are broken or have collapsed, with slabs toppled and sliding, their engraved names disappearing into nothing. At the bottom of the hill, fields unroll before us in ancient patchwork.

'Isn't it lovely?' Mum says to me. We listen for the faint midday bell at the grand church in Branstock and stare out as a fast commuter train to London zooms across the Woodholt viaduct.

Tess

I wait until Max has kicked off his school shoes in the porch, flung down his rucksack, his lunchbox clattering on the stone floor, and grabbed a glass of orange squash and a packet of crisps from the cupboard. Only then do I ask him to come and sit with me on the riverbank. If he's surprised, he doesn't show it, but follows me without question out of the house, still crunching his crisps, and onto the bank where the grass is brittle and dry, and a lack of rain has made everything look golden, including the alder, whose leaves ripple as the light catches them. Whenever I look at the river, even now when it's at its lowest and cowers from me behind a screen of thick vegetation, goosebumps prickle and the pain in my chest deepens. Perhaps this isn't the best place to do this; a walk may have been easier. I should have let him lead me through the woods to see if that bird hide of his is empty. It shames me – I've not taken a walk alone with Max since Sonny left us and can count the number of times before that on one hand. It was always Sonny who dragged me off to walk the miles of footpaths, to explore uncharted droves, leafy lanes that, though beautiful, led us nowhere. Max only ever seemed to need his brother's company. And me? I needed to make myself less visible.

On the other side of the moor runs a thin strip of darkening rain clouds. Max leans against me and his arm alongside mine feels light, as though my presence is the only thing that keeps him from dispersing like the fluffy white willow seeds floating around us. The past weeks of sunshine have tanned his cheeks, forcing melanin hidden inside his skin to make an appearance so I glimpse the underlying spectre of Sonny's face and there . . . in the bone over the brow, is that my father? But why should it surprise me? The baby feels heavier today, pressing on my pubic bone as it becomes someone substantial who refuses to be denied. I'm half hoping my observant son will look down and notice, without me needing to spell it out for him, but he's enthralled by two parties of ants, one black and one red, who war against each other on a piece of shrivelled driftwood.

'So, Max,' I start. 'I know you've been worrying about me lately. That I've been unwell and . . . unhappy. The thing is . . . well . . . Max? Are you listening to me?' Max shakes off the ants that have crawled onto his fingers.

'It's fine, Mum, I know. You're having a baby.' His sad eyes look into mine. 'Sonny already told me.'

Richard

Although last night's brief rain shower finally cools the heatwave, the polytunnel's small ventilation flaps still need opening. Condensation weeps down its plastic walls, but Richard is too distracted by thoughts of Tess and by the letter clenched inside his fist – another one from the county council, this time more forthright, informing Richard of an imminent inspection and, in bold font, possible enforcement. Some bureaucrat's signature is chicken scratch at the bottom of the page. This is not the first time Richard has run into this kind of trouble; there was that officious planning officer who objected to his rough, but logical, hand-drawn plans for the extension, claiming he would only consider designs created by a professional architect. Like Richard had access to that kind of money. Tess stepped in, reawakening her brain and retrieving her collection of rulers and pens, a large T-square and a half-used A3 pad of draft paper from a black bin bag stashed behind the wardrobe. This house was as much her creation as his. Now, if he is to make any progress, he will have to manage by himself.

The black and white scan photo blazes in Richard's mind like the afterimage of a bright light bulb. On seeing it lying there out of context on the kitchen table, he was baffled – where had it come from? *Whose was it?* Was it even real or just a cryptic bit of advertising from a magazine that Tess was using as a bookmark? Her panicked reaction when he asked her about it took him aback; she said it was hers, but rather than explain what she meant, she fled as though the idea of talking to him was unthinkable. Suddenly all those jumpers she wore made sense.

Much of the morning was wasted with him glaring stunned into space, so Richard puts his foot down hard, and propels the van through the lanes with little care for oncoming traffic. Crates rattle, spilling out new potatoes. Thankfully, punnets of precious red gooseberries are packed tight between rolls of newspaper. It is Brian first, at the Bird, who will be wanting his salad greens and tomatoes ready for the lunch run of ploughman's. Richard speeds towards the village centre past a new, temporary twenty-miles-per-hour sign, which flashes at him accusatorily.

Brian can only have just unbolted the heavy door but already one of the stools is occupied by Moocher, uncle to Marge on her father's side, who nurses a pint of Guinness, his customary breakfast and, as he has told Richard on several occasions, a complete meal in a glass. They nod their usual greeting.

'Brian? You about?' Richard calls to the empty bar, deter-mined to ignore the strong smell of stale beer that pulls at his taste buds.

'In here,' comes a shouted reply. Resting the crate on his hip, Richard flips open the side hatch and steps behind the bar then out into the cellar, where Brian is changing the barrels. 'Got a skittles match tonight, us versus them fools from the Swan. They'll be here at half four so thought I better put on some extra lager just in case,' he says, by way of explaining. Richard deposits the salad crate on the floor.

'Good plan,' he agrees. 'Least the weather's cooled down a bit. It'll make it easier for you.'

'Yeah. It was like a furnace in here last week. Just wish I had more help. Had to lay off young Lucy Winslow only yesterday. Can't afford to keep the staff. Anyway, that's by the by. Stopping for a half?' Brian asks, already reaching up to the shelf for a glass.

'Not today thanks, Brian. Got too much to do to stop.'

'I can imagine. Well, it's not likely to get any better soon, is it? Not now you got another little 'un on the way. Heard Beryl Meade telling Janet in the shop this morning. Glad you and the missus sorted things out in the end. We all thought you had your eye on someone else. Would've been a terrible shame.'

Richard delivers the rest of the crates in a daze, incapable of his routine small talk. *Had my eye on someone else . . .* He cannot understand how anybody could come to such an absurd conclusion. He slams his foot down on the brake. *And how is it everyone knows about this baby apart from me?*

Several parcels are waiting to be unpacked in the shed. Richard kicks them all aside, sending their 'This way' upwards arrows whirling. 'What's the fucking point?' he asks and slumps upon the worktop with a violent dizziness. On the wall, the clock ticks soothingly and Richard finds himself thinking of when he took Tess to the hospital for that first scan, how nervous they had been and excited. On the way home in the van, they had not been able to stop laughing, clutching at each other's hands, and predicting whether they would have boys or girls or maybe one of each. Impulsively, he thinks of heading back to the pub, it will only take a few pints to quash these unwanted feelings, but, exhaling slowly, Richard instead gathers up the parcels, loads them tenderly into the wheelbarrow and pushes them up the garden path. From all sides, there is the evidence of tasks left unfinished; even the leeks look woefully neglected and have gone to seed, shooting out lengthy tough stalks. He wedges open the door of the polytunnel and is calm for a moment, enjoying the mollifying smell of warm soil, but is brought sharply back by the alarm call of a blackbird somewhere nearby, followed seconds later by the escalating sound of Mrs Bulmer's scornful voice. Dressed in her habitual riding get-up of jodhpurs and padded vest, though she has not owned a horse for well over a decade, she stands on Barbara's side of the wall talking, as Richard quickly determines, to the prospective new owners of the Gables.

'... the neighbours? Oh no, can't vouch for them ... no, the polytunnel shouldn't be an issue. God only knows what's in there – it's been reported to the council. Yes, hard to believe the Hembrys used to be respected farmers around here ...'

Sonny

Can you hear those village drums *drumming*? The thrush finishes his evening song as whispers travel down the lanes. When the sun sets, I'll step my brown feet beside those of the bargemen and look to see the ships arriving at Bridgwater. All those broken bricks pile up along the quayside. Smoke from our clay pipes threads through the trees like silver mist. A mead moon rides the dusk sky with Venus. Don't you know? The cracks let in more than light. Overgrown withies collapse under their own weight. Mum won't go any further than the school gate. Eyes down, she's gone in a flash before they can be sure she was ever there. Look, Dad, never mind unspoken words, it's all just gossip anyway. Tales have a way of undoing in the retelling. Let's close our ears and weave ourselves into a family-shaped basket, strong enough to carry the mud dredged up from my quiet riverbed. Let's daub our wattle, build up our house and beat down our dirt floor. Replace mud with stone and stone with brick. See the endless fingerprints pressed into the wooden lintels. Mum has left her own mark along with the others.

Tess

Place the fish heads and bones in the Dutch pot – seems I'm making soup. I must thank Les and his son for the second bag of mackerel. Mama calls it fish tea, even though this hot weather calls for cold cuts. Something ... no, someone inside me craves more heat. Add water and boil for a few minutes. I wait for him to confront me, I've worked out the words I'll have to say, but there's been nothing from him but his usual silence. He talks to Max, as do I, but we're afraid of each other. I make the soup the way Mama taught me. Strain the stock until the broth is clear. Discarded fish bones are thrown in the bin. Why do I never slice enough onion? No okra or green bananas, but I've learnt to make do with potato and carrots, and a few of those shrunken sweet green peppers he stripped off the plants to let the bigger ones ripen. I see him walk past the kitchen window, past my orange irises. He doesn't see me here. Where's the mixed herbs? Really, I should cut some fresh, but then I might run into him. My belly bumps softly against the cooker's hand-rail. Now for the flesh of the fish. Are those footsteps I hear stepping close behind me – a smaller palm pressing onto the back of my hand?

Mama takes the news surprisingly well and doesn't launch into her customary 'Jesus wept, child' tirade but, instead, maintains 'God is good', and that a new life is a blessing for the family. I'm not to lose any sleep over David's offer of a job – it was a kind gesture for old times' sake more than anything else – nor am I to return the money she's gifted me as there's no doubt I'll need it, whether it be for a rental deposit, college fees or simply for the baby, wherever I choose to raise it. As though England can never be hot enough, even with this July hitting well over thirty degrees Celsius, Mama tells me to wrap up warm, not to walk on the kitchen floor barefooted, to eat plenty of spinach and, most important, I'm not to let *dem people* rub my belly unless I know for certain they are good people. Of course, there's some annoyance that I'm only just letting her know, but she understands how the words will have been hard for me. Seems I'm that difficult child who brings as much anxiety as they do happiness. Maybe to save my dignity, she doesn't voice her opinions about Richard, but it's now that she offers the invitation I once longed for – if London isn't really what I want and there's no home for me here then, perhaps, I should come home to Jamaica and to her. In the loneliness of my bedroom, I try to imagine myself beside her, but can only visualise a series of scenes, each perfect, but static and remote. The both of us technicolour bright, vivid against a scenic tropical back-drop, while the sun irons out the creases on our brows and our tired mouths remember how to smile.

I bend my head closer to the mirror so I can see each parting clearly as my fingers massage olive oil onto my scalp and out through the length of my hair, which has grown into a full-blown afro, soft and light, encouraged by sunshine and surging hormones. From the wardrobe, I choose a sleeveless green dress I wore during my pregnancy with the boys, simple in design, but which will leave no one in doubt over my enlarged waistline. *Is there too much skin showing?* Today I'm nervous, so spend far longer in front of the mirror than I do for my usual *chuck it on and go* approach. I take an extra step and put on mascara, a smear of plum-coloured lipstick, and a pair of silver studs. The small gold clock on my bedside table tells me to hurry up.

Richard waits with the engine running. He sits rigid, with his face immobile, staring straight ahead, and the moment I've fastened my seatbelt takes off, but at a steadier speed than his usual breakneck haste. Even this we couldn't arrange by ourselves; it was Max this morning who asked over his bowl of bran flakes, almost slyly, with his fair lashes shielding his eyes, if we would *both* be coming to collect him from school, seeing as it is the last day of term – his last day of primary school to be exact. And so, here we are together inside the van trapped by our inability to communicate. Richard coughs to clear his throat and I wonder if it galls him to be thrust into such close contact with me. Does he worry about what the recipient of all those secret phone calls would say about our mock display of a relationship? *He still hasn't said a single word about the baby.* School's only a five-minute drive away, but it feels more like half an hour. We keep our gazes fixed, him on the road and me turned away towards my window letting sunlight stream onto my closed eyelids.

A boisterous mass of parents and onlookers congregates outside the school, where a tractor and its attached hay-bale-filled trailer have been decorated with balloons and streamers ready to take the Year 6 leavers for their farewell victory lap of the village square. The fuss begins the second I step out of the van. Heads crane, with some openly pleased, while others struggle to hide their surprise at seeing something so unexpected, but, as always, there are still those few who look through me dismissively as though I'm not worth their notice. Amy strides over to offer me moral support, leaving Richard with no other choice but to follow.

'You look smashing,' she whispers into my hair as we walk into the packed playground.

Max

The cockerel at Marge's is already crowing, but the stars haven't gone yet. I should be asleep, like everyone else in the house, but today's the first day of the summer holidays and I'm too excited. I sit up in bed so I can look at my school shirt again. Both the front and back, and part of the sleeves, are covered in marker pen where some of the kids in my class signed their names. Ruby put hers inside a green heart and Daniel drew a little dragon beside his that's breathing out fire. There are even a few names on here from children in the lower years who wanted me to remember them.

Yesterday was one of the best days ever. Mr Reid let us play games all day and there was a tractor waiting for us outside the school gate. The whole village came out to wave us off. It was epic! I can't stop thinking about it. Mum was so pretty in her green dress, and it looked like parents were queueing up to give her a hug. Dad was stood on his own but cheered with everyone else and took photos on our camera.

I roll over to look across at Sonny, but I think he's still sleeping. While I wait for him to wake up, I imagine what it will be like at Combe Hill Secondary. There's a bus that picks up the teenagers from our village, so Mum and Dad won't need to do the school run. But when we went to the open day, Mum said she couldn't believe that out of a thousand kids, not one of them wasn't white. I'll be the only black person there, though Nathan would say *Quit your beefing, cuz, you look no different from the rest of them.* Some of the older Combe Hill kids hang out in the park. They're always there on a Sunday afternoon when there's nothing else to do. They smoke and kiss and touch each other round the back of the tennis pavilion and under the climbing frame. There are flattened cider cans chucked in the hedge, and behind the scout hut always smells like pee and cigarettes. It scares me to think I'll become one of them.

There's a splash. Outside in the river. It was so loud I could hear it through our wall. Maybe it's a huge pike jumping, but it sounded much bigger.

'Sonny!' I pull his sheet back and poke him until he moves.

Mist hovers above the ground like a soft white blanket. It creeps slowly through the garden like it's alive and crosses the road to join the other morning mists collecting over in the fields. By the time the sun comes up, they'll all have disappeared. When we get to the river, there's not even a ripple. Now it's not muddy, we can get right to the water's edge without getting our feet stuck.

'I told you. It's just the pike jumping,' says Sonny. He's cross because he wasn't ready to leave his bed yet. Lately, it's getting harder and harder to get him to do anything I want. He'd much rather do stuff by himself or disappear completely.

'It was definitely bigger,' I insist.

'It was nothing,' he says, but then changes his mind. 'Or maybe it was the sound of an oar hitting the water.'

'An oar? What are you on about?'

Downy mallard ducklings race away from me as I push

342

through the reeds. If she sees me, their mother's quacks will wake everybody up. We must go careful; the nettles are thick now and we're out here with bare legs. I use the very tips of my fingers to pinch the nettles' tasselled flowers and lean the leaves away out of reach. Under each leaf are clusters of teeny green eggs put there by red admirals. By my feet, I find the crinkled shell of an oyster that still smells salty like the sea. I turn to show it to Sonny, but he's gone off somewhere. 'Sonny?' My shout sets all the ducks off quacking. Fine, let him be like that. I'm not going to look for him. Reed warblers pip in the hedge and there's a cuckoo that should have left for Africa by now.

Sonny's not in the kitchen when I get back to the house, but Mum is, wrapped up in her dressing gown even though she must be too warm. I wait for her to tell me off for sneaking out, but she just asks if I'd like some breakfast. While bread's toasting, I get the honey from the cupboard. Mr Brewer's bees made it. They've spent all summer on our lavender. Mum scoffs her toast down real quick, then takes a glass bowl sealed with cling film from the fridge. Inside are raw portions of chicken covered in Nana's spicy marinade. We've just had breakfast and already she's thinking about making tea. The longer it cooks, she says, the better it tastes.

'Want me to teach you?' she asks when she sees me watching.

Sonny

A tidal overflow washes over your bones. Listen – hear horses snorting steam as they wait for morning on the towpath. Sunrise explodes cherryade pink. Plastic caravans clog the lanes, while the dead sing under apple trees. Mum and Max make cook-down chicken and a summer pudding with raspberries from the garden. Harvest mice race through the maize to beat the teeth of the combine. In the Scots pine, the barn owl's talons are empty. Chickweed sprouts through the bleached skull of a weasel. Would you like to see where the deer have made a soft grass bed, or shall we go into the pasture and look for field mushrooms and blewits? Let's fry them up with bartered sausages. I'll give you a dozen chicken eggs for a jar of honey. Bees murmur it's time to lift the onions. Soon there will be sloes and damsons. Along the hedgerow, blackcaps pick off the haws and mistletoe berries. Young swallows strengthen their new wings. In our orchard, russets, pippins, royal Somersets and Bramleys turn deeper greens and browns and reds.

Tess

In the mellow heat, I feel myself expand so grief sinks into my marrow to become hard, as close to the underside of my skin as bone, yet soft, deep, melding like the sinews that support my pelvis, which ease and stretch as I move about the house. The breeze floods in through every open window and brings me the heady fragrance of warm grasses, lavender, my roses in bloom, peach and yellow, and whispers from my son. There he is again, telling me of woodlice that run along the skirting in the midsummer mornings. I hear his laughter reverberate inside the sun-kissed walls. His dark eyes stare out at me from every mirror, every polished surface, be it bathroom tap or Rayburn hotplate cover. We talk of everything – whether it will rain today or stay gloriously blue-sky hot, shall we have cream or custard, did we remember to collect the chicken eggs this morning, is there enough bacon left for a quiche, we could make two and drop one off at Marge's, will they see me and know I *jus come from foreign*, will they jeer at my bodged attempt at patois, how lonely it feels to live as an outsider. *Oh, Sonny, would I know myself as me in Jamaica? Won't I miss the seasons and the way time turns here?*

Richard

Richard fumbles through his chores. He promises himself that in the afternoon he will sit down and make the phone calls needed to keep the council off his back. Using the sharpest of the secateurs, the red ones, as Sonny used to remind him, he cuts back the early raspberries seeing as all the fruit has been picked and loads the cuttings into the wheelbarrow bound for the compost heap. It is rhubarb next, which wants earthing up a few inches, and trays of potting mix wait for him on the bench inside the greenhouse ready for another run of basil and flat-leaf parsley. A blur of brown, white and pink thrashes against the glass, striking each pane in wild desperation as it ricochets through the greenhouse. Richard waits for it to stop, its tiny beak gasping, before taking up a sheet of green netting and using it to persuade the bird in the direction of the open door.

'There you go. Just needed a bit of help, didn't you?' he tells it.

'A chaffinch!' Max's face appears in the doorway in time to see the bird escape.

'Yeah, a juvenile. My fault. Forgot to hang up the netting. Here, seeing as you're standing there, see if you can hook it up for me.' Max grapples with the netting while Richard continues sowing herb seeds. It is peaceful, just the sound of their breathing and the faint babble of cyclists out on the road. It's not long before Max comes and stands next to him, looking triumphant.

'I've done it,' he says.

'Great job. You don't fancy giving me a hand with something else?' Richard asks, hopeful, but aware the answer is unlikely to be a yes. Of course, Max would rather play at being with Sonny. 'No, actually . . . it's fine. Don't tell me. You're busy.' Richard smiles mildly at his son, with the knowledge that this is one of many problems he might never be able to solve. He starts out of the greenhouse and back down the garden path only to find, when he looks over his shoulder, that Max is behind him, flicking with his fingers at the feathery fronds poking from the ripening ears of sweetcorn.

'No. Sonny's busy, but I'm not. So if you want, I can help you instead,' his son volunteers, head bent now to the ground as he examines a stippled wasp beetle. Afraid of breaking the spell, Richard continues slowly along the path, pausing just once, without turning, to listen for the soft tread of Max's following footfall.

Emptied of their summer stock, two of the vegetable beds have been cleared in preparation for kohlrabi, winter cauliflowers, turnips, cabbages, and a second round of potatoes that will be ready in time for Christmas. Richard hands his son the rake and shows him how to start up in one corner and comb the dark, rich soil towards him – steady, not too fast or too hard – making the earth smooth and level, and loosening any compacted lumps. Max watches delighted as small orange centipedes squirm to the surface. Pebbles and stones are towed into heaps at the edges, where Richard uses the larger of the forks to scoop them into an old, cracked bucket. Low white cumulus clouds cruise over as they work, casting both shadow and light.

'Dad?' Max is the first to shatter their easy silence. 'What will happen when the baby comes?' The question jolts air from Richard's chest. Max stops raking. 'Dad?'

'Um . . . I'm not sure, to be honest, but . . . I know it will be fine.'

'But are you looking forward to it being here?' Max asks with more persistence. Richard worries with the heel of his boot at a stone embedded in the soil. Only a sharp corner protrudes, but he knows from the feel of it there is much more buried underground.

'I guess so,' he ventures as both happy memories and painful foresights collide. Max pushes the rake away, then pulls it back again.

'I wasn't,' he says, 'but now I think it might be okay. Maybe, when she's bigger, she can sleep in my room with me cos it's lonely in there now.' Richard's eyes burn and a pain he has been trying to avoid for so long begins to crush him. 'Wish Mum had told me sooner though. I've been so worried about her. She cries so much when you're not here.' It is not meant as an accusation, but Richard can take it no other way. Worry clouds Max's face. Richard reaches out and holds his son close. 'Dad, you're not going to leave us, are you?' Max whispers into his chest.

Sonny

Without their fleeces, sheep shiver in the cool morning air. Deer burst white-tailed through the hedge and leap away across the withy beds. Mum's thoughts shout and Dad's silence bellows. In the quiet, everything is so much clearer. Listen – can you hear my brother crying? In the village square, the ice cream van chimes Oranges and Lemons. Grasshoppers *chirrup* away all other sounds. No Maggi? Don't worry, Mum, we can use soy sauce and a drip of golden syrup. Let me help you fold the clean tea towels. The river tugs impatiently, but I'm not quite ready. I spin on its surface, a black whirligig beetle, half an eye keeping watch, while the other half looks down at all that life. Under pondweed, the water scorpion hunts a stickleback. Tears flow downstream. Max searches for me, but I hide under the butterburs where he can't find me. I take my oyster shells and sharp-edged river mussels and slice at the bond that ties us. Like Cyril says, 'two sides of the same coin'. Nana told us, a day will come when you pickneys must go your own way and be independent. But don't worry, your roots will sustain you. Now, there is no *we*; he is Max, and I am Sonny, keeper of bones and fossils.

Max

Mum has an appointment at the hospital, but Mason's mum turns up to take her before Dad gets a chance. He looks disappointed, but says, 'Never mind, we've got stuff to be getting on with here,' and calls John on his mobile, rather than going down the road to talk to him in person. Sonny's barely talking. He either sits on his bed or stares out of the landing window. He says he's listening to voices calling from the riverbank. Maybe those people are nosying round next door again, but I've not seen anyone over there except that man last week, who was outside taking photographs over Barbara's wall. He didn't look like an estate agent, not like the one that came last time. This man's suit was plain black, and his tie was boring.

John arrives carrying what I think is a large birdcage covered over with a spotty towel. Twittering comes from inside it. Dad's scratching at his head, which is what he does when he's worried.

'Managed to get you a breeding pair, so you might get lucky.' John smiles so wide his lips disappear completely into his beard. 'Max, this here's to be your responsibility, seeing as you're the bird lover in the family.'

'Me?' I ask, so surprised. I must be getting budgies like John's Fred and Ginger for my birthday. Under Dad's arm is a small white cardboard box he picked up from the village shop this morning. Ted and Janet ordered something in for him. I'm guessing it must be something he wrote down inside their Requests book. At first, I think it's food, maybe Turkish delight or shortbread, but when I get up closer, I can see the box has tiny holes punched in it. The words on the top say 'Caution – Live Animals'.

For once, the door of the polytunnel is propped open. John sidesteps in with the cage and Dad follows, leaving me alone on the garden path. But it's fine. I know I must wait until my birthday arrives, otherwise it won't be a surprise.

'Max, where are you? Aren't you coming in?' calls Dad from inside the polytunnel.

'What?' I shout back.

Dad sticks his head out. 'Come on. I've got something to show you.'

Tess

He pinches the fish the way I used to, by the tail between forefinger and thumbnail, wary, afraid it's going to wriggle alive at any moment. Mama would tell me to hold it firmly, head end down under the cold tap, with its slit belly gaping so the running water can flush out the muck and guts.

'Argh, Mum. That's disgusting,' Max says, making me laugh – that's my childhood voice coming from him.

'Stop being squeamish. Get your hands in there. You're not going to be one of those people who only buy things already boned and filleted,' I tell him like my mother told me – I wonder, when did I let the hardiness I learnt leave me? I was taught never to shy away from anything, which is how I found the courage to move out here in the first place. Max lets me guide his fingers inside the fish's cavity. I teach him how to use the knife to scrape off its scales, so the water directs them towards the mesh trap covering the plug hole. 'Careful! You're pinging them everywhere. Make sure you're scraping downwards,' I explain. His smile, when four cleaned fish sit neatly on the plate, thrills me and I don't see Richard, but my son Max, with his unexpected Hembry eyes and Sullivan little-boy crooked teeth. Spending time with him brings me a joy I wasn't able to handle. He's spending more time with his father too, helping with the veg, voluntarily, which is the strangest thing – he's never liked gardening. But the flip side of this means there are fewer and fewer mentions of his adventures with Sonny.

It is a good thing, I tell myself and the baby inside me jerks in agreement. I say 'baby' because its gender is still unknown – how could I ask, with no Richard there beside me? Though Max, for some bizarre reason, swears with no uncertainty it's going to be a girl. Mama would say, 'Him having a feeling'.

'What's next?' he asks, prodding at one of the fish's bulbous eyeballs.

'Your choice,' I tell him. 'Do you want to fry them like that or fillet them and cover them in something? Breadcrumbs? Or we can make up some flour with seasoning.' He decides on breadcrumbs, but with a sprinkling of paprika, turmeric and chilli powder, my fallback trio. Turns out he's a natural, with Mama's cunning knack for guessing the right quantities for the best flavour. We remove the heads and I show him how to lift out the spine and larger bones and how, before the breadcrumbs, each piece of fish must first be bathed in beaten egg. Max pulls off each step with his face locked in concentration. *How did I not know this about him?* Suddenly, I can see it – him and me making a go of it *wherever*, here or in London or even somewhere as far away from everything he knows as Jamaica.

'Max—' I begin.

'Mum, look! There's that man I told you about.'

Max

Mum washes the smell of fish from her hands and makes sure her dress is on straight. The man is now standing inside our garden ready with his camera. Two more men come through our gate to join him. They all look very important in dark trousers and white shirts. Me and Mum wait but there's no knocking at either the back door or the front one. The men walk straight past the kitchen window, through the garden towards the back of the house. I know where they're going.

'Call Dad!' I shout back to Mum as I run outside.

The garden path is hard to see under Swiss chard and dark green kale leaves so the men have to go in single file until they reach the polytunnel.

'No! Don't go in there!' I yell. They stop for a second to glance back. I hear Mum running up behind me. Why isn't Dad here when we need him?

When Mum catches up, she's breathing really hard and holding up her tummy with both hands. 'What on earth's going on?' she demands. The men look at each other, embarrassed.

'Mrs Hembry ... is it?' The one with the camera says to her. 'Yes? Ah ... I'm Mr Walmsley. Simon Walmsley from the county council's Planning and Development Department. Sorry to disturb you. Your husband should have been expecting our inspection today as several notifications were posted out to him. We've had reports of a commercial structure being used without permission on residential curtilage . . .'

But while he's speaking, one of the other men wrenches the polytunnel door open. He's going to ruin everything.

'No! You're not allowed in there!' I yell, feeling braver than I've ever felt. 'It's Mum's garden that Dad made her. It's not finished. No one's supposed to see it yet!'

Sonny

As the sun climbs bright above the topmost branches of the alder, I tiptoe between these plastic walls and whisper one last time to the flower buds. Never mind the way life is shouting. Wake up, *Hedychium coccineum, Hibiscus sabdariffa, Portlandia grandiflora.* It's time to show Mum her home is right here with us. We mustn't let the cold darkness of winter make us forget. Dad, hurry. Snip back your bindweed and throw open your precious chrysalis. Despite everything, your plants are still thriving.

Tess

A garden ... for me?

I'm stunned, and strangely nervous. Ignoring my son's pleas for him to stop, Mr Walmsley takes a couple of steps inside the polytunnel, only to jump back out in alarm as two birds bolt past his head.

'No ... no! Now they've escaped!' Max is shouting and Mr Walmsley starts going on about how the council will need to inform pest control, but I'm not listening. It's those birds. I recognise them. I watch them fly away over the river, fleeing into the distance, then slow and circle round and round before coming back to land in a nearby thicket of willow. I'd know them anywhere. Parakeets – true London natives, no longer tropical migrants. Their screeching takes me back and all at once, I'm a child again, heart racing, desperate to catch a glimpse of brilliant green flashing overhead.

Richard

Unfamiliar cars are parked along the road when Richard returns, and he is forced to park the van in front of the Gables and sprint back to the house. Tess's message has him panicked. Thank goodness he was already on his way home after finishing the deliveries. 'Shit!' he shouts. This is not how it was supposed to go. He spent months planning everything down to the very last detail, has played the whole thing out inside his head night after sleepless night when he sat in the shed as broken as his deckchair, has spent every waking moment and every penny he earned on trying to achieve perfection, to the detriment, he realises now, of everything and everyone around him. He was supposed to bump into her, most likely in the kitchen, unintentionally of course, and ask if he could show her something. If she said no, he would have talked her round *somehow*, made her walk with him through the garden and he would have opened that polytunnel door with a flourish so she could instantly understand how much she means to him. Richard knows this was pure idiocy – there was never any chance of his dream unfolding so effortlessly. He would have been nervous, terrified, certain Tess would push him away, that nothing he could ever give her would be enough to lessen her grief or numb his deep-rooted guilt.

'Dad ... *hurry*!' Max screams as Richard flings open the gate.

Tess

There are raised voices outside, but inside the stillness of the polytunnel, glossy leaves of ginger lilies spill open onto the path, and I'm astonished by plumes of intense pinks radiating from their centres. Jamaican swallowtails, which I know from a postcard Mama sent Max, float past me on rhythmic gold and black wings. More beautiful still are the bell flowers that hang in soft swirls of painted silk above my head. I stroke hesitant fingers over petals soft as velvet. Their fragrance is spellbinding. I'm lost. There's the warmth of a small hand and Sonny's dark eyes pull me in.

Richard

He sees her in profile, motionless, as though captured in still life, as exquisite and breathtaking as the yellow hibiscus flowers surrounding her.

'What's this one called?' she asks and gently lifts a spray of rosy magenta.

Richard steps closer. 'You'll like that one. It's ladies' fingers or . . . kiss me over the garden gate,' he tells her.

Tess smiles and Richard watches the shy movement of her lips.

'And this?' She points at an impressive plant growing up between the fan-like spread of ferns.

'I thought you'd notice that. Magnificent, isn't it? They call it *Heliconia bihai aurea* or red palulu.'

'Red pa-lu-lu,' she repeats, and he cannot help but move a little closer. 'Oh, I know this one.' She points again, this time down at a low-growing shrub with delicate leaves and little yellow flowers. 'Cerasee. My dad managed to grow some once, back in Lewisham. It was only a small plant, nothing as big as this. Mama used to make me drink the tea when I was poorly. God, it tasted awful.' Tess laughs, a rare and beautiful sound, and Richard takes another step, so there can only be a few inches now between them. 'I didn't think you liked growing flowers,' she says, looking up at him with wet eyes.

'I didn't think I did either.' He touches her now and takes both of her hands in his.

Tess

Flowers are not the only thing my secretive husband has been growing all these months. Seems I now have my very own kitchen garden, complete with ginger, with its enlarged golden roots visible just below the surface of the soil, masses of delicate coriander and callaloo, and calabaza, only a few plants, but whose leaves spread wide hiding the small pumpkins forming underneath. Okra, Mama's favourite, grows upright through dense bushes of West Indian thyme, whereas cho cho hangs from two small trees, the palest green, rather like the unripe quinces in the orchard. Richard shows me yams, white and yellow, with heart-shaped leaves, and sweet potatoes, neat rows of purple scallions, chillies too, so many different varieties, though I'm able to pick out scotch bonnets and habanero. Unfamiliar are the fountains of lemon grass, and who knew turmeric grew such beautiful white and pink flowers?

Oh God, Peaches won't believe me when I tell her.

Although I'm under no illusions – only the hardiest will endure the dampness of autumn, even less the inhospitable cold of coming winter, despite my husband's efforts and his makeshift heating system, which it seems most of the neighbours have had a hand in – for now, sunshine blurs away impossibilities and Richard says if we keep replenishing the plants, there's hope some might establish permanently. There's nothing to stop us adding a few things to the veggie boxes, shake things up a bit. 'But what if people don't know what to do with them?' I ask him, and he laughs and says then I must teach them – maybe I could make up some recipe cards he can pop into the crates. We could expand the business, I could host a cookery class . . . or two, match the dishes to the seasons. Optimism floats me out of myself like a raft soaring over the moor in flood.

Sonny

Tough Jamaican roots grow deep and thick in English soil. See them thrust downwards to huddle with vervain, milk thistle and marsh mallow. Can you smell the meadowsweet, so sweet, like honey spread on warm toast? Listen – the reeds are murmuring. Feel the eddies twist and flow, towing shredded rushes, shards of heavy timber, and old plastic milk cartons over sunken bones. I let the river *sip, sip, sip* at my toes. We both know in which direction the bargemen should go. Watch how I blend into the landscape. See me skip across the water, a child's perfect skimming stone. I'm woven like dog rose all through the hedgerow. You'll find me buried deep beside those ancient village gravestones.

Max

Finally, the neighbours have gone, so Mum can relax and walk with Dad again through her new garden. Word's already got out and someone from the *Gazette* is coming to do a story on it. Dad's pleased – he reckons the publicity will be good for business.

Mason and his mum stopped by when we were in the middle of eating my birthday breakfast fry-up. There was plantain, sausages, fried dumplings just as good as Nana's, and eggs and baked beans. Mum made loads, so Mason and his mum stayed and ate with us for a bit. Mason didn't talk to me much, but he gave me an MP3 player for my birthday, so I can listen to music when I'm on the school bus. Les brought me a homemade withy eel trap. Edith came with another itchy jumper, and that pink and white blanket thing she was knitting was for Mum and the baby all along. Edith said she had a feeling it would be needed. At lunchtime, Mum lit the candles on my chocolate cake and we drank Marge's elderflower champagne. Turns out Cyril left a present for Mum and Dad too. Stashed away, unopened, behind Dad's radio was a letter from Cyril's solicitor. We're not going to be rich. Not like Oliver, who gets to go skiing in France every year. But Mum's getting her own car so she can get around the village and drive to London to see Aunty Peaches whenever she wants to. Best of all, we're all going to Jamaica at Christmas time to see Nana and show her my new sister. I can't wait. There'll be loads of creatures I've never seen before.

Summer turns the moor green and lush, nothing like the scruffy swamp we live beside all winter. It looks much more beautiful, but there are fewer birds for me to spot. Everything changes, even the sky, which gets larger, so the horizon seems further away. Though Mr Reid told us there's no *real* horizon, it's just imaginary. The edge of the planet looks different depending on who's looking and where they're standing. I stand on the riverbank and let my toes wriggle down into the long grass. Thistles don't bother me because I know where not to step, although Mum'll still say I ought to put shoes on. Blue damselflies, beautiful demoiselles, dance together in pairs over the water. If Sonny were here, we'd sit and listen to the buzz of insects and small fish blowing bubbles on the river's surface. The church bell across the moor at Meare chimes just once. Means Daniel will be here any minute now for my birthday sleepover. It'll be the first time he's come to my house. We're going to stay in the tent Dad put up for us in the orchard and set up the awesome wildlife camera Aunty Peaches got me that's got night vision and motion detection. Maybe we'll catch a badger or a fox cub or, if we're lucky, the black panther I know hides in the hedges.

Cyril's present is the only one I've got left to open. It's heavy. When I shake it gently, something, or maybe two things, rattle inside. Dad says he'll have given me something special, but I don't see how because Cyril couldn't get to the shops and didn't know how to order things off the internet. Not unless Gillian helped him. I make space at the water's edge so I can sit beneath the Himalayan balsam. My legs vanish under marsh buttercups. Coots, who nest on the other side of the riverbank, are diving for froglets. When I tear away the present's newspaper wrappings, two identical wooden boxes sit side by side. Inside the first, rolled up in cottony blue fabric, are the golden animal figures from Cyril's dresser. The jaguar's pointed teeth gleam like treasure. I squeeze it tight before pushing it deep into my pocket. Inside the other box, protected by layers of tissue paper, is the megalodon tooth Sonny so desperately wanted. It feels cold and smooth in my hand, and when I run my fingers along the serrations, they're still sharp. Seagulls call from somewhere and a swan paddles closer to take a look at what I'm holding. There's been a full moon and the high tide's turning. This is the best time for fishing, when the water that was pushing upstream and bringing us all the flotsam from the estuary slows right down until it stops. It's almost like the river's waiting. Pulling my arm back, I fling the tooth far out and wait to hear it splash. Another fossil to add to his collection. Beyond the large wide leaves of the butterburs, I watch the tide turn and begin its journey downstream.

Acknowledgments

Thank you to Karolina Sutton for believing in me and this book, and to everyone at CAA and Curtis Brown. A huge thanks to my UK editor Louisa Joyner for her warmth and understanding. To Jordaine Kehinde, Josh Smith, Hannah Marshall, Rachael Williamson and the rest of the Faber family. Not forgetting Lesley Jones. Thank you to the team at Henry Holt, in particular my US editor Retha Powers. This dream wouldn't have been realised without The Bridport Prize, so a big thank you to Kate Wilson and Max Riddington, and to the judge of 2021 *The Peggy Chapman-Andrews First Novel Award* Victoria Hislop. And thanks to my former classmates at Bath Spa University for all those hours of workshopping, especially Ananda Cresswell, Mirte Meeus, Jenny Hayes and Ria Newman, and to my tutors Richard Kerridge and Lucy English for the ongoing support they give to me and my writing. And to the awesome Natasha Pulley for her endless enthusiasm, advice and encouragement. Thank you to the early readers of extracts from this book, in particular Zoe Gilbert and Aminatta Forna. To the writing community I've befriended along the way, including Kim Squirrell, my Zoom sister-in-arms. A special thanks to Lucy Willis for her imperturbable feedback and stamp of approval. Heather and Berni Williams, ballet aficionado and rural sage, thank you for everything, for reading, feeding, babysitting and hugging away tears . . . it's time to get the sloe gin out!

To my dearest friends Donatela Dashchi and Esther Anglow, thank you for holding my hand every step of the way. Thanks also, to my brother Michael Green – surprise, I wrote a book! And to my godmother (Aunty) Lorna Graham, my mum knew what she was about when she chose you. And, of course, a heartfelt thank you to my mum, Shirley Eunice James, for her infinite love, wisdom and empowerment. Thanks to my children Red and Jaida for keeping me grounded and providing me with oodles of inspiration. Last, love and deepest gratitude to my husband Joseph (Jo) Williams, without whom this book would not exist.